"You make me different, you make me want to be different."

A startled glow went through Janina. She blushed for the first time in…well, it felt like forever. Maybe it was. "I—I don't know what to say. Thank you. You—I—"

The oh-so-gentle tip of Russ's forefinger touched her mouth. "Dance with me?"

"Yes."

The one word was like magic, as though she'd said "Abracadabra." Just that quickly, the outside fell away, she was in his arms and the music and Russ's heartbeat were the only things she heard, felt, *knew*. The rhythm of her heart keeping time to Russ's was what she moved to, the feel of his body against hers was all the cue she needed, the slightest pressure of his hand in the small of her back, of his thighs against hers, his knee between them while they swayed.

She reached her arms around him as far as they would go, to hold him, hold on to him. Make sure he was really there. "Neither one of us is dreaming. We're both really here. Together, same wavelength. For a change."

Dear Reader,

No doubt your summer's already hot, but it's about to get hotter, because *New York Times* bestselling author Heather Graham is back in Silhouette Intimate Moments! *In the Dark* is a riveting, heart-pounding tale of romantic suspense set in the Florida Keys in the middle of a hurricane. It's emotional, sexy and an absolute edge-of-your-seat read. Don't miss it!

FAMILY SECRETS: THE NEXT GENERATION continues with *Triple Dare* by Candace Irvin, featuring a woman in jeopardy and the very special hero who saves her life. *Heir to Danger* is the first in Valerie Parv's CODE OF THE OUTBACK miniseries. Join Princess Shara Najran as she goes on the run to Australia—and straight into the arms of love. Terese Ramin returns with *Shotgun Honeymoon,* a wonderful—and wonderfully suspenseful—marriage-of-inconvenience story. Brenda Harlen has quickly become a must-read author, and *Bulletproof Hearts* will only further her reputation for writing complex, heartfelt page-turners. Finally, welcome back Susan Vaughan, whose *Guarding Laura* is full of both secrets and sensuality.

Enjoy them all, and come back next month for more of the most exciting romance reading around—only from Silhouette Intimate Moments.

Enjoy!

Leslie J. Wainger
Executive Editor

Please address questions and book requests to:
Silhouette Reader Service
U.S.: 3010 Walden Ave., P.O. Box 1325, Buffalo, NY 14269
Canadian: P.O. Box 609, Fort Erie, Ont. L2A 5X3

Shotgun Honeymoon

TERESE RAMIN

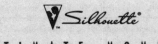

INTIMATE MOMENTS™

Published by Silhouette Books

America's Publisher of Contemporary Romance

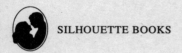

SILHOUETTE BOOKS

ISBN 0-373-27380-0

SHOTGUN HONEYMOON

Visit Silhouette Books at www.eHarlequin.com

Printed in U.S.A.

TERESE RAMIN

The granddaughter of an Irish Blarney Stone kisser (who, lowered by her ankles to do so, kissed it last at the age of ninety-six) and the oldest of eight, Terese Ramin has been surrounded by kids, chaos and storytelling all her life. At the request of her siblings she told outrageous stories late into the night, which caused a great deal of giggling among the kids and aggravation for her parents, who merely wanted them all to Go To Sleep! Terese lives in Michigan with five dogs, three cats, two kids and a husband who creates sawdust.

To all the waitresses who have waited on and fed me
throughout the years, especially the ones at
Little Chef in Brighton, MI. You guys are the best.
And to the gang in the BT Bayou:
thanks for the silliness factor.

For my darling daughter, Brynna, who goaded me
into writing a different book from the one I originally
had in mind. I love you with all my heart. Also for
C. Rita Brigham, friend and student, who at eighty-plus
may be full of vinegar but has failed miserably at
turning into it. To shared laughter. Love you, my dear.

Acknowledgments
My sincere thanks to the following people:
Annette Mahon, Cat Brown, Kristi Studts,
and Karen K.—Arizona. Lillian Stewart Carl—title.
Special thanks to Intimate Moments authors
Melissa James, Lindsay Longford, Vickie Taylor
and Linda Wisdom, who responded to a friend in need.
As ever, all leaps of faith, lapses of reality and
flat-out mistakes are wholly my own.

"Like newborn calves we will not be afraid of tigers."
—2000 Chinese men's Olympic gymnastics team motto

Prologue

Winslow, Arizona
July 17. Thirteen years ago

The worst nights didn't start with a body on the ground. They began with a dispute that could end with a body on the ground, possibly his.

Russ Levoie, nineteen, and only three months out of the police academy, had known this going in. He'd seen it up close and personal on the Havasupai reservation where he'd grown up—not in his own family, but in too many of the other families. Poverty begat fear begat the need to numb it begat drinking—or some other form of self-medication—begat dispute begat violence. And the cycle didn't alter with the scenery, it simply changed addresses. Nevertheless, here he was, headed into a trailer park on his own on a "see the woman" domestic-violence call because no one else was close enough to take it with him. And hot damn, didn't that just make him feel peachy-safe.

On the other hand, if he'd really meant to feel safe for the rest of his life, he'd have chosen another line of work. But this was all he ever remembered wanting to do. Adrenaline pumping, he parked his car, radioed in his position, alighted and slid his nightstick into place on his left hip before unsnapping the holster flap on his right.

Across the dusty street, he saw a white curtain flutter back into place. The neighbor that had called in, he guessed, peeking out to see who'd arrived. He headed in that direction. The door was cracked open and a hand beckoned him through the chicken-scratch front yard. "They've stopped now," the woman behind the screen said. Her voice was hushed as though in deference to the dusk. She carried a cigarette to her lips, lit it, inhaled and blew smoke from the corner of her mouth back into her trailer, away from Russ. Crossed an arm beneath her flat chest and propped her other elbow on it. The hand that held the cigarette to her mouth trembled.

Behind her, almost hidden in the shadows, was one of the young waitresses from the diner he frequented almost every evening before he went on duty. Janina. Young, pretty, everyday made astounding by a pair of huge heavily fringed mahogany eyes and a thick, roughly halved mane of hair the midnight side of brown. His heart and libido did the same damn telltale hop-skip-and-pucker it'd done any time he'd wound up in her vicinity lately. *Damn* because at maybe sixteen and still in high school Janina was jailbait. Still she was a cute little thing. He hoped her future would be more attractive than her present appeared to be.

"I don't get involved," Janina's mother recalled his attention by saying, "but this time it's bad, worse'n I ever heard. Hadda call, y'know? Lotta bangin' around—someone gettin' hit, like. Body hittin' walls, furniture bustin' 'n all. Then I hear her scream and she runs out the house all bloody. Her brother runs out after, drags her back in. Their old man's waitin' for 'em in the door, hits her good in the stomach 'afore he and the boy throw her inside an' it sounds like they start goin' on her again."

Russ flicked a glance at the teenager who nodded slightly in frightened confirmation. Russ's mouth thinned. Nobody's kid should have to live in a place like this.

No woman of any age should have to live here, either.

Once again his attention stuttered. His libido loosed its hold on him, turned over to his youthful heart. One regulation-clad foot slid him protectively nearer to the screened door and the young woman inside the trailer. Her eyes flared at the movement, lit with something akin to...

Welcome, worship, recognition...

Skittishness.

And more insight than he wanted her to possess.

Russ felt his Adam's apple bob, his sliding foot stammer and slip back where it belonged: under his control, no longer betraying him.

Or his seditious heart.

Deliberately he returned his attention to the mother. She put the cigarette between her lips and dragged hard. "Little while later I hear this sound, *pop-pop*, like that. Then it comes again, *pop-pop*, an' I see the old man run out the door lookin' like he don't believe what happened. I see he's been shot, 'cuz he's bleedin' down the side of his head somethin' fierce. Don't slow 'im down none, though.

He just gets in that old car 'a theirs an' takes off. All the while I hear this *pop-pop-pop-pop* goin' off over there. Then it went all quiet. That's when I called you."

The demon of Russ's temper battered his temples, demanding release from the cage in which he kept it. He short-chained it to the floor. "You waited until *after* to call?"

The woman nodded. "Seemed safest." She cast a suddenly wise glance over Russ that seemed to take in his youth and his lack of backup. "Fer ever'body."

Except the woman in that trailer, he wanted to snap at her. But didn't. Instead he asked, "There was only the three of them in there?"

She nodded again. "Far as I can tell. Three of 'em's all there ever is—'cept when they bring in paid company t'bang on that girl. Wasn't none of that today though."

"And you haven't heard anything more from inside?"

"Nope."

"Do you know their names?"

The woman shrugged. "Ever'body knows 'em 'roun' here. Girl's kinda the local hooker. Her daddy an' her brother bring guys to her. Don't think she likes it none, but she ain't got much choice. Name's Maddie Thorn, her brother's Harold, daddy's Charlie—"

"Damn." At Maddie's name, Russ yanked his handie-talkie off his shoulder and radioed for help, crossed the street and unholstered his gun before crashing through his former high-school classmate's—his best friend's, his prom date's—front door.

And damn her to hell for not asking him for help.

As Russ crossed the narrow street, Janina Gálvez flew across the room to lift her absent father's ever-loaded Winchester down from its rack on the wall. Weapon in hand, oblivious to her mother's weak protests, she fled out the far door to carefully work her way around the edge of the trailer.

She wasn't stupid. She kept to the shadows behind the propane tank and beneath the awnings as much as possible. She knew how to handle herself and her daddy's gun and she really couldn't let that boy-cop go out there alone. She just couldn't. If anything happened to him, she wasn't sure she could bear it. Not when she'd only just made up her mind three weeks ago that the instant she could, she intended to marry one rookie police officer named Russ Levoie, the most wonderfully gorgeous hero she'd ever laid eyes on. And if he got himself killed trying to save Maddie Thorn again, why she'd…

Janina swallowed. She didn't know what she'd do. The only thing she was certain of was that she intended to save the taciturn hero from himself for herself.

Period.

Chapter 1

He lived like a freaking monk.

Frustrated and furious with himself because of it, Russ Levoie slammed through the door of his trailer, causing it to bounce on its hinges. For the first time in his thirty-two years he was really sitting up and taking notice of all the things he'd never done, didn't have in his life.

What he noticed most was that he was damn-it-to-hell lonely in a way he'd never felt before.

All because of his brothers and their wives.

Damn them and bless them.

Jamming a fist through what there was of his neatly trimmed hair, Russ made his way to the refrigerator, yanked it open and grabbed a beer. For an instant he studied the unopened can, then loosed a virulent oath and threw the brew the length of the neat-as-a-pin trailer. The can burst against the far wall, spewing beer floor to ceiling, and spraying the sofa he spent most nights sleeping on—alone, always alone—as well as the table and chair beside it.

"Damn."

He viewed the mess tiredly. He rarely lost his temper, and certainly not like this. Not that he didn't have one. No, he had a decided temper. He'd simply learned young that allowing it to have its way with him tended to frighten people and got him nowhere.

Of course, holding it in check all the time wasn't necessarily the best alternative, either.

Cleanliness is next to Godliness. His elderly sixth-grade teacher, Sister Ann Henry, niggled across his memory. Turning, Russ grabbed a couple of rags and a bottle of spray cleaner from under the kitchen sink, strode across the trailer and began to mop the beer off the industrial-grade tile flooring he'd put down a year ago.

Judas-stinking-Billy-goats, he was envious of his brothers. Shoving air between his teeth in disgust, Russ caught up the exploded beer can, drained what remained of the beer in a long swallow then angled his body to pitch the can the length of the trailer. The can bull's-eyed the kitchen sink, clattered briefly about the stainless-steel sides and settled. He grimaced. He hadn't been a three-letter jock in high school for nothin'.

Tiredly he turned back to the job at hand. He'd never before envied his brothers anything. Guy, Jeth and Jonah were all younger than him and there'd never been anything they'd had that he'd wanted. Sure, he'd occasionally wished he could be as laid-back about life as Guy, and once, he'd wished for a little of Jeth's recklessness, but he didn't remember ever wishing for a bite of Jonah's loose-cannon hotheadedness. He had enough of that commodity of his own to worry about.

Not that he let anybody see it. Hell, you couldn't be a hothead *and* maintain your cool as one of only two local police lieutenants.

But his lack of sibling envy had been before Jeth and Guy had gone off and found themselves wives.

Russ moved up to scrub the wall paneling. He'd known before he'd gone out tonight that he should never have agreed to have dinner with the lot of them. He'd needed tonight's guys-only annual blowout, dammit, but not the way Guy and Jeth had set up this particular so-called remembrance day.

He never liked remembering what had happened thirteen years ago today, what he'd walked into the middle of in that trailer. So much blood, the terrible disfigurement Maddie had suffered—the nightmares that hadn't ended there but begun. But this year was worse than most. This year he'd had to go tell his best friend that her psychopathically abusive, pedophile of a father had been released from prison and was looking for her. She'd spent the past twelve years learning to feel safe for the first time in her life, learning to *have* a life at all, because Russ had assured her Charlie would be permanently incarcerated for the things he'd done to her. And now he wasn't. Because Russ had missed one parole hearing in twelve years and the psychologists and psychiatrists had gotten their way.

But of course, he couldn't back out on his family. *They'd* expected him. *They'd* done the bar thing for him tonight. Instead of it just being Guy, Jeth, him and a rip-roaring drunk to the destruction they too often saw on the job, they'd all been there, including Jonah and their brilliant oldest sister, Mabel, who hated boredom, dabbled in herbs and did investigative work for the state's forensics crime lab when she wasn't needed elsewhere. Including Jeth's glowing-with-new-pregnancy wife, Allyn—now teaching marine paleontology for the University of Arizona in the field at her grant-approved study site not far from Havasu Falls—and Guy's nearing-delivery pregnant wife, Hazel. Even his youngest brother, Jonah, the newest addition to the Levoie law enforcement legacy, was present. The only one of his siblings who was missing was the youngest, Marcy, killed on this date several years ago during a kid-napping gone wrong on Jeth's watch. It had taken them all a long time to get over that one, Jeth especially, and then only with Allyn's help.

Russ knew Marcy's murder at age ten was part and par-cel of what ruled him now where his life on the job was concerned, this annual drunk he and his peace officer brothers went on "in memory" of both their baby sister and the piece of his soul Russ had lost on this same date thir-teen years ago when he'd burst into Maddie's trailer and seen for the first time what her father and brother had been doing to her for years.

Life was not always as easy as it seemed in a small town, especially for a cop whose best friend was both abuse vic-tim and whore. Suspicion followed one like gossip, and these annual nights out with his brothers were a lifeline he needed to keep him sane, grounded—and also, sometimes, to keep him from thinking too much.

Thank God they'd left Guy and Hazel's adolescent daughter, Emily, and Jeth and Allyn's almost-four-year-old son, Sasha, at home. If they'd brought the kids, too...

It would be one thing if he envied his brothers the love they'd found or their subsequent happiness, but he didn't. No, his envy was far more complicated than that.

What he envied was their contentment.

With a snort of self-derision, Russ gave the wall a final swipe and returned the rag and spray to the kitchen. The blinking red light on the counter caught his eye. He punched the button to listen to his messages. A reminder about a meeting in Gallup scheduled for the following morning. A suspiciously timed call from his mother telling him she hadn't heard from him in too long. A circumspectly inquiring message from Jeth and a follow-up one from Guy, neither of whom had missed the tension vibrating through him by the time he'd left the restaurant.

And finally a voice almost too deep and husky to be feminine, though it was: Maddie. His best friend since as long as he could remember, his first adolescent crush, his prom date—and the child-girl-woman he'd spent most of his life trying to rescue and protect from more horrors than he cared to remember.

Maddie Thorn, who'd been abused unmercifully by her father, before he had finally attempted to kill her that night thirteen years ago…

"Russ?"

She sounded edgy, as though she looked over her shoulder while she spoke. Not at all the way she'd sounded three weeks ago when he'd let her know that her father was going to be released from prison early because the psychologists and psychiatrists who'd been working with him thought he was rehabilitated enough—medicated enough—to walk about in polite society again despite his track record as being, well, *not*.

Russ, who'd seen the man over the years, listened to his rambling assertions on having found religion and wanting to set things right with his daughter, had told Maddie that Charlie might be looking for her. Maddie, truly and completely happy for the first time in her life and with other things on her mind, had more or less blown him off.

And now here she was, exactly as he'd known—as he'd *felt*, with that strange extra sense with which he'd been gifted, with what his brothers called his spider sense— she'd be.

"God, Russ, where are you? I need to see you. You were right about him. He found me. He said you—" She broke off suddenly. He heard her breathing, raggedly. Afraid. *"No,"* she whispered, though not directly into the phone. *"Oh God, no. He can't have. He couldn't—no."* Then a deep, steadying breath and more strongly, firmly, *"No!"* And into the phone again, *"I have to go. But God, Russ, please. Be there. Please."*

The receiver on the other end of the line clattered into place hard, and Russ's machine beeped once and announced, *"End of messages."*

Russ could only stare at the message light for a moment. He'd come in not quite thinking about her, his heart on Janina—the woman he'd wanted across almost every single hot cup of coffee she'd served him for the past thirteen years—and the current Maddie-involved reasons he'd yet to act on his longings for her.

And here Maddie was calling him.

Needing help again.

Palms flat on the counter to hold himself erect, he gave her call for help some thought. Whispered "screw it" to the cupboards because he knew there was no way he'd ever walk away from Maddie, no matter what happened.

Maddie had been a different person when they were younger, a messed-up abuse case beyond what even he'd realized at that time. And he'd been the only friend, only *person,* to see her, know her and love her for who she was.

And now she'd gotten herself together and found Jess, the life partner who made her happy and…

Now this.

All of *this.*

Her father out of prison and looking for…something. Revenge, maybe. Reconciliation, he'd said, but Russ didn't believe that for an instant. The cop's gut in him crawled, remembering Charlie's eyes. The man in him, the *friend,* simply unhooked the chain that held his temper and withdrew any pretext of masking the savage within the trappings of civilization should Charlie get too close, legally released from prison or not.

Russ rubbed his hands hard across his eyes. He didn't know what he was going to do. Because as well as he understood Maddie, as good as he was at working with wounded females, he was no damn good at emotions, or at figuring them out. Not his own, and not women's. Particularly not while Maddie needed rescuing by him yet again, and Janina—who constantly tortured his dreams—seemed to him about as obtainable as the moon.

Always had been, truth be known.

Emotions. Geez-oh-Pete. God save him from female best friends, who pulled themselves out of hell by their toenails when offered the slimmest of chances, feminine soul mates with nerves of steel and hearts of gold and courage as raw as anything he'd ever seen—yeah, Janina thought he didn't know about her shadowing him that night thirteen years ago, right? *Wrong!*—and freaking, obfuscating emotions.

With an oath, Russ turned his back on the kitchen and headed for the small room at the back of the trailer that should have been his bedroom but was now where he kept his silversmithing and lapidary equipment. He opened the heavy safe he kept there, withdrew the envelope he'd placed inside six months prior and emptied its contents into his hand. It was a sort of Guinevere-style ring he'd designed in platinum with a single large not-quite-square piece of green Baltic amber canted diamondwise in the center and offset by a small but exquisitely cut and flawless diamond at each of the amber's points. The wedding ring lay heavy in his palm, spoke to him of plans and cowardice, a life lived in faux courage.

Oh, he could take down bad guys, face bullets, walk into domestic quarrels, go through fire with the best of 'em—hell, he'd even had enough chutzpah, damn it, to make her a ring—but put him in front of Janina and say anything remotely having to do with a you and me—a we—and ha! It came out sounding like, "I'll have today's special and coffee."

Dating was simply beyond his limited verbal capabilities.

Russ started to drop the ring back into its envelope, putting Janina away for another time once again in favor of seeing what he could do to help Maddie, always Maddie. Suddenly he felt the hair on his neck stand up and stopped, hand poised.

Even before the knock came low on his screen door he knew Maddie was there.

Nerves alight, he shoved Janina's ring into his pocket and went to push open the door.

"Hey, Maddie," he said quietly, and stepped aside to let her in.

"Hey yourself." She crossed the threshold with a shaky laugh.

Then she flung herself forward, threw her arms around his neck and hung on for dear life.

Without further thought, he folded his arms around her and held on tight.

No matter how hard she worked at it, no matter how disgusted she got with herself, nor how unrequited she knew her feelings were, every time she saw Russ Levoie, Janina Gálvez Carmichael fell smack-dab right back head over heart over heels in love with him again.

Had ever since the first time he'd walked into the Fat Cat Diner thirteen years ago when she was a sixteen-year-old waitress and he was a fresh-from-the-academy rookie working his first evening shift for the Winslow P.D.

It still happened now that she was a twenty-nine-year-old working-her-way-through-college-a-class-at-a-time waitress who'd been around the block a few times and who damn well knew better than to fall for a guy who carried a torch for someone else and who wasn't going to budge from that path no matter what.

The idiot.

Him *and* her. Meaning not only her as in herself, Janina Gálvez Carmichael, but as in *her*, that blasted Maddie Thorn that Russ couldn't seem to let go of long enough to notice the girl with the heart-on-her-sleeve look who'd served him coffee, flirtation, offhand friendship, advice and good humor almost every day of the week for the last thirteen years.

Geez, what a fool.

Both of them.

No, make that *all* of them, because though she seemed to count on his friendship like a lifeline, Maddie'd never really given in to Russ in a one-on-one love-me-tender-and-forever way, either. Which was pretty damn stupid of her, in Janina's oft-considered and far-less-than-humble opinion.

Fuming, Janina watched Russ seat himself and the ice-cool Sharon Stone look-alike, wearing the expensively cut slim white designer sheath, at his usual back booth. His concern for the beautifully coiffed and manicured blonde was plain, spelled out something subtle to the green-eyed monster Janina knew she wasn't entitled to harbor yet harbored anyway. Maddie'd had to scrape and scrap hard to pull herself out of the hell she'd grown up in, Janina knew that. Once Maddie had made her own way through beauty school—with Russ's help, damn it!—she'd gotten a job, worked hard, paid him back and she was now one of the most sought-after stylists in Phoenix.

And that was not to mention the time Janina knew Maddie put in at a couple of Phoenix battered women's shelters doing corrective makeup and makeovers for girls and women trying to get out of situations similar to her own past.

Janina also knew that Russ never brought women into the diner. In fact, she'd never seen him out with anyone other than his brothers or other cops unless it was in a crowded social situation like a community barbecue. And even then he never paid particular attention to anyone special.

Especially not to her, Janina Carmichael née Gálvez—and chalk *that* married name change up to one truly witless mistake. Damn it.

On all counts.

She grimaced wryly at herself in the revolving dessert-display cooler mirror. Russ was thirty-two years old, for pity's sake. He had a life, presumably. She didn't own him, more was the pity. And other than the little time they spent flirting when she waited on him, Russ probably barely thought of her or remembered she was alive.

Another glance at Maddie Thorn made Janina growl unintentionally under her breath.

A half snort, half chuckle at her shoulder made her catch herself, realize what she was doing and redden. In self-defense she snatched up a pot of coffee and a rag, preparing to head over to the table to greet Russ and his...

Guest.

"Don't say anything," she said without looking back.

"He's got a friend tonight," Tobi Hosey observed, ignoring her. Tobi usually ignored Janina when Janina wanted Tobi to say nothing. It was the basis of their friendship. Tobi spoke her mind regardless of the tact involved and Janina swallowed it and spoke her own back, no baloney involved. Which meant they each had someone who'd laugh at their bouts of temperamental stupidity.

Which was exactly what Tobi was doing now.

Which was exactly what Tobi did each and every time Russ came in and left without Janina saying one word to him about going to a movie or dinner or anything else that resembled something that might turn out to be romantic or relationship-developing—or that might at least get him home and into Janina's bed. Because they both knew that Russ Levoie did not do casual in any way, shape or form. Hell, the creases in his uniform and even his jeans were knife-edged. Of *course* he didn't do casual—*any* kind of casual. And if you wanted confirmation, all you had to do was ask his brothers.

Janina and Tobi had each, in fact, casually dated—as in "hung out with" not "bedded"—all three of Russ's younger siblings. And enjoyed themselves tremendously in the process. But Janina really wasn't interested in casual dating anymore. She was interested in Russ, pretty much constantly, nonstop.

But there had been moments in her life when she got intensely, out-of-control lonely and had to do what she had to do to keep her sanity intact. These were past tense, of course. Still, they'd led to the smart-girl-doing-stupid-things someone had written the book about.

Like letting herself be flattered into her first romantic relationship with and then marrying that good-for-nothing bruiser Buddy Carmichael a couple years after high school just because she thought she'd finally gotten over Russ, lost her mind and fallen for Buddy, let him have her virginity and then thought he'd gotten her pregnant.

Which would have been a mistake of gargantuan proportions even if he had, which he hadn't. Because not only had she not been pregnant, but Big Man on Northland Pioneer College's Campus, Buddy Carmichael, had turned out to be a drinking-man's wife beater with friends in high places and an ability to manipulate the system to his own ends.

And so much for doing what some desperate mutation of yourself thought you had to do to keep yourself from being lonely!

After the Buddy idiocy Janina had started hanging out with Russ's brothers, almost exclusively. They were fun and they didn't stray beyond boundaries they all knew existed but none of them mentioned.

True, they weren't Russ by a long shot, but they shared

minor similarities and were a fairly safe substitute for, not to mention a good source of information on, the real thing.

Foolish, but there she was.

Head high in refusal to succumb to the truly moronic things she knew about herself, Janina slung a pair of brown coffee mugs from a finger and sashayed out from behind the counter, hips swinging in her best "I don't give a damn what you're doing or with whom, Russ Levoie" style.

Not that he'd get it, but that wasn't the point.

At least not entirely.

"Damn the torpedoes," Tobi suggested helpfully, grinning.

"Shut up," Janina retorted and, head high, huffed off.

"I don't know how I can help you, Maddie," Janina heard Russ say as she approached. She watched him run a hand over the back of his freshly shorn neck in a gesture of frustration with which she was all too familiar. He accepted responsibility for the world, and when the world didn't cooperate, it got to him. "It's not like—"

"I know you don't have jurisdiction, Russ," Maddie said, not quite able to keep the panic out of her voice. "I just thought maybe…" She swallowed, drew herself together. "*Hoped* maybe there'd be something…" Her voice trailed off.

Janina paused, watching.

Maddie's face grew shuttered, her troubled hazel eyes clouded, and the perfect bow mouth took on the edgy shape of self-derision. "I don't know what I hoped. Aside from—from…" She swallowed convulsively, clenched her fists and looked away, at the table, at the window, anywhere but at him. "Aside from the other stuff…m-my fath—Charlie getting out an-and coming for me…" She ran her tongue around the inside of her mouth. Shrugged. "Other than that, I dunno. Maybe I hoped partly that you'd changed your mind about what I asked you. Or something."

She looked at him, suddenly in command of herself again. "I'm sorry, this was stupid. What am I thinking? You'd think I'd have learned how to rescue myself by now, wouldn't you?"

"Maybe not from this," he said quietly then eyed her directly, hard. "But is that what you're here looking for, Maddie? A knight-in-shining?"

Maddie laughed without humor. "Wouldn't that be a kick if I were. Why? You looking to joust windmills again, Russ?"

Russ shrugged. "We all need a little rescuing once in a while."

"Even you?"

"Not by you, Maddie." The comment was terse, accompanied by an unconscious, half-reflexive glance that skimmed the room and brought his gaze to rest for half a second on Janina.

She stopped dead in her tracks. He needed to be rescued, but not by Maddie. Not by *Maddie!* And he'd looked at her—*her, Janina!*—when he said it. So he *did* notice her—maybe. *If* she was reading correctly the signals he might not even be aware he was sending.

A frisson of—Janina wasn't sure what—shimmied down her spine. Fear and anticipation, caution and recklessness, pure unadulterated and exhilarating hope.

In less than a heartbeat, hope changed the "I don't give a damn" swing of her hips into a "come-hither" sway-and-roll, turned her step into a glide, sparkled her eyes, instinctively curved her mouth into its most welcoming and flirtatious "hey-how-you-doin'" smile, and focused her entire attention on Russ.

In just longer than that same heartbeat, and seemingly from out of nowhere, a large, booted foot shot out and tripped her, sent her sliding and sprawling across an empty table that tipped and dumped her, the burning-hot coffee, the mugs and the chair she smashed into, crashing to the floor.

Somewhere off to the right the air filled with raucous, full-bellied, hatefully familiar, cruelly delighted laughter surrounded by shocked silence.

Half-stunned, Janina lay in the middle of the mess, feeling the bruises gather and the coffee scald its way through her skimpy pink uniform. She couldn't quite find her right wrist, and the left fingers that had carried the coffee mugs felt pinched and a trifle slick.

The spiteful laughter lasted for less than a moment longer before Russ jerked Buddy Carmichael out of his seat by the throat, slammed him backward into the wall, tripped him face-first onto the floor beside his ex-wife and handcuffed his beefy wrists behind him.

Oblivious of her expensive white designer sheath, Maddie knelt amid the debris beside Janina and gently began to feel for broken bones. Tobi arrived at Janina's other side almost simultaneously to do the same.

Not far from Janina's face, Russ gripped a hank of Buddy's hair and lifted his head, forcing him to look at Janina. "This what you think's funny, man?" Fury tightened Russ's voice to a whip crack. "Seriously, man, you find this *funny?*"

Apparently unaware of who had him pinned, Buddy sneered, unrepentant. "Yeah."

Russ dragged Buddy up farther, hard, by the hair. "What?"

Buddy's smirk wavered hardly at all. "Yeah—sir."

The chains on Russ's temper seemed to snap. Even as the rolling *whoop* of sirens filled the air outside the diner, he dropped Buddy's face onto the floor and hauled him up for another go.

Suddenly, Buddy was neither cocky nor smirking. He also no longer found what he'd done to Janina funny, and croaked that to Russ through bruised and bleeding lips. Hardly satisfied, but knowing it was the best he'd get, Russ removed his knee from between Buddy's shoulder blades, released the man's hair, jerked a nod in his brother Jonah's direction as he came into the café and moved to squat beside Janina.

Casting a wry look at his oldest—and tallest—brother, young officer Levoie went to collect Russ's prisoner.

Gently, Russ touched Janina's cheek. "How you doin'?"

She tried a wobbly smile on for size. The man had reduced her ex to pulp for her, *for her,* the least she could do was smile at him and say thank-you. Because no one had ever done that for her before, had even *tried* to rescue her.

Janina blinked. Her eyes watered and tears spilled. Russ stroked her cheek and she'd never known a man's hand to feel so gentle, so calm, when less than two minutes ago he'd been Buddy's terror from hell. Why had she never asked him for help when she'd been married and needed it? He'd have given it. But she hadn't asked because she hadn't wanted Russ Levoie, of all people, to know how stupid she'd been over a man who wasn't *him*.

"Hey," Russ whispered, spotting her tears. He pulled a clean hankie out of his back pocket and blotted her cheeks awkwardly. "It's okay. You're okay now. We've got you, Janie. You'll be okay. It's only friends here now."

It's only friends here now.

The problem exactly. Because of all the people in the world with whom Janina didn't want to be "only friends," Russ Levoie was at the top of the list and had been for the better part of a baker's dozen years now.

Unable to contain her multihued emotions, Janina let the sobs loose. Without thought, Russ sat down on the floor, carefully gathered her into his arms and held her close while the EMTs checked her over and Janina cried into his chest.

Chapter 2

July 18

Janina stood in front of her closet and surveyed herself in the full-length mirror.

"Very attractive," she muttered, taking in the fuzzy, yellow Woodstock-the-bird slippers on her feet, the overly warm plaid flannel magenta pajama bottoms, the Remember 9/11-2001 emblazoned in navy and white on red alongside the U.S. flag on her ragged-edged, oft-worn, long-sleeved gray T-shirt, the bright turquoise Ace-wrap peeking out from the pushed-up sleeve on her right wrist and forearm that protected the slight sprain to her wrist, and the green tape wrapping the stitched-up fingers on her left hand. "Absolutely blasted ducky brilliant."

She studied her face, the small, relatively minor bruising below the eye on her right cheek and beside it the butterfly bandage where she hadn't needed stitches to close a laceration. Then she examined the lumpiness on her upper lip where it had taken a plastic surgeon a surprising number of stitches to close the small but deep cut inside. "You look stinking beautiful. No wonder he had to leave. Sheesh."

Or rather, sheesh and damn. Because the reason Russ had given for leaving after he'd brought Janina home from the hospital three hours ago was so he could see *Maddie* home.

Maddie, who'd refused to leave Janina's—or Russ's— side and tagged along to the hospital with Tobi while Russ rode the back of the ambulance with Janina.

Maddie, with whom Russ had been in love since he'd been, oh, six. And twelve. And sixteen. And forever.

Maddie, who lived in Phoenix, which was in the neighborhood of one hundred and eighty miles away.

Seeing her home. Yeah, right. His trailer home maybe. Where he didn't take anybody.

Which she knew because Jonah had told her.

Janina fumed.

Then she eyed herself in the mirror again, stuck out her tongue at her reflection and decided to act. Because by the time Russ had brought Janina back to the apartment she shared with Tobi, Jonah had turned up to see Maddie off to wherever. Right?

Right. So Russ had gone home by himself after all.

Groggy or not at the time, Janina had made a clear note of *that* smidgen of information. Which meant that whatever Russ had said when he'd left, it was an excuse, pure and simple, a means to leave her alone to…

Get some sleep and recover from her ordeal, let's say.

She tried to purse her lips—a painful move—and considered that thought. As thoughts went it had real merit, showed tremendous consideration by him for her welfare and boded well for her desire for a relationship with him.

And it had absolutely no Maddie in it.

Especially, no Maddie *and* Russ. As in together, paired up, in the same place, where there might be a bed.

Janina breathed out, an action of both decision and courage, and took the thought a step further. Actually, she took it several steps and a leap of faith further.

She might have a slightly sprained wrist and be on mild painkillers, but she was sober, she hadn't been told not to drive and Tobi was asleep. Right?

Right.

So, darn it, she was going to see him. Russ, not Jonah. Now.

Because clearly though he was the kind of guy who might want a girl—she hadn't imagined the look he'd sent her tonight right before Buddy had tripped her—but he was also the kind of guy who was damn s-l-o-w about getting to what he wanted. So if the girl had mutual feelings for him, then she'd better do something about it herself.

Like go and attack him, or at least throw herself at him and tell him exactly what she wanted of him. And how often. And for how long. And maybe, while she was at it, say something about forever. With him.

Or something like that.

Oh, geez. Janina covered her face with her left hand— gingerly. Maybe she shouldn't drive, she thought. She wasn't making sense anymore, even to herself.

She checked on Tobi to be sure her roommate was sleeping then got dressed anyway, makeup and all, then found her keys and purse, and headed out to find Russ.

* * *

Two cars were parked outside of Russ's trailer, one of which was Maddie's—Janina swallowed jealousy—but neither of which was his.

Surprised, she pulled over to the side of the road and studied the darkened trailer. She was pretty sure she knew everyone Russ knew, knew their vehicles, or so she thought. If Maddie was inside, where was Russ?

Hope sang through her in a low thrum. Maddie was inside and Russ's car wasn't there. Somebody else's was.

Janina's mouth trembled. She almost smiled. Almost. She wanted to. But she was afraid.

A Winslow police cruiser coasted up beside her car, startling her. Janina grabbed her heart, winced when her hands objected, then, recognizing Jonah, rolled down her window.

"You supposed to be out 'n about?" Russ's not-so-babyish baby brother asked.

Janina looked at him. Lightning-quick onyx eyes set in a deceptively youthful native nutmeg face stared back. As usual, Jonah's straight ebony hair stood on end because of his constant need to do something with his hands, attesting to the lack of stillness that was both his strength and nemesis. Though he was shorter and slighter than his brothers, his slim, wiry body made him quicker than any of them, had stood him in good stead as a wrestler in both high school and through the academy. Didn't matter the size of the prisoner he put a hold on, if Jonah Levoie didn't want to let someone go, they stayed held on to.

"Fine," Jonah said. "Let me rephrase. You're looking mighty dressed to kill for someone who maybe oughta be home in bed. You stalkin' my head-case brother?"

Janina blinked. She'd handled Jonah before. He was

merely an outspoken, sometimes arrogant, frequently youthful hothead. Silence on her part would trip him over his tongue sooner than byplay.

Jonah sighed. "I ask because *if* you were stalkin' him and *if* he was here, I'd open the door for you because I think he could use a good dose of takin' care of you right now, and vice versa. Get Maddie out of his system but good. But since he's not here and I dunno why he asked me to run extra patrols past his place tonight, I can't do that."

"Where is he?" The question was out before Janina could stop it.

Jonah grinned. "Knew you were interested."

Janina, the would-be grown-up of the two of them, stuck her tongue out at Russ's baby brother.

Jonah laughed. "Can't hide, Janie. You've been hot for him since before I knew you. The only reason you went out with me was to get closer to him."

"Not true," Janina protested far too vehemently and transparently. "But a girl can't sit around all her life waiting for Russ Levoie to get it into his head to ask her for a date."

The mild painkillers must have made her tongue looser and her head muzzier than she'd realized. "And if you tell anybody I said that…"

Jonah didn't laugh. He smiled slightly and nodded, two months to twenty-five and grown-up for a change. "Mum," he said. "Heard nothin'. But…"

Janina glared at him. He grinned slightly and shook his head.

"Nope, no strings. Just thought I'd mention I think I saw Russ's car parked down at the Bloated Boar an hour ago. My guess, I'm gonna get a call to haul him out of there in about twenty minutes. He'll be on his feet, but he won't be drivin' anymore tonight. And…" He hesitated, looked Janina over as though making a judgment call. Shrugged and gave it up. "He'll need a place to stay because he said he won't be stayin' here."

Janina's breath flipped in her lungs, and her heart hit the back of her throat. Something in the early-morning air made her unaccountably dizzy. "He will?" she said.

Jonah nodded. "Yeah. And he took tomorrow off."

"Oh." Janina swallowed. Fear, anticipation, excitement, hope, nerves—readiness. "Thanks." *I think.*

"Don't thank me yet," Jonah muttered almost too low for her to hear.

Hands tense on the steering wheel—she needed to hang on tight to something right now—she watched Jonah sketch her a two-finger salute and peel his cruiser into a tight U-turn, returning to his third-shift prowl. Then trying not to wonder what Jonah had meant by his last cryptic remark, Janina, too, pulled back onto the road and made tracks toward the Bloated Boar Saloon.

The Bloated Boar Saloon.
July 18, 3:17 a.m.

Nothing and everything about the Bloated Boar was unique.

Situated off a dirt track in the middle of nowhere and a goodly distance from anywhere else, the Bloated Boar boasted a badly taxidermied mascot protected behind a scarred, bulletproof Plexiglas shield below the carved sign that bore the saloon's name. The shield was bulletproofed because of weekend revelers intent on trying their luck at taking out the mascot's shiny glass eyes.

Contrary to the stories they put out, the owners did not hail from London or anyplace resembling it, but had once had a great-aunt who was an Anglophile and who'd willed them enough money to open the Bloated Boar if they called it the Bloated Boar, decorated it to her specifications and gave it the legend she wrote for it. Tall-tale-tellin' Texans, the lot of 'em, they'd willingly complied with the great-aunt's request, and the Bloated Boar was now in its third generation of fake Cockney-accented or East End-accented Texans.

At various hours of the day the saloon was peopled with busty serving wenches and unsavory-looking serving pirates. There was also a full-figured barmaid who often chose to dress the part and a six-foot-six-inch ruddy-cheeked swallow-tender barman who also acted as the saloon's bouncer.

Any number of colorful "plants" among the customers added to the atmosphere when tourists—who found the out-of-the-way place in surprising numbers—were present. Janina knew the place well as it was a favorite haunt among the locals, too. The Boar opened at 7:00 a.m. for breakfast and closed only briefly twenty-one hours later. The food was good and plentiful, the drinks ran freely, and it was a rowdy place in which to have a good time.

And for the life of her, Janina couldn't believe Jonah had sent her to find Russ there. She'd have bet money that the overly intense Russ Levoie didn't believe in rowdy good times, or relaxing good times, or maybe even just simple good times, come to that. She wasn't even sure he knew *how* to relax and have a good time. Janina wheeled her vintage Chevy wagon into the Bloated Boar's parking lot. Sure enough, parked well away from the scarred display box and sign sat Russ's immaculate white Jimmy. Though a classic with a removable hard top and hardly new, the vehicle always managed to look it, despite the rough and dusty country Russ drove it through. Spoke to the man's character, Janina was pretty sure.

She simply found an empty parking place, took a deep breath, released her seat belt as she exhaled, and launched herself on her search for Russ.

He was difficult to find in the dim light, despite the waning number of patrons left inside the pub. When she *did* spot him, Janina nearly dropped her charmingly crooked teeth in astonishment. Because there was Russ Levoie as she'd never thought to see him: relaxed, a pint mug of dark ale in one hand, head thrown back in laughter, with one of the lustier-looking saloon waitresses perched on his knee.

Janina saw green at once. Green-eyed monsters, green-eyed fury, a murky, jealous green haze. She also felt green moths floating in her stomach and a hot green fire roiling up through her veins. The bastard's brother had thought he might be drunk, but if this was what it took to get him to pay attention to a woman…!

Then Janina remembered who the man she'd long wanted—forever longed for—was, who the Russ Levoie she knew was.

Swallowing hard, she made herself locate his other hand. Sure enough, it was curled loosely in a fist on the table and nowhere near the girl, who shoved herself out of his lap with apparent regret and offered him a slip of paper. He shook his head. The waitress pressed what must have been her phone number on him anyway, bending forward and tucking the bit of paper into the left front pocket of his shirt.

Janina watched something flicker across Russ's face, not quite regret, less than revulsion, a jaw-tightening away from awkwardness, then it was gone. His lips twisted, a travesty of a smile to someone who knew him at all. The waitress twitched her hips at him as she walked away. Russ blinked and grimaced at the woman's departure, and downed his drink in a long gulp.

Janina breathed deep and went to the bar to order two large dark beers. God help her, she was stupid when it came to Russ. She should have tackled him the way she'd done everything else in her life: head-on and face-first and a long time ago. Then she'd have known one way or another about that long-standing "if," and she wouldn't be standing here worrying about whether or not she had a shot with Russ. Plus, she wouldn't be jealous over nothing if she didn't have a chance with him.

Well, maybe she would, but then there'd be a reason for it, instead of this nebulous sensation of "get away from him, he's mine" when actually he wasn't. Yet. Or maybe ever.

No, she told herself firmly. Yet. Yet. Yet. Yet.

Be careful what you wish for, Tobi's demon whispered in her ear.

"Go to hell." Janina barely moved her lips but the barmaid eyed her askance. Janina tried a grimace, winced when the stitches pulled and shook her head. "You don't want to know."

The barmaid grinned. "Bet I do."

Janina shook her head. "Trust me."

"You got it for that one?" The woman lifted her chin in Russ's direction while she pulled Janina's beers.

"Mmm." Janina sighed. "Obvious?"

"Only to someone who reads the signs." Another flashing grin from the woman tending bar. "Good luck. He's waitin' on something. Though he doesn't seem to know what. Won't cotton to anybody here, fact. Most of the girls have tried."

"They have? He won't?" Hope soared. She gave the barmaid a crooked smile. "Thanks. I feel like I'm in seventh grade asking for info on the varsity quarterback."

"Eh, s'okay." The other woman shrugged and winked. "I was in seventh grade myself last night. Good to know I'm not there alone." She nodded at Janina's hands and face. "Wasn't him did that to you, was it." Not a question exactly.

Janina's smile tumbled in her belly, felt tremulous on her mouth. "No. He saved me."

The barmaid grinned happily, as though Janina had confirmed something she'd long thought—and hoped. "Don't look like you can manage these. Why don't you go sit. I'll bring 'em over. I'm Shelley, by the way."

"Janina."

Sending Shelley a grateful smile, Janina did as she'd been told, preceding the woman across the room to slide onto the bench beside Russ even as the beers were placed on the table in front of him. He didn't even glance up.

"Thanks, but I'm still not goin' home with you, Marg," Russ said slowly but firmly. His words didn't slur, but he definitely sounded too comfortable to either be the real Russ Levoie or to be Russ Levoie sober. "Doesn't matter how many drinks I have. Told you it wouldn't be fair to either of us, I got somebody else on my mind."

"And I'll bet she said it didn't matter to her whether you've got someone else on your mind or not, didn't she?" Janina asked. She thought she heard a tinge of that green-eyed thing in her voice but she couldn't be sure. If Maddie was the other person he had on his mind what the hell was *she* doing here?

"Janie?" Russ cocked his head and looked at her. "What're you doin' here? You're supposed to be home takin' care of yourself. I knew I should've come back and made sure you did."

Damn straight, Janina agreed silently. *Saved me a trip out.*

"Couldn't sit still," she said aloud. "Needed company. Wish you had come back. I wanted to say thank-you. Anyway, I went out looking for you, and Jonah told me you might be here, so here I am."

Russ smiled. "That's good," he said simply. "I'm glad. I wanted to see you, too, but I didn't know how to ask and I didn't want to wake you if you were sleepin'."

Janie's heart flipped, and knocked aside any common sense she might still have possessed. "Really?" she whispered, as shy as she would have been if he'd noticed her way back when, hero to her hero worshipper.

Inhibitions lowered by the amount of alcohol he'd consumed, Russ turned to look at her full on. His eyes were dark, smiling, full of promise. He reached up to trace the uninjured right side of her mouth with the tip of a forefinger in the lightest of caresses. "Oh, yeah," he whispered, so close she could taste his breath on her lips, feel the heat of him on her skin, know the touch of him throughout her body by the single contact the pad of his finger made at the edge of her mouth. "Very much. Definitely."

Janina's eyes drifted closed. Opened. She had to watch him. She swallowed and her own mouth seemed to float gently closer to his yet not close enough. He played with her mouth without touching it, moving as though to nuzzle her smile, teasingly pulling his own mouth back until she thought she'd go mad, until she was breathless with laughter.

"Russ," she murmured, "what are you doing?"

"I don't know," he said. "I've never done this before. What *am* I doing?"

"What do you mean?" She couldn't think. She didn't want to think. She'd known being with Russ would be special and this was only a kiss, not even a kiss. "Please, Russ. You're making me crazy. Are you going to kiss me? Please, Russ, kiss me."

"Might." His mouth came closer to hers and withdrew slightly. The tip of his forefinger drifted across her mouth, barely tracing the outer edge of her lips, finding the bruises, investigating more gently and carefully than she'd known it was possible for a man to touch a woman. "Don't want to hurt you. You've been hurt too much. Never want it to be me who hurts you."

The simplicity of libido fled in the face of something else entirely.

Startled senseless by the tenderness of touch and statement, Janina blinked. Her eyes burned with sudden emotion and a lump lodged tightly in her throat. The butterflies and moths that had been churning up her stomach suddenly fuzzed into warmth at the same time that the rest of her body became suffused with the loveliest sense of chills and confusion and warmth and safety and...

And a whole lot of something more. She blinked again. The world, made up of Russ's face, swam before her eyes. The lump in her throat dissolved, and whatever toughness she'd developed through the years puddled in Russ Levoie's hands. Tears ran down her face and collected along the lump at her lip.

"Oh, Russ."

"What?" His surprise was the genuine surprise of a

drunken man. The distress was a drunken man's distress, too. Normally Russ knew exactly what to do with crying women—or seemed to. "Janie, don't cry. I don't know what to do."

"Oh, Russ." Laughter and wry despair mixed with the tears this time. Janina placed her less injured left hand against Russ's chest. "You always know what to do."

"Don't." He was thoroughly helpless.

She lifted her face, smiling, and snuggled into him because it seemed like the natural place to be. "Do."

He turned toward her. His arms pulled her close, instinctively seemed to claim her, the same way he'd wrapped her up and taken her in earlier at the diner. "No, I don't." He bent his head to rub his cheek against hers. "Doesn't matter though. I can learn. Just don't let me hurt you."

"You won't hurt me, Russ," Janina whispered against his throat. "You can't. It's not in you."

"I could," Russ warned her honestly, enunciating each word with care. "If I wasn't drunk I probably wouldn't even be able to talk to you."

Janina lifted her chin to look at him, gave him a slow, woman-for-her-man-only smile and nuzzled his jaw. "Then drink your beer," she murmured suggestively, sliding the two not-taped fingers on her left hand inside between the buttons of his shirt. "And let's go back to my place 'n see what we can do about making you comfortable enough to still be able to talk to me tomorrow."

Chapter 3

They didn't make it to Janina's place.

Instead, Russ smiled his slow, sideways smile down at her and once again didn't quite brush her mouth with his. Then he released her, downed half his beer, sauntered over to the big, old-fashioned jukebox, fed some coins into it and punched a few select buttons that he didn't seem to have to look for.

Everything inside her, every nerve, every sense, every particle of her being zinged alert, alive, *awake*. As though she'd been sleeping every moment before in her life.

Awake.

Electricity charged through her, then exhilarated pulse points, titillated nerve endings, thrilled along her spine and laid a fuzzy, sizzling pool of restlessness in the small of her back.

Whatever leftover aches she had from her bruises fled

and she blessed Buddy for unwittingly giving her a moment she'd never otherwise have had the courage to pursue.

Then Russ hooked a glance at her over his shoulder and all thought fled.

He stood in front of the jukebox for a long, drawn-out moment during which Janina's heart felt as if it beat in some sort of slow-motion animated suspension. The pure masculine intent in the look he sent her snapped the suspension. Her heartbeat turned staccato, her breathing stuttered and the safety that had flooded her moments before fled, to be replaced by a flood of liquid heat, a sense of pure elation, a knowledge and anticipation of a danger she couldn't wait to face. Want coursed through her veins, sang a tightening song through her lungs, pushed like wildfire into her belly.

He wanted her.

The rawness of what he wanted was written on his face. Her beneath him, her atop him, her around him. Her with him. Her.

And more than that, he needed her.

She read need in his eyes, on his face, and it wasn't just anybody he needed. It was her, Janina.

Janina caught her breath and rose unsteadily to stand between the bench and the table. He was coming for her. Not Maddie. Not Marg. Not anybody else who'd offered or thrown herself at him.

For her.

Only.

She saw the "only" written on his face, too, and stopped breathing. She couldn't take her eyes off him. She couldn't...

And then he was there, leaning down to grab his beer,

draining what remained of it before he cupped his palms beneath her elbows and carefully lifted her out of her prison to stand in front of him.

"Liquid courage," he said regretfully. "I'll be sober in the morning. If I don't do everything I've always wanted to ask you to do now, I may never get around to it again. Okay?"

She swallowed. "Okay?" It came out as a question because nothing in her life could have prepared her for the way he made her feel.

He grinned. "It won't hurt, I promise."

She laughed nervously. A teenager if ever she'd been one. "I know. It's just...I've never seen you...like this."

He shrugged. "I'm never like this. Sober, I don't know how. Drunk, I don't usually know how either. Tonight's different. You make it different. You make me want to be different. You make it special."

A startled glow went through Janina. She blushed for the first time in what felt like forever. Maybe it was. "I— I don't know what to say. That's good. Thank you. Both of them. You—I—"

The oh-so-gentle tip of Russ's forefinger touched her mouth quiet. "Dance with me?"

"Yes."

The one word was like magic. Just that quickly the outside fell away, she was in his arms and the music and Russ's heartbeat were the only things she heard, felt, knew. "When a Man Loves a Woman," she thought the song was, but couldn't be sure because the rhythm of her heart keeping time with Russ's was what she moved to, the feel of his body against hers was all the cue she needed. His hand drifted upward through her hair, his head bent to hers, his tall, muscular body stooped low to accommodate her shorter height and much softer curves. "Perfect" was the only word that came to mind when any word did, and even that single word was a wisp of smoke in the fog of the moment.

"Janie." His breath was warm, moist against her neck, his whisper disbelieving in her ear.

"I'm here, Russ." Heedless of the protests in her right wrist and both hands, she reached her arms around him as far as they would go. To hold him, hold on to him. To make sure he was really there, too. "Neither one of us is dreaming. We're both really here. Together."

She felt him smile into her neck and fold her tighter into his embrace. "Good. My dreams are vivid, but I usually only imagine I can feel you, touch you, taste you, smell you." He shifted his lower body uncomfortably and groaned.

She gasped and laughed softly when the same charge that beat through him coiled hard through her, pinching her breasts and spinning wildly, almost violently into her belly. Want, need, more, infinitely more—she'd never felt this before. And whatever it was, he made her feel it by just saying a few words.

"It's okay, Russ. Me, too. My imagination is pretty vivid, too."

He lifted his head slightly. "You're hurt, it's not okay."

She kissed a spot as near the center of his chest as she could reach, nuzzled his jaw, brushed her cheek across his. "It is, trust me. I'm not that hurt. Really. Some bruises, a couple stitches, a mild sprain. Nothing to prevent us from what we both want. Together. Now let me take you home, okay? So I don't have to worry about you."

Hesitation was plain. "Janie, I don't... I can't—"

He stopped. He might be drunk, but he had self-imposed

rules that wouldn't be broken easily. Janina planned to break them all if she could.

"You can't drive yourself, Russ," Janina reminded him. "Jonah said you needed somewhere to spend the night. It was my long weekend even before Buddy tripped me, so I'm not working tomorrow."

"Janie—" Again he said her name and stopped.

And capitulated.

"All right," he agreed. Then his lips twitched and he offered her a rueful grin. "Just don't say I didn't warn you, all right?"

"'Bout what?" Janina, reaching for her purse, looked back at him.

Russ picked up the remains of her beer, raised the mug to her in what was halfway between a salute and a silent apology, drained it and shrugged. "The drunk and relaxed man you take home with you tonight will not be the sober, somewhat anal man you wake up with in the morning."

Janina laughed outright at him. "Russ, I know that man, too. I've seen him almost every day for thirteen years and I've wanted to take that man home with me longer than I've wanted the man I'm with tonight, so I don't see the problem."

"You might tomorrow," Russ muttered darkly.

Janina slid her arms around his waist. "Tomorrow, if I put my arms around you, will you tell me to stop?"

The slow, sideways smile tilted Russ's mouth. "Prob'ly not."

"Then shut up about tomorrow and let me drive you home."

"Because tomorrow I'll be too inhibited to open my mouth and say anything to you," Russ finished belatedly, deliberately baiting her, and ducked away laughing when Janina swung at him.

"You—"

Grinning the charming, devilish Levoie grin that Janina associated with his brothers but couldn't remember ever seeing on him, he offered her a broad, two-handed, supremely innocent shrug. "What can I say? I was an Eagle Scout. Honesty is bred in the bone."

"That sounds like something your brother Guy would say," Janina returned dryly.

"Where d'you think he got it from?"

She found herself laughing up at him, astonished herself by teasing him. "Not you."

Russ draped an arm around her shoulders. A natural move from a man who never made this kind of move naturally. "Yeah, me."

Janina found herself sliding easily beneath his arm, fitting close against his side where she'd been made to fit, born to belong.

She wanted to touch him, to have as much of him as she could in the here and now, but she couldn't comfortably fit an arm around him so she settled for pulling his hand down where she could hold on to it, could at least keep her left hand in his.

Could feel every bit of warmth, every pulse in his fingers in the way his fingertips tickled her palm, traced the inside of her wrist, seduced and tempted and... She closed her eyes and her stomach tightened, body vibrated, became heavy, turned to liquid.

And suddenly her panties, that sexy, almost nonexistent scrap of a silk thong she'd put on in hopes of finding him, of being with him, was...wet. *She* was wet.

For want of him.

From simply imagining him.

"You sure?" She sounded breathless, and was.

The look he sent her from those deeper-than-midnight, clearer-than-the-full-moon, more-powerful-than-any-tide eyes of his when he said, "I'm sure," made Janina lose her grip on his hand, drop her own to his waist and tip her head up to his.

Her eyes widened when his released fingers quite casually, naturally, instinctively grazed her nipple, brushed her breast, then closed over it to gently squeeze.

And her body burned with awareness, with desire, with excitement…with need. And with the sudden, absolute and potentially embarrassing recognition of where they were and the fact that she wanted complete, utter and immediate *privacy*. Where was not a factor, so long as it was right now, at once, instantly and without delay.

"Russ?" Urgent, a plea.

He offered her a slow smile. His fingers played with her breast, found her nipple once again. She lifted into the pleasure of his touch, pressed into it, and her breathing grew ever more shallow. They were in public and she couldn't make herself—and didn't want to—step away. But heaven help her if she wasn't alone with him soon…

"We have to get out of here." The effort it took to manage seven short syllables was amazing.

Without taking his eyes off her face or his left hand off her breast, Russ pushed open the Bloated Boar's outer door.

"We're outta here," he promised.

"Oh." Stunned, Janina drew a half breath and swallowed the taste of dawn. She'd been so mesmerized she hadn't even realized they'd been moving. "Good."

Russ's laugh was deep, his voice gravelly with need. "Take me home, Janie."

Urgency became a frantic blast of something beyond want, beyond desire, beyond simple need or even passion, became quite suddenly a critical piece of her existence, a fundamental element of survival, of life. Her life, his life, *their* life. One life combined. One life only.

"Yes." Her voice shook, her heart grew three, four, ten sizes—grew big enough to hold a man who stood six foot four-plus inches in a barefoot slouch, but who never slouched. Her knees were jelly. She fumbled for her keys. "Yes, Russ. I will. I am."

"Good." He folded to nuzzle the side of her face, her ear. "The night's short, dawn's shorter and there's a lot I want to do with you before I wake up and turn into a pumpkin again, ya know?"

Janina turned her face into his mouth and kissed him furiously, pouring all of herself into it. "It took me a long time to get up the gumption to do it, but I found you now, Russ Levoie, and I'm not letting you back off. So consider this fair warning. You're making me believe in magic right now and I want it and everything you've got to give that goes with it. So you go shy and tongue-tied on me tomorrow, it won't matter 'cuz I know who you are underneath and I know you want to be with me. So I won't let who you seem to be intimidate me. You got that?"

Dazed and bemused, Russ ran his tongue around his mouth to taste the kiss she'd left there, then touched the tip of his finger to the stitches in her upper lip. "If we kiss again, will that hurt?"

"It'll hurt more if we don't," Janina whispered, sliding her arms, sprained wrist and all, around his neck.

"Good," he muttered, "because you taste incredible. I've never tasted anything like you, and I really have to kiss you again." Then he caught her around the waist, lifted her high against his chest and did just that.

His kiss was careful, mindful of her bruises and almost, Janina realized somewhat fuzzily, out of practice.

Then she stopped realizing anything at all, stopped being able to think, stopped *being* and simply became absorbed in and by the kiss.

Thrilled to it.

The instant held beauty, power and enchantment, oneness and an absolute absence of alone. Breath shared became needed oxygen, air and life, a place beyond passion and pleasure, an existence within heart and soul, pure, complete, without boundaries.

It was a place Janina had never before been.

Arriving there left her breathless.

It made her afraid.

And she never wanted to come back from it.

"Janie." Russ broke the kiss, raised his head and gave her what she'd craved since she'd been a starry-eyed but not-so-innocent sixteen-year-old schoolgirl ready to worship and adore her tall, dark and hunky hero. "I-40's right out there, it's not five hours to Vegas. Four hours with a cop in the car, maybe less." He groaned when she wrapped her arms more securely around him and her belly rubbed provocatively but unintentionally against his. His muscles went taut, his breathing went harsh and ragged, his arms contracted around her. "Definitely less. Has to be less. We could go, find a chapel, not an Elvis one, though, and—"

"Yes," Janina interrupted, wild and giddy from the magic, the enchantment of the moment, the pure unadulterated impossibility that made her sure she should pinch herself to see if she was awake. She had to be dreaming because this was what she'd wanted since the moment she'd picked up her mother's shotgun and skulked after him without him knowing it to make sure he'd be safe until help arrived the night Maddie Thorn had shot her father and killed her brother in self-defense and Russ had gone to rescue Maddie, the always-victim, again.

But Maddie wasn't here and Russ was thinking of her, Janina, and only of her. Of her, *Janie*. And that was what made Janina look deep into his midnight eyes, touch her nose to his and know she wasn't dreaming. That's what made her repeat, "Yes," breathlessly, with her heart in her throat, and then again, shouting, joyous, loud, clear and strong, "Yes, yes, yes!"

Then, laughing and oblivious to her bruises, to the consequences of dreaming without a thought to what came after you woke up—without a nod to anything but the unbelievable reality of having achieved your heart's desire— she wriggled out of his arms, grabbed his hand and made a beeline across the Bloated Boar's parking lot to her car.

And no, she didn't listen to that far-off whisper, that superstitious mother-warning fading in the desert dawn: *Be careful what you wish for because you just might get it if you don't watch out.*

By 6:30 a.m., they'd stopped for gas on the other side of Seligman, and Janina was feeling more than wild, beyond anxious, outside of nervous. Russ was no longer quite drunk, but he showed no sign of swaying from the path they'd set out on.

His hand resting on her thigh while she drove had

played havoc with her concentration, her pulse and her blood pressure. The hand, the fingertips on her thigh had roamed up and down the inside of her leg, just high enough under her short dress to sketch ticklish, teasing circles that claimed her attention and made her catch her breath before stroking back down to the inside of her knee and letting her almost—almost!—relax.

Then he'd settled his arm around her shoulder, slipped his hand along her collarbone, over her throat, caressed the delicate skin there and slipped his fingers inside the deep neckline of her scooped-neck sundress to draw patterns along the top of her breasts, never quite touching where it ached.

And all the while he leaned close to her ear and told her to mind her driving, to watch the road, to concentrate on the horizon and not on what he was doing to her….

Thank God there'd been little traffic to speak of.

Even though she'd done as he'd instructed and kept as much of her mind as possible on the road, if he touched her again, she'd explode, she was sure. Because by telling her to concentrate on something else, he'd heightened the suspense, sensitized her awareness of him at the same time that he kept her focus elsewhere, sharpened the surprise behind what he did to her, and intensified the sheer eroticism and anticipation of what he *didn't* do to her.

She was beyond needy, beyond ready, beyond…fevered. Her body wept to hold him, cried for his touch, begged— no, *pleaded*—to take him in. Literally ached to do so.

She had to do something about that. *Had* to. For her sake, his sake and the safety of any other driver on the road, she had to find some quiet little private nook and do something to relieve that ache.

Soon.

Russ glanced up at her from under the hood of her car and his hot gaze lingered on her mouth, her breasts, her legs, her thighs—the places he'd touched and the places he hadn't quite—and Janina's breath tripped, heart hammered. She felt the heat everywhere his gaze touched, as though he made physical contact.

She had to have more than his teasing.

Quickly.

The corner of his mouth tipped up. He knew, damn him. And then she didn't care what he knew. Because he gently closed the hood, leaned on it to make sure it snapped tight and moved toward her. And backed her into the side of the car, between the open driver's door and the back door he also opened to keep them out of the way of prying eyes.

Belly to belly, loin to loin, they rocked together lightly. Frustrated, tormented, tempted; his breath on her neck was ragged, and then his mouth closed on her pulse, his hands molded her rump, hoisted her against his erection and he ground himself against her. She whimpered softly and her body quickened instantly. She arched her throat then hooked an ankle around his calf both to balance herself and to give him better access to the center of her need.

His need.

Her entire body sang, from her belly outward, inward, hot and hotter, seeking flame to flame…when Russ abruptly gasped and raised his head. Untangled himself and thrust her away.

Separated himself from her, breathing hard.

"No," he said emphatically—and more to himself than her, "Not yet. I promised. Not yet."

Dazed, needy, frustrated and more than a little bewildered, Janina could only blink at him, reaching to draw him back. It didn't matter where they were, he couldn't leave her—*them*—now. He couldn't.

"What? Russ, *please*. I need to finish this. We need to—"

He looked at her, stunned, and ran a hand over the side of his face, trying to collect himself. "I can't, Janie, we can't. Not yet. I promised myself I wouldn't do that to you. Not yet. Not *here*."

"Why, Russ, why? Please. You don't know where you're leavin' me hangin'. I need you."

His snort of laughter was short and harsh. "Trust me, you don't know what need is till you're standin' in my skin. If I can't have you soon…" He shut his eyes and swallowed.

She'd dated, been married, and there'd been other guys. A few at least. It didn't matter. When he'd met Janina she'd been too young and too innocent, and he'd never quite been able to get over thinking of her that way.

He'd known that no one else would satisfy, no other woman would do since very shortly after he'd first seen her. Known it so hard that he'd been Celibacy R Russ because he didn't want anyone but her.

But he also understood that most people wouldn't understand things the way he did. They wouldn't believe that he, a man—and not a particularly tame one at that—could live his life in so-called innocence—or at least without the trappings of sex—while the woman he craved seemed to live hers on the other side of it, because marrying Buddy certainly hadn't kept Janina *innocent*. But he didn't see it that way.

Because the one thing he knew after a lifetime of living, of friendship with Maddie, of growing up Indian on the reservation in Supai long before he'd become a Winslow cop, of watching people and being a cop was, that *innocence* was not a by-product of virginity the way the romance novels Mabel was always reading suggested. Janina had been married to a bully and dated and probably had sex, but compared to him...innocent of the world's evils didn't begin to cover it.

He knew in his heart which of them was innocent and which of them had never been. And sex and virginity had nothin' to do with it.

Wherever she'd been, whatever she'd done, Janina had managed to come through it with hope, faith and self-possession intact. For whatever reason, he'd been born wearing the raw material of an adult: uncertainty, cynicism, irony, a sense of desperation and fear. And he knew gut deep to the soles of his feet that she would be better for him than he could ever possibly be for her, and that if she ever figured that out...

She couldn't be allowed to ever figure that out.

He shut his eyes, rested his forehead on hers, put an infinitesimal distance between the length of their bodies with great care and cupped her face between his palms. "Just leave it at I promised myself I wouldn't do that to you. Wouldn't use you. Wouldn't be anybody else you might...know. That for us—*between* us—it'd be different than...anybody else. Any other guy and you. That we'd be married first. Do you see?"

"No." She couldn't understand anything yet. Her body was still too focused on what *it* wanted and needed from him. She caught his hand, held it, grounded herself. Her body was still on high alert, strung taut, but her immediate concentration was on him. "No, I don't quite see. No."

He swallowed and looked down at their joined hands then turned his gaze to the desert for several long moments before bringing it back to her face. The sober man was taking over and the Russ who'd seduced her at the Bloated Boar fought him valiantly, warred to communicate with her still.

And then he did.

"I promised myself a long time ago to wait to bed my woman until after our wedding," he said simply. "We're getting real close to me breaking that promise and I don't want to, not with you. You've been hurt enough. You've had enough promises made to you and broken. I don't want something to happen to get in the way of the wedding even for a minute, so…" He hesitated. "I want you badly. I also very much want to marry you. But I don't have a lot of control left on the *want you* part. So if we could just get in the damn car and break the speed limit to Vegas I'd appreciate it."

Chapter 4

Puzzled, Janina stared up at her fiancé, trying to sort out the subtleties of what he hadn't said.

And then she did.

Stunned, dumbfounded, she swallowed. Hard. *Waited*, had he said? As in *waited*? As in there was *nobody* before her? Not even…

Maddie?

With all that history, all that time, all that everything?

She looked up at him for confirmation. He shrugged.

"Why?" Not, perhaps, the most sensitive thing she might have said, but her mouth wasn't taking orders from her brain at the moment. "How?"

He snorted. Grinned. "Opportunity. Desire. Your lack of availability at the…ah…fitting moments. My lack of verbal…um…eptitude in the dating game. Never got around to it I guess."

"That's not a word." Obviously she was in shock and couldn't be held accountable for what she said.

He canted her an odd glance. She deserved it. "What's not?"

"Eptitude."

Another snort. "Sue me. It fits."

"But, Russ, what about Maddie?"

"Who?" The uncharacteristic looseness, the remaining uninhibitedness brought about by his beer consumption faded. "What?"

"Everybody said…they knew…they *thought*—" She floundered, lost in repeating gossip from the trial.

Thirteen-year-old gossip that had followed him from the moment he'd started defending Madelyn Thorn from an overabundance of small-town speculation. Because he'd known Maddie since long before either of them came to Winslow.

He went rigid beneath her hands. "Everybody knew nothin'," he said harshly. "Everybody *knows* nothin'. Not about Maddie, not about me. What they think or thought's got nothin' to do with anything."

She was trembling under his hands, the wide brown eyes looking up at him, the same brave but frightened ones that had peeked out at him over her mother's shoulder, her body half hidden behind her mother's skinny, unprotective frame. Oh God, he'd never been able to get past that picture of her, of the girl who'd taken down a shotgun and followed him to make sure he didn't get hurt when he went into a lethal situation alone.

Of the woman who didn't know he knew what she'd done for him. And therefore by default for Maddie.

"Ah, screw it."

"Russ, don't. Wait—"

Shaken, sobered—and sobered up—he released Janina and slammed shut the wagon's rear door, shoved himself away from everything he wanted-needed-craved, and turned to long-leg-it to the highway's edge. Emptiness crossed by electric lines and black ground spotted by straggles of vegetation and lumps of sandstone against a spectacular rising-sun backdrop—Arizona at its finest—spread out before him. He saw it and didn't.

"Russ!"

He heard but ignored her.

"Russ, damn it."

She was angry, but still he didn't turn. There'd been reasons beyond simple choice he'd kept body, soul and self to self where women—and Winslow's women in particular— were concerned since he'd taken Maddie's father down.

Since the publicity from the trial had raked him and his lifetime connections to Maddie over, dissected him and them, and changed him.

There was more that he'd protected Janina from than him simply thinking she was too innocent for him.

More that he'd forgotten in his annual drunks with his brothers than he realized.

When he'd burst into the Thorns' trailer that night to find Maddie disfigured, torn up and bleeding to death, he'd also found her holding the bloody weapon that had been used to shoot her brother over—and over. Cherry on the job that he was, he hadn't thought about gunshot residue or anything else that might clear her—he'd thought only about the horror in front of him, and he'd taken the weapon from Maddie, cleaned her fingerprints off it and thrown it into Lake Havasu on his next trip home to the difficult-to-reach Havasupai reservation he'd grown up on. He and Maddie had never talked about what had really happened, because she couldn't remember, so he simply covered up what he assumed happened at her hand. She'd suffered enough—nothing could be proved....

But the suspicion he'd brought on himself by standing by her, being her friend, had been considerable. She'd been used, abused and pimped out by a pedophile since she was twelve and Russ hadn't known, but the looks he'd gotten when the defense got him on the stand and asked him about Maddie, about knowing her in high school, about the things she'd done for his football, basketball and baseball teammates, and that they insinuated she'd done for him when she hadn't because he wouldn't let her, had been enough to label him for life.

The term *conflict of interest* had been flung about when his captain found out about Russ's past relationship with Maddie. *Cover-up* was what the newspapers wondered when it couldn't be proved definitively one way or another whether or not Maddie had killed her brother that night in self-defense, or someone else had done it.

Small towns had long memories for gossip and innuendo and Winslow was no different than most. The couple of times he'd gotten his verbs together in coherent order and thought about dating respectable town women way back when, he'd been discouraged from it in no uncertain terms by "right-thinking" moneyed types like Buddy Carmichael's father, who'd...

No. He didn't like remembering what he'd worked hard to put aside. He didn't want Janina thinking what others thought—used to think—about him, ever. He didn't give a flying fig in hell about anyone else and never had, but Janina...

Was standing in front of him. Slapping his chest with the edge of her fist—she winced—and kicking him once in the shin with the side of her foot for good measure to get his attention. He looked down at her, bemused.

"Hey," she said, almost loudly enough to wake the dead. "You got a problem I oughta know about, maybe you should tell me before we get to Vegas."

Russ frowned and canted a brow, remained silent. He was good at silent. Best to stick with his strengths in unfamiliar situations.

Janina sighed. He'd startled her with his admission and she didn't do surprise or silence well. Both were designed to elicit comments that could leave her with her foot in her mouth. This time she had a feeling she'd stuck them both there.

"So." She tapped a foot, wondering where he wanted to be. To go. Trying to decide where she should be. Because reckless or not, the road to Vegas with Russ Levoie still looked like the most awesome, and the most right, ride to her. "I take it you've suddenly sobered up and gone taciturn on me again?"

Russ tried not to smile. Tried to maintain a straight face and not to acknowledge the question at all. If you wanted to call failing at both by giving in to lip tugs and twitches some kind of success, he almost succeeded.

"Yeah." Janina gave him wry face. "That's what I thought." She considered the space between them for a moment, opened her vista to take in the light khaki tan of his neatly pressed short-sleeved shirt, the triangle of white T-shirt showing where he'd left his collar buttons open, the healthy expanse of native bronze skin above where she wanted to place her open mouth, leave her unmistakable "do not poach" brand....

She shut her eyes on a half smile, half grimace, shook her head at the ground. Looked up at Russ. Who waited. "You ever see yourself in the mirror?"

"I don't want anyone else, Janie," he said simply. "I never have."

"But—"

He gave his head a negative tip. "You tie up my tongue. I can't think straight around you. All that old stuff…you shouldn't be part of it. We can go back."

She stared at him astonished—and miffed. Which meant her tongue got away from her again. "The hell we are!"

His grin was startled and genuine this time.

She took it as an invitation to let her tongue get away from her some more, and poked him in the chest, backing him toward the car. "We're not goin' back, mister. We're goin' forward."

His grin widened. He nodded. "Forward."

"To Vegas," she affirmed, just in case he had any doubts about what *forward* meant. She pushed him backward another few steps. "Go west, young man."

"West," he said, casting a glance over his shoulder in the direction she was herding him that was certainly not west. "Toward Vegas?"

"Don't be so literal," Janina ordered, catching the amusement. "You know what I mean."

"Get in car, go west, through Vegas." Russ's eyes gleamed with unholy light.

"*Stop* Vegas," Janina said. Patiently. She was, perhaps, working with an idiot, aka a man, albeit one she liked a lot, after all.

"Ah." He fetched up against the driver's door of her wagon. "*Stop* Vegas." He mimicked her inflection perfectly. "Got it."

She planted herself in front of him. "You were a handful when you were a child, weren't you."

His teeth showed when he grinned. "Me?"

She cleared her throat of a snort. "Yeah. And no girl's ever told you they wanted to lie down because when the gene pool spit you out, you got all the breaks."

He shrugged. Turned and backed her against the car. Did the tall-man slouch to surround her, bringing his mouth within range of her ear. "Told you. Never wanted easy. I want you."

Which could mean any of a variety of things, but when he nuzzled her lips apart and kissed her as though she was the answer to a quandary he'd long been seeking the solution for, Janina forgot to wonder what he meant.

The giddiness started in her toes. Laughter gurgled through her and the smile that spread after it was brilliant, joyous. Her heart sang. Her soul soared. Her palms started to sweat.

Impossible as it seemed, she believed him. He was all hers.

And he wanted her badly.

At once.

As soon as they were married.

She wanted him now. But she'd settle for the minute they were married.

Which meant...

She pushed out from underneath him, heart pumping crazily, breathing hard. "I take it you're sober enough to drive?"

His smile was slow and muzzy, sleepy, desiring of darkness and the back seat instead of the front. "Yeah."

"Good." She slipped through the driver's door and slid across the seat only as far as she had to in order to give him room to drive. "Then do it."

Russ ducked into the car, glanced at where she was sitting—essentially half in his seat and pressed tight to his thigh with her arms ready to wrap around his neck—and his smile widened. "Better buckle up," he advised, "because until we get to Vegas, I'm peggin' this baby out."

The marriage license bureau was just open by the time they reached it.

Impatient, nervous and excited, eyes on Russ searching for signs of doubt the entire time, Janina went through the formalities, showed her driver's license and signed at the X as required. Her sprained wrist was nearly as shaky as her breath.

Russ's, on the other hand, was as firm and bold as the grin he tipped her and the prolonged kiss he planted on her mouth before picking up the pen.

Janina sighed and calmed at once, sank into the rock-solid strength of him while he swiftly and surely assigned his life to hers. Something significant had happened between them at that gas station this side of Seligman. She couldn't name it, but she recognized "it" as an *event* and clung to it along with Russ.

Then they took their license, paid at the cashier and headed for the Strip.

The argument started almost as soon as they left the marriage license bureau.

Russ was in favor of raiding the nearest cash machine, then taking enough time to book a chapel for a little later in the morning or early in the afternoon while they spent a few hours preparing to do their wedding up right.

Janina objected instantly. Now that they'd arrived she wanted to get the wedding over with so there'd be no chance of anything getting in their way. She remained absolutely adamant on that score, until Russ pulled her close, linked the fingers of both his hands oh so carefully through hers, dropped a most fiancé-like kiss on her nose and suggested in a hot whisper that shivered through her nape hairs and fuzzed heady suggestions down her spine that he planned to have only one wedding in his life and only one wife, *her,* and consequently he didn't want her to regret anything…like not wearing white, or not getting her one opportunity to see him in a rented tux, or having a double-ring ceremony, or…

Her mouth began to curve reluctantly upward at one corner at *shopping for her wedding dress…*

Her smile went shy with delight and widened.

…*picking out wedding rings, one of which he intended to wear for the rest of his life…*

Her smile trembled, her eyes burned and blurred with tears, and she capitulated.

Just like that.

Well, just like that after she turned her head to find his mouth on a searing kiss that was as deep as the ocean and bright as the moon, hot as the sun and breathless as the wind, and that made more promises than a false lover ever dreamed of, because neither the kiss nor Janina had any intention of playing Russ false.

Ever.

"Platinum," Russ said firmly when Janina dithered over the fourth tray of wedding rings, unable to decide. "Platinum is the purest and the best, that's what we want."

Janina eyed him worriedly. "It's too expensive. We don't need to start out this way, really."

A trace of something Janina recognized as typical Levoie amusement twitched the corner of Russ's mouth and settled in his eyes. He swallowed it valiantly. "Trust me. Do you like the ring?"

Janina hesitated. Trust him? Oh Lord, she wanted to, she did. Heart, soul, body, mind, instinct and intuition. All of her wanted to trust all of him. And the ring…the ring was…

Beautiful. Exactly what she'd choose for him—*them*—if her brain would disengage and she didn't have to think.

"Yes," she said quickly, before she could change her mind again. "Platinum. It's wonderful. I like the ring."

Russ grinned. "Good." He nodded at the jeweler, who pulled the rings in question and put the other trays away. "Now." Russ rested his hands on Janina's shoulders. "Why don't you go find your dress so I don't see it before the wedding. I'll finish up here, pick up my tux and meet you back here in…"

"An hour and a half," Janina supplied then planted a laughing kiss on Russ's mouth. She might feel dithery, but no way did he get to dictate it all.

"An hour and a half," he agreed, smiling. "Or less." He looked down at her and his eyes darkened and grew hot, and everything inside Janina liquefied. "I think I'll book a room near the chapel," he muttered hoarsely.

Unwilling to trust her voice, Janina merely nodded. Then because she couldn't seem to stop herself, she pressed her body the length of his, flattened her right palm along the nape of his neck, ignoring the twinges in her wrist as she did so, and lifted her face to his.

His parted lips barely touched hers before he set her away from him with a molten, "God, Janie, don't tempt me, not here. I don't know if I could stop."

Dazed, Janina blinked, half smiled, blushed when she realized how far she'd unintentionally teased and tormented him. Then the woman in her wakened and brazenly decided she had nothing to be embarrassed for. So on a heated, "See you soon, babe," she brushed an alluringly seductive hand across his mouth and down his chest, turned and sashayed provocatively away, leaving Russ staring after her slack-jawed, heavy-loined and damn uncertain of his own name.

She hadn't anticipated finding the perfect dress at the perfect price in the perfect amount of time, but she did all three and despite being hampered by her injuries when she wanted to try things on.

The dress was a two-piece affair, ivory and slim with a sleeveless, deep-cut bodice of lace and some stretchy-but-gorgeous fabric Janina couldn't identify offset by a faux closure of pearl buttons behind which lay the real hook-and-eye closure. Her skin heated when she imagined Russ fumbling to open the bodice and she immediately promised herself matching ivory lingerie, too.

And she'd worry about getting herself into the hooks and eyes once she got to the chapel later.

The skirt matched the bodice exactly, though without the stretch. When the two pieces were put together, they looked for all the world as though she wore only one piece.

A rack of hand-painted, beaded shawls caught her eye and she allowed herself to splurge on one bit of color to go with her dress, before finding a small beaded purse that she was quite sure she didn't need then turning her attention to shoes. They were a bit more difficult to find as her feet were narrow and she hated heels, but she finally reconciled herself to the lowest pair of heels she could find—two inches—and decided it was time to make the decision about what to wear on her head: veil, no veil, hat, flowers.

When she found the sun hat with its long filmy ivory trailer about the crown and its bunch of Arizona wildflowers tucked into the band, she didn't look further.

Russ had been waiting nearly an hour by the time Janina returned with her purchases.

The time without her had sobered him—again—plenty, nearly returning him to his usual, reserved and downright reticent self, but the sight of her glowing face and her arms loaded down with purchases brought him to his feet with a grin. When she pressed into him immediately upon reaching him and leaned into him for a kiss, the grin widened and softened to something far deeper.

"Hi." He nuzzled her ear. "Welcome back. I was about to send out search parties."

"Hmm." Her murmur was unrepentant. "I promise I'll be worth the wait."

"I know that." Russ's whisper was hot. "I just don't want to lose you before you find out whether or not *I* am."

Then before Janina's body could recover from that promise, he relieved her of her bags and caught her elbow to steer her toward the car.

It was time to head for the chapel.

With her heavily lashed mahogany eyes, the creamy olive skin courtesy of her Spanish heritage, and rarely tamed halo of brown-black hair, Russ had always found Janina beautiful. But the sight of her dressed to wed him rocked him on some visceral level, stole his breath and left

him more speechless than usual. She'd grown into the
promise her features had presented at sixteen, taken on
character that went far beyond simple prettiness. Soft
teenage potential had grown into the phenomenal power
that was woman: exquisite, electric, peerless.

Russ swallowed. No longer merely beautiful, she was,
simply put, stunning. He couldn't take his eyes off her.

Unused to and unsteady on the two-inch heels, she
walked toward him carefully, unconsciously graceful, her
body swaying, floating forward in time to some inner
music. Her color was high and her entire being seemed to
glow. Her eyes were alight with anticipation and fire,
steady on Russ's as she drew opposite him before the minister. The only evidence of nerves was the dart of her
tongue along her stitched lip and one corner of her mouth,
the faint swallow that drew Russ's attention to her throat
and down to the medieval cross done in silver with green
Baltic amber stones that nestled just above her breasts.

The sight calmed him. Metal and stone always did. It
was one of her favorite pieces of jewelry, he knew; she wore
it often. She'd purchased it at a Renaissance fair outside of
Santa Fe a couple of years ago. He knew, because the piece
was one of his. He doubted she knew he'd designed and
smithed it, but it didn't matter. He'd designed and made the
wedding ring after seeing how often she wore the cross.

He touched it now with an index finger, tipped a smile
at Janina, folded her hands gently into his and nodded at
the minister.

The "you may now kiss the bride" part was nearly a di-
saster, at least as far as the minister's embarrassment level
was concerned.

The trouble started when Russ fumbled out the rings—including the one he'd made for her and still had in his pocket after Maddie showed up—and Janina had to put his on his middle finger because it was too big for his ring finger. Russ blinked at her, clearly taken aback by his mistake. He recovered quickly, and told her they could either return the ring and exchange it or get it sized, not to worry. Then he took her hand to slip her ring onto her finger.

Janina took one look at the ring he'd designed and brought with him from home, misunderstood what was happening, thought he'd bought it when he'd shipped her off to find her dress, grabbed her hand back and opened her mouth on a furious protest to tell him that of all the things they couldn't afford for him to have done, this was chief among them.

He hushed her with two fingers to her mouth, reclaimed her left hand firmly and told her in the fewest possible words as he deliberately fitted the ring to her finger that he hadn't *bought* the ring, he'd made it for her. That's why he'd suggested she choose a platinum band for him. She stared at him openmouthed for a moment, then burst into tears and wept happily for the remainder of the ceremony.

Which meant that by the time they got to the "you may kiss the bride" statement, things were already a bit out of hand and, given permission, Janina simply launched herself bodily into Russ's arms, hooked her elbows around his neck and kissed him as though her life depended on it, and showed no evidence of stopping in the near future.

Russ didn't seem keen on the idea of letting her go soon, either. Still, he retained enough presence of mind so that when the minister cleared her throat loudly for the third or fourth time and suggested that they carry on *in a room,* he came up for air, swung Janina into his arms and got them both out of the chapel as quickly as his long legs could carry them.

Chapter 5

The hotel-room door bounced hard open against its stop then held wide when Russ and Janina slammed into it together, breathing hard. Janina was already shimmying her skirt up her hips and had reached for Russ's fly by the time he kicked the door closed behind them.

"Janie, *Janie!*" Laughter was harsh, guttural, strained. "Slow down, please. I'm too close to gone. Slow down or I guarantee things'll be over before they start."

"As long as you're inside me when it happens I don't care." The tension, the need in Janina's voice was as raw as Russ's, if not more so.

Russ tried to hold her still. "I do. I care. I've dreamed about this too long. I want it good for you, for both of us. Premature is *not* the way this is going to happen."

Janina stilled for an instant then drew a long shuddery breath. She reached up and traced her green-taped, stitched-up fingers along her new husband's jaw. "How many times have I heard you or one of your brothers say, 'Trust me'?" she asked.

Russ simply watched her. *Trust me* was what he and his brothers said when there was nothing else to say, when they didn't know if they were coming out of a situation or not, and sometimes when they didn't trust themselves in a plan. They let someone else do the trusting, have the faith, bring them through when they weren't sure they could do it themselves. He was pretty sure that wasn't where Janina was going with her question.

Maybe.

The very corner of one side of her mouth curved. She nodded and began to tug him deeper into the room, toward the king-size bed that was its focal point. "You guys say it a lot, you especially. I've always trusted you, Russ, and every time you say it, I know it's true. It's a Levoie saying, right?"

He flicked a glance at the bed, brought his gaze back to her and dipped his chin once—cautiously.

Her smile widened in anticipation, invitation. Her breath moved visibly faster in her lungs, causing her breasts to swell provocatively above the low-cut, heart-shaped bodice of her wedding ensemble. Her eyes were liquid, dark…a summons Russ could not ignore.

"I'm a Levoie now, too," she said hotly, and pushed him onto his back on the bed. "Trust me." She crawled onto the bed over him. "I need you badly *now,* but nothing's going to happen before it's time."

For a moment Russ could only stare at her, mesmerized. Then the unholy grin Janina had only seen twice before on him spread across his features and put the devil in his eyes.

"Trust you," he said. Not a question. Laughter and something else filled his voice.

"Trust me," she repeated, moving farther up him.

"Because you're a Levoie now."

"That's right." Why did she suddenly have the feeling she was getting in over her head in this conversation?

No time to think about that now. Russ caught her legs and slid his palms up her thighs to her hips.

"I trust you," he said thickly. "Panties off."

"Not wearing panties." Janina swung astride him and quickly freed him from the confines of his trousers and shorts.

"Good—aaah…" Russ's groan was primal and harsh when she rubbed against him, naked sex to naked sex, for the first time. His member thickened and strained upward, his lower body bucked. "You're so wet."

"I told you I was ready." Janina's laughter was both smug and husky. She rose on her knees, undulated her hips and stroked him again with her body. Reached between them to trace the tip of him with her uninjured ring finger. Again he thrust upward and expanded, and a few latent drops beaded beneath her finger. She smiled a deeply feminine smile and stroked them down his length, circled as much of his broadness as she could. "You're ready, too."

Russ's fingers curled hard on her thighs. Sweat beaded his forehead. "I thought we'd already established that." His laughter was tight, painful.

Hers was breathless, giddy. She shifted forward, her grip on him firm. "A woman likes evidence." She teased him lightly with her entrance.

In a rush, Russ turned the tables on her, hooked his hands around her hips and ended the play. "Put me inside you," he commanded. "Now."

Janina's eyes widened, her breath caught. Then, belly already tightening, heat already beginning to coil and flare, she sank onto him.

Leaned forward onto her hands to take him deeper, faster—and winced.

Russ caught her shoulders and half rose to sitting, mood forgotten. "Janie, are you all right? I should have my head examined. This can wait. You need—"

Janina groaned and shut him up with a kiss that was highly explicit, mostly tongue, and exceedingly deep. "I need you," she said against his mouth. "Hard, inside me, now. And if you pull out, I will scream with frustration. But I can't ride you easily the way I want to at the moment, so if you'd put me on my back and do the honors?"

He wanted to be convinced, but all those years of needing to make sure no one hurt her, and especially not him, got in the way. He hesitated. "Janie…"

She knew, somehow understood his hesitation. She didn't know how she knew, especially now, but she did. Perhaps because it was Russ and that was the only thing her intuition needed to cobble it all together.

She framed his face between her injuries—between the green-and-blue wraps that he hadn't even noticed when she'd stood before him and said "I do," because he was the kind of man who'd seen only *her* in that moment—and kissed him again, this time with passion and something purer, deeper than mere carnality.

"It was twinges in my wrist, Russ, that's all. Nothing life-threatening. Painful but not deadly, isn't that what you say? Not…interrupting. A matter of changing position so my wrist doesn't hurt, not stopping altogether. Okay?"

Russ said nothing, only studied her face for what

seemed eternity, canting his head from one side to the other and drinking Janina in visually and unreadably. When he'd seen whatever he'd been looking for, he shifted her a bit, raised his knees behind her back and began to rock. His fingers went to work on her bodice.

"If we're going to take our time, we're wearing too many clothes," was all he said.

Janina gasped and *Mmm*'d, and swayed into the rhythm he set, wrapping her stockings-and-garter-clad legs around his hips and lifting her chest to his fingers as he undid hooks and eyes.

"I'm not letting you out of *me* just so you can get undressed."

Russ stopped opening her bodice, leaving her breasts bound, and dipped his head to lick the corner of her mouth, gently tracing the curve of her lips over to her stitches with his tongue. "Is that a challenge?"

"Only if you feel up to it, rookie."

Midnight eyes glittered. "Trust me."

Janina bit her lower lip and smiled almost shyly. "My pleasure."

"That's the plan."

Russ crossed an ankle over a knee behind his wife's shoulders, leaned in to sandwich her tight against his chest while he nibbled his way down her exposed neck to the pulse point and left a long, openmouthed kiss there. Janina arched her throat and sank readily, greedily into the pleasures he evoked, barely conscious of each of his shoes and socks hitting the floor in turn even when he switched ankles behind her back.

Her hands were on his face, his neck, bandaged and protected fingers clumsy on his collar studs, shirt buttons.

She'd wanted him, needed him, loved him for so long.

Her tape-thickened fingers fumbled, stumbled awkwardly and stalled, unable to make his buttons and studs work the way she wanted them to. Janina yanked at his shirt and growled in frustration.

Russ slicked a smile across her throat and up to her lips. His hands prowled her back, tunneled through her hair, feathered heated caresses along her legs and up her sides but never quite curved, molded, traced in far enough when they reached her bustline, her breasts, where she ached for him to touch. He was too busy slowing things down, setting a pace he could control, making her wait. "Problem?"

Janina tapped his shirt. "Get rid of this."

"In a minute."

"No." She caught his face, his wandering attention between the heels of her hands, forced his gaze level with hers. "Now."

The single word was fierce, rife with intent, demand, command. His hands worked, hers did not and therefore they must accommodate them both, be available to both, please both—be commanded by both.

In the space of two heartbeats Russ understood what Janina didn't say. His breathing hitched, the control he'd fought for and won seeped away, the blood in his heart, arteries, veins heated, pounded south and pooled, causing him to lurch upward, swelling painfully hard inside Janina.

Who rolled her hips and arched into him, gasping appreciatively. *"Yes!"*

Sweat beaded on his skin. He dropped his forehead against hers and clutched her hips to hold her still, afraid of spilling his seed then and there, and groaned. "Janie. Wait."

Her voice was a searing breath against his lips, the side

of his face, "Trust me," then she was forcing his attention to hers again, commandeering it, telling him to look at her, into her eyes, and not to stop even as she tugged at his wrists and urged him to get rid of his shirt.

Quickly.

His turn to find his fingers fumbling, stumbling over his buttons and studs while her lips skated his jaw—and her gaze returned to claim his—urgent, hot, dark, liquid.

Sultry.

Hungry.

Russ tore his shirt open and let the pieces hang wide, framing his chest. Janina smiled. Shut her eyes and dropped her chin, opened her eyes and looked at his chest. Drew a shallow, appreciative breath. Mmm—*damn,* he was beautiful. Copper-bronzed, sculpted, with not an ounce of spare anything, anywhere. Built for her alone to touch.

The thought made her smile go wide enough to make her cheeks ache.

"What?" Nerves and pulse points alert to any movement, touch. Greedy for them.

Janina shook her head, laughed lightly and lifted her Ace-wrapped right hand to run the pads of her fingers carefully down the center of his chest. "Mine," she whispered.

"God, yes." He flinched and groaned, his muscles contracted, nipple tightened when she rolled it between her thumb and forefinger. His sex flexed hard inside her. "Janie, *geez.*"

Her laughter was throaty, wicked. She tilted her head so she could watch him watch her as she bent forward and slicked an openmouthed kiss across to his right nipple, nipped it, then suckled lightly. He inhaled sharply and went utterly still, as though hanging on to sanity or self-control by a thread—and then he simply let go of the thread.

Janina saw it happen, and it still stunned her. She saw his midnight clear eyes turn as smoky as the desert sky gathering a storm before going suddenly, untamably black. Saw him release whatever fetters tied him the same way he rid himself of the remains of his shirt: one moment it was there, the next it was gone and she couldn't say where it went, or how it happened. And then he'd scooped his hands under her and risen, juggled her briefly, and his pants and boxers were gone, too.

Before she could catch her breath, he'd spun about, dragged a pillow off the head of the bed and come back down on the bed with her beneath him and the pillow underneath her hips.

"Russ." His name left her throat on a moan of shocked pleasure when the move seated him even more deeply within her.

His answering rasp was guttural, dark, strangled. "Janie, I can't…ah…I can't…wait. I'm sor…r…y…"

"It's okay, it's all right, I don't want you to wait, I can't wait anymore eith—" Janina tried to tell him, but he was already moving.

It took him an awkward, jerky moment or two to find the rhythm, but then instinct took over and he was stroking into her high and hard and fast, and without warning, Janina felt as though she'd been struck by lightning.

One instant she was simply relishing the pleasure of having Russ Levoie, her husband, her teenage fantasy, the man of her dreams finally making love to her, and the next she was soaring, part of something grander than herself, blown asunder and coming to bits in more pieces than she could possibly ever put back together again.

It was the most frightening thing that had ever happened to her—and the most remarkable. She struggled against it, afraid of losing herself, losing some identity that she couldn't quite remember at the moment but one that she might miss tomorrow or the next day if she let it get swallowed up here, in this.

In him.

But then Russ lifted himself on his arms above her and called her name, sounding nearly as unsure as she felt. Janina looked up at him and knew she'd never seen him look so beautiful or so vulnerable, his darkly handsome features cast in passion, his emotions lost in her. Without thought she cast her own fears aside and reached for him, framed his face once again as best she could between her bandaged hands and drew him down to her. He came with a growl, trapping her head between his forearms and winding his hands tightly in her hair. She wrapped her legs more securely around his hips, her arms about his neck, and they went together into that place of light and no tomorrows and no looking back.

There were no mere fireworks, no stars, not even simple bliss, but something further and beyond, more astonishing—if Russ but knew it. An exceedingly amazed and bewildered Janina did.

With their hearts, souls and bodies wrapped securely about each other, what they found within their extraordinary, extended and explosive burst of ecstasy was peace.

Russ's release was massive, prolonged. His entire body shuddered with it. He'd waited forever to give himself to this one woman, and he had no other way to do it than this, not enough words to ever let her know what she meant, this meant. But he had this.

So he lifted himself on his hands to look down at her and let his body move, hoping it would show her everything his tongue might never say.

But then she whispered his name and reached up for him and something happened. To him. Within him.

He'd always had an innate ability to connect with wounded creatures, especially female ones, whether wild or domestic, had inherited a strange empathy for them, an uncanny gift for understanding language that wasn't spoken, for communicating in a way that was beyond thought or description but that simply existed. That was simply a "knowing."

But it only worked if he banged into a situation and didn't think about what he was doing.

It was a gift he took for granted, had never tried to explain. Some things he simply knew. But he'd never been close enough to another person to experience anything like what was happening to him now. This was…

Connection. Complete, whole, soul to soul, spirits bound by being unbound and undone. Connected. United.

Married.

The minute Janina touched his face to draw him down to her, Russ felt it, fell into it, into her. What she knew, felt, experienced, he knew, felt, experienced, too. Everything she was, he became.

When her body clamped around him, he shattered, his heart engulfed in hers, both the lightning and its cause, its victim.

He saw what she saw, as though he were within her eyes and his own at the same time—and it broke him, tamed him, set him free.

Face buried in her neck, against her ear, he spoke to Janina in his mother's tongue, a language he rarely used, and even then, as he used all verbal language, sparingly.

He didn't remember what he said, but it hardly mattered. Janina responded to the tone, to the movement of his body within hers, the heartbeat that was one with hers, and the simple terrifying, wondrous, earthshaking knowledge that the world as she knew it, and they understood it, would never be the same again.

He breathed out, she breathed in and vice versa; oxygen shared and exchanged, life blended, entwined.

Intermingled.

Magic.

At some point that neither of them would remember specifically but that Janina would never forget, Russ finally undid the rest of the hooks of her bodice and removed it. His response to his first sight of her unbound breasts was mesmerizing, reverent. His eyes burned with heat, his already warm skin went hot, and his touch...

His touch proclaimed her a tabernacle at which he was a barely worthy worshipper. But worship he did, with hands and fingers, lips and teeth, tongue and mouth. Then with his body he adored her again and again and again.

And yet again.

And still it wasn't enough.

So they slept entwined, woke and loved, then feasted, feeding each other from the room-service cart until food hunger melted to other darker, more urgent hungers and their bodies simply slipped together, found each other, and loved—and *loved*—some more.

At last, five days into their overextended-without-notifying-anyone-of-their-whereabouts three-day-long weekend, there came a moment of…well, not complete satiation exactly, but of contentment and sweetness, of idleness and saturation, of softness and…

Exhaustion.

Sprawled across Russ's belly, Janina practiced signing variations of her new name with a hotel pen—"Janina E. Levoie" or "Janina Elena Levoie" or "Janina Gálvez Levoie"—above each of his pectorals in turn. Under her, Russ stirred lazily awake and smiled sleepily down at her.

"What are you doing?" he asked, stroking her hair.

She wrinkled her nose and studied her handiwork. "Either autographing your pecs or figuring out which name I want to use when I get my new driver's license," she said. She signed "Levoie" with a satisfying flourish and capped the pen tight, amazed by how little her right wrist twinged today. Attaining one's heart's desire was a marvelous drug. "I can't decide."

Russ craned his neck for a better look, did a double take, and started to laugh—hard.

Surprised by the sound, Janina shyly peeked up at him from beneath her lashes. She'd never heard him laugh this way, even in the company of his brothers: freely, uninhibitedly, completely relaxed and thoroughly enjoying himself. She chuckled, pleased with herself for eliciting the response—until she realized he was laughing at her or something she'd done.

She sat up and poked him in the chest none too gently. "What? My handwriting's neat. What's your problem?"

Unable to respond through his laughter, Russ simply caught her offending fingers in one hand and gestured inadequately at his torso with the other.

Janina shrugged her entire body and gave him a hugely mystified look. "What? I don't see anything. What is so funny?"

Russ looked "I don't get it" at her and doubled over, buried his face against her hip and howled.

Janina wrapped the sheet around herself, slipped out of bed and stalked across the room muttering, "I know you're hell at communication, but this is ridiculous. The least you could do is *point* at whatever you think I've done, for God's sakes. Married forty-some hours and to what, I ask you—"

"Janie," Russ managed through his laughter, interrupting her.

His wife turned and eyed him. "What." It was not a question.

To give Russ credit he tried—oh *God* how he tried!—to maintain a straight face while he swept a hand from Janina's autographing on his chest and stomach to the neatly—and boldly—printed legend below his belly button but above the curling black hair: "FOR THE EXCLUSIVE USE OF JANINA ELENA GÁLVEZ LEVOIE" with an arrow indicating Russ's manhood. Then in smaller print, the line below that read: TRESPASSERS WILL BE EXECUTED AT ONCE AND WITH EXTREME PREJUDICE.

"Oh," Janina said in a small innocent voice.

"So." Russ stuck his tongue in his cheek and tried valiantly to control the urge to lose control of his mirth again. "How much of this stuff washes off?"

"Well, um..." Janina said faintly, backing away. "Um...the stuff on your chest...um, well, um...that—that might. That's just, I think, pen. But the other stuff, um...we-ell..."

Russ looked at her, looked at the darker, *bolder* lettering at groin level. "Janie." Her name was a warning.

"Ah, well…" She used delay to dance farther out of his reach. It might have worked if her legs were longer or if he was shorter.

Or slower on the uptake.

"Janina Elena Gálvez Levoie."

A bound had her within reach. A grab had her squealing and stripped of her sheet, in his arms and headed for the shower.

"How long will it take for you to scrub it off?" he asked mildly.

"I'm maimed," she reminded him.

"Ha," he said. "We'll bag your fingers and take off your Ace and you can scrub me to my heart's content. Now, how long?"

She batted her eyelashes and tried to look seductive. "Well," she said, although *hedged* might be closer to the point, "it's laundry marker. I think it'll have to wear off."

Russ swore, then grinned and started to chuckle again. "At least it's where no one'll see it."

"They'd better not," Janina warned him firmly.

"But I think I'll have to make you pay for it."

"Oh?" Janina raised her eyebrows suspiciously. "How?"

Russ grinned his bad-boy-Levoie grin. "Trust me," he promised. "I'll be creative."

By the time they left Vegas, Janina had paid for her "crimes" several times, much to her—and their—eminent satisfaction.

She also, however, bore the indelible legend low on both her belly and backside: "PROPERTY OF RUSS LE-

VOIE" and "ABSOLUTELY NO TRESPASSING," in Russ's decidedly male script.

Secretly, the turnabout delighted her no end. She had always wanted to be his exclusively, lock, stock and world without end. No way on earth was she about to argue with unwashable ink.

Smiling to herself, she slid closer to Russ, dropped her head to his shoulder and wrapped her arms around his right bicep and hugged it to her breast while he drove. He grinned and brushed a quick kiss in her hair, returned his attention to the road, but not before she nearly blackened his jaw when she suddenly sat up straight and clunked him in it with a panicked, "Oh my God, driveways. Russ, pull over. We haven't talked about driveways."

Despite provocation, Russ Levoie did not lose control of the vehicle. He had not earned his lieutenant's bars due to a propensity to panic in the face of unforeseen circumstances. Which meant that he did not fluster now when the beautiful woman who tongue-tied him on a regular basis popped him in the chops with her head and incomprehensibly announced that they had to stop in the middle of the infamous Route 66 to discuss driveways.

Instead, he very calmly and infuriatingly said, "What?"

To which Janina responded by getting the best grip she possibly could on his lapel and shaking him…well, it…and almost yelling, "Driveways, Russ, houses. We didn't talk about them. Where are we going to live? We can't stay at my place, Tobi's there. And your place…I don't know. Can we live there? At least to start?"

"No," Russ said calmly. "I sleep on the couch."

"What?" Janina asked, wild-eyed. "What kind of life is that for a grown man?"

"I did wonder," Russ admitted, "until I got drunk and you came along."

"What?" Janina repeated, staring at him, wondering when she'd lost control of the conversation. "What kind of answer is that? Have you lost your mind?"

"Possibly. There's probably no other way to explain this."

"Russ, really, I'm trying to talk to you about driveways and kitchens and beds and things, and if you're not even going to be coherent, this marriage isn't going to survive to Winslow."

"Beds," said Russ innocently. "I'm with you now."

"Why do I so doubt that?" Janina queried blackly.

"No, really." Russ gave her earnest. Guileless. "Beds. Excellent topic. Speak. I'm listening."

"Why," Janina asked him, "do I get the feeling I'm going to prefer you when you *don't* communicate?"

Russ's lips twitched and he blinked at her but said nothing.

She sighed, took a deep breath and calmed down a trifle. "No, really, Russ. I want to know where to come home to after work tomorrow. I want to know where you'll be sleeping so I can crawl into bed with you and vice versa. I want an address to put on my new driver's license and all that jazz, you know? So will you pull over so we can figure this out? I can't think at eighty miles an hour."

Russ's wry, thoroughly amused grin told her he was pretty sure she could do otherwise at quadruple the speed, but he pulled off onto the shoulder and canted sideways to rest his elbow on the back of the seat so he could stare at her, waiting.

Patiently.

Which made Janina want to kill him.

Or something.

Then he smiled that slow, lazy, first-thing-in-the-morning-last-thing-at-night-and-anytime-in-between smile at her and *or something* took precedence and shape. Her brain puddled to jelly and landed in a heated pool in her belly, slid eagerly to that place that fitted him so perfectly between her thighs.

Only it wasn't really her brain, it was her heart.

Janina sighed.

And reminded herself firmly that the side of I-40 in full view of the passing world was probably not the optimum place to remove her panties and straddle her husband's lap and make love with him yet again—no matter how badly she, her heart, her brain and her body wanted to.

Were willing, ready and able to.

Shouted, screamed and cravenly longed to.

As if he read her thoughts, Russ's smile deepened. He dropped his free hand lightly to her knee, drew idle circles into the crease that hid the back of it.

Janina bit her lip against the ready tension and unflexed her leg to allow his tickling fingers access. She suddenly caught her breath on an *"Oh rats"* and crossed her legs to trap his hand when she realized he'd successfully sidetracked her and said, "No you don't." Then glared at him when he laughed, thoroughly male, thoroughly pleased with himself for arousing her so easily.

Hand still trapped, he only wiggled his fingers against the back of her knee and laughed harder when she tensed and whimpered and unintentionally eased closer to him, then gritted her teeth, uncrossed her legs and shoved him away—hard.

"Will you get serious?" she demanded. "We got married without thinking. We need a driveway. We need a *plan*."

Already doubled over, Russ lost it entirely.

Janina studied him, mystified. "Thirteen years I thought I knew you. I felt sorry for you. *Em*pathized with you. I thought you were the serious one, the lost one, the dark one, the intense one, the one who *never* laughs. Your brothers didn't warn me. Jonah didn't warn me. He just said, 'Go find Russ, you'll be good for him.' Ha! I'll kill him. And you! Clearly I don't know you at all."

"You married me because you felt *sorry* for me?" Laughter faded, replaced by curiosity and something far more vulnerable.

Janina quieted, suddenly aware of precarious ground, of an uncertainty she'd never before seen in Russ, wasn't aware he was capable of.

She backpedaled, correcting misconceptions, fast. "That's not what I said—that's not what I meant. I married you because I wanted to. I've always wanted to. I've just apparently always wanted to under false pretenses—or rather misconceptions of one sort or another, which—" she held up a hand to forestall the baffled look V-ing his eyebrows "—isn't necessarily bad. It's just…unexpected. *You* are unexpected. I'm going to have to get used to you."

He snorted and glanced at her, implying without words a similar fate for himself.

She grinned modestly. "Yeah, well. But that still brings us back to…"

"Driveways?" Russ suggested.

"The need for a plan," Janina said firmly.

An unholy gleam came into his eyes. Janina had the rapidly sinking, and yet oddly secure, feeling she recognized it. She was sure the moment Russ opened his mouth.

"Trust me," he said.

Then he checked for oncoming traffic and let the tires spit gravel getting them back onto the road.

It was too easy—his wedding, this not-quite-five-day-old marriage, his sudden ability to play with, laugh at and talk to Janina…all of it—and Russ knew it. In hours, minutes, seconds, he would revert to his former self and screw it up. Somehow, without meaning to.

But he didn't do it.

He'd watched Janina long and well. He'd listened to her tell her dreams to Tobi—hell, to him—when they were both on the late shift and he was in search of a pick-me-up and the diner was slow and she was in search of company. An ear.

He'd always hoped she'd come looking specifically for him, *his* ear, not merely any handy and available company.

But whatever, he'd listened well. He knew what she dreamed, wanted, hoped for. So his "trust me" held a wealth of meaning he'd never let her in on. She'd seen the devil, not the thought behind it.

Which was what he meant for her to see. Sucker for her though he might be, emotion was not the place he went to easily. Putting it on display was not so much his first choice of action to take.

He gave himself a mocking half grin.

So strong-arming away the sense that Winslow was closing in on them and their new relationship far too fast, Russ sped toward a few houses in town that Janina recently had mentioned liking the look of. He preferred acreage outside of town himself, room to spread out, expand the house as they needed to when the kids came along— land on which to keep a few horses, some sheep if she wanted to, since he knew that would go along with the textile, spinning, weaving and wool-dyeing classes she'd been taking, and a small garden. And he had the place already—thirty-five acres of ranch land outside of town, backed up against the Apache Sitgreaves National Forest and bounded by canyon on one edge. What putting in her driveway might entail… He grinned slightly. That might prove interesting.

But he was willing to go along with whatever Janina wanted in a home. She was the one who'd never actually lived in a house before in her life. He had—low-income reservation-style though his family's home had been, it had still been a "house," and it had certainly been "home." He doubted that the trailer she'd shared with her mother ever classified as home. She'd left it the moment she'd graduated high school, as he recalled.

Which meant, he understood instinctively, that she was the one who needed to feel that what they built together was theirs and theirs alone, not his, not something *he* chose. But something, frankly, he supposed, that she did.

A place for her to…nest.

He wondered if she'd thought about the ghosts that came with living in someone else's house. Breaking the news of their marriage to his family would be interesting enough without dealing with the phantoms of someone else's family or history on top of it.

Yeah, okay, so maybe he was superstitious, sue him, he was Indian. The damn Jesuits hadn't weeded everything out of him—and hell, because the Pai had precious little left of their own culture to weed out, he'd tried especially hard to retain what he could. So it was some blasted bit of uneasiness about other people's ghosts that he might not even have actually gotten from his own culture but from someplace else, so what? He'd live with the damn specters if he had to.

On the other hand...

Perhaps he would just tour her by his land on their way back to Winslow, point out the fact of it, the convenience of it. Slip in the idea that they could get a trailer out there fairly quickly, set up a generator and be downright self-sufficient in a week, maybe ten days at the outside, especially with help from his brothers. But he wouldn't pressure her in that direction if she was dead set on a house in town. No. That would be wrong.

Absolutely. Wrong.

Especially when simple coercion—er, make that *subtle persuasion*—would work as well.

"What?" Janina asked suspiciously, not trusting the glint in his eye for an instant. She knew better than to trust "innocent" when it came to a Levoie.

Russ merely grinned, squeezed his wife's knee, winked at her and drove.

A community with a young median population, Winslow was like many smaller communities: looking to attract business and industry with prime development sites. Situated in western Navajo County in the Little Colorado River Valley, it was a place where water was precious and mention in an Eagles' song had made it famous long after it was a minor way station along the Route 66—now I-40—corridor. It was a good community in which to live, work and raise a family—something Russ looked forward to but had never before seriously considered in his cards.

He'd participated in town events from the inside for years—you did that as a member of a small community police force—but he'd never had a chance to participate from the family side, as the parent of a marching-band member, athlete, equestrian club member, 4-H clubber. Never attended the parades with a kid on his shoulders, balloon in hand, wife at his side....

He looked forward to that side of town life, town celebrations, to life with Janina.

He glanced at her when he made the turn that would take them out to his property—make that *their* property.

Without thinking he caught up Janina's hand and carried it to his mouth, placed a fervent kiss in her palm.

Heart in her eyes, Janina studied him. "What?" she asked again, breathless, worried...and falling heart over head in love all over again.

Russ offered her a half smile and shook his head, kissed her knuckles and folded her hand back around his arm. Then he drove steadily over back roads for about thirty miles, turned easily onto a beaten track for a rougher ten-mile jaunt and finally pulled up in front of a run-down gate with broken fencing trailing off on either side of it. A faint, nearly legible dirt track that Janina thought might charitably have been called a road at some point led away from the gate and into the land beyond it. Russ swept a hand at the view.

"There're thirty-five acres. I—" He glanced sideways at her. "Make that *we*—" he emphasized the word and she stifled a smile "—own it. There's water, I made sure. The land backs up to the Apache Sitgreaves. I figure we can sink a well, move my trailer out here and get another trailer with a generator to live in while we build. What d'you think?"

Janina stared from the land to him and back for a moment. And started to laugh. "This is your 'trust me'?"

He shrugged. "We can go look at the ready-built houses in town if you want." He sneaked her a sidelong peek.

"Very subtle." Janina didn't bother to contain her amusement. He didn't fool her for an instant. This was what he wanted, and frankly, she'd only considered something small in town because the homes were affordable from her pocketbook. But with combined resources on land he already owned... "No—no, that's okay," she said magnanimously. It didn't hurt to *appear* to compromise early in a relationship. Especially if you were getting exactly what you wanted anyway. "Far be it from me to ask you to live in a cracker box with no yard. I think we should consider getting a trailer and building first."

"Hunh," Russ grunted in disbelief, but let it drop. He'd thought she'd like the idea, and if she hadn't...well, arguing about it wasn't the first thing on his mind.

A well, a generator and a trailer with a bed in it, those were the first priorities.

After he came up with a place for them to stay in the meantime, where a bed was the center point with Janina the nucleus of his universe.

"You want a better look?" he asked.

She eyed the dirt track with misgiving. "It's not going to tear up my car, is it? I need this car."

His grin was wide and full of the devil.

"Yeah, yeah." She rolled her eyes and laughed. "Trust you."

He tipped his head. "There you go," he said and left the car to pull the gate out of the way.

Janina had never thought much about owning land, any land, anywhere. Always before it had just been a place she rented because she had to make a home somewhere. And after growing up in her mother's less-than-perfect trailer, she wanted the nicest home she could afford. This was different. This was beyond her imagination's ability to comprehend.

When Russ parked the car, got out and came around for her, led her to a spot he'd staked out with flags and string, showed her "the front door" and turned her to face the view that would bring them each morning's sunrise then bent to nuzzle the hair away from her ear and whispered, "So what do you think of our home?" She couldn't speak, she could only show him what she thought with hands and mouth and skin touching skin.

And the hell with the dirt and the scrub and the grit. She wasn't in the mood to notice it.

Neither was he. So they didn't.

The man with the binoculars scrubbed his free hand over his balding, clean-shaven head. He was back, finally. That boy—the cop—the one who'd looked after Maddie. That was good. That meant they could get on with it now. *He* could get on with it.

The cleansing.

He turned at the sound of a whimper behind him, eyed the doe-eyed brunette he'd had to pick up yesterday when she'd run from the trailer where Maddie was staying.

He knew that boy was the first person Maddie would run to; she always ran to him. And it wasn't as if the boy had been hard to find. Small-town cops weren't. The little brunette was out of the picture now. She couldn't keep Maddie from seeing him anymore. She'd bring Maddie to him, in fact. That's all he wanted. Maddie back.

He turned back to the binoculars and the cop below. Stood to reason from the looks of things that, should the need arise, the dark-haired woman lying atop that boy would bring him running, too.

If he wouldn't come on his own.

The man scrubbed his head again, trying to hold on. Trying to hold his thoughts in. A man had to do what he had to do in order to cleanse his soul before the time came to move on.

Sometime later, thoroughly disheveled, eminently pleased with themselves and each other, and in need of food and a shower, Russ and Janina went into town and took the Mary Colter Balcony Room at La Posada for a very short interim in order to prolong their honeymoon while they got things situated for the short-term move into Russ's cramped trailer before they moved that out to the property.

Russ, frankly, had misgivings about the two of them moving into his trailer for any length of time, but Janina shushed them. As she pointed out with a sly smile and a timely wriggle, "living on top of each other" was pretty much what honeymooners did. Janina living on top of him was *so* not the problem but telling her what was…Russ didn't know how to do that.

Because how did you tell the woman you'd just married—the woman you wanted beyond anything and had since always—that the reason you didn't want her to move into your trailer with you was because your best friend—your best female friend—was already in residence?

When they were finished at La Posada they stopped by the walk-in clinic so Janina could have her stitches removed then went house-trailer hunting. Janina also wanted to run by the DMV, and the social security office to take care of the updates to her numbers, but they settled for a stop at the bank and another meal.

By the time they headed out to the Bloated Boar to collect Russ's truck not long before twilight, the newest Mr. and Mrs. Levoie had a joint savings and checking account using the current location of Russ's trailer as their temporary address, and they'd pretty much decided on a trailer to move out to the property. Things were going well....

Until the moment they arrived at the Bloated Boar to pick up Russ's truck and all hell broke loose and their all-too-brief honeymoon came to an abrupt shotgun end.

Chapter 6

The problems began before Russ and Janina arrived in the Bloated Boar's parking lot. In fact, they began a couple of days before.

"Damn it, Tobi," Jonah said, attempting to avoid the pot of coffee Janina's best friend and roommate threatened to upend over his lap. "There's nothing I can do about it. You don't know where Janina is and I can't find Russ. So we've got to turn Buddy loose. Way it is. You see her before I do, tell her to get a restraining order so he can't get near her again."

"Yeah, well," Tobi retorted, "you see that brother of yours, you tell him I'm lookin' to clean his clock since he can't show up to keep his assault prisoners where they're supposed to be."

"Get in line," Jonah advised her. "Russ made a few other promises he didn't keep."

"Maddie?" Tobi guessed.

Jonah shook his head, not talking. "Just tell Janie what I said, huh?"

That had been two days and several hours ago.

Jonah flipped his left wrist so he could read the watch face. Damn it to hell and back. Where in thunder was Russ? He'd be damned if he'd stake out Russ's unblemished classic vehicle for another fifteen seconds let alone until his never-before-wayward brother took it into his head to show up on his own. Buddy Carmichael was on the loose and hardly happy with Lieutenant Levoie, and Charlie Thorn was out of prison with a major bone to pick with Russ as well. And nobody'd seen Jonah's numbskull senior male sibling since...

Since Jonah had sent Janina after him in the wee small hours of the eighteenth. Which meant if somebody had them, they probably had them both.

"Damn." Jonah whacked the dashboard with his fist. He did not do "still" well.

Maybe he should put out a call and have somebody check to see if Buddy Carmichael was alive. Just for the intellectual exercise.

Or the entertainment value.

Jonah was trying to decide which, when the near-distance crackle of tires over gravel drew his attention. A glance down the highway gave him a view of headlights on what looked like Janina's station wagon. Two figures were silhouetted, features almost visible in the front seat. He didn't need a clear sight line to recognize the bigger, taller of the two.

Jonah picked up his cruiser's handset and called in his brother's location to the department switchboard.

"Piper time, Russell," he said quietly to the air.

And grinned. There were just some small sibling pleasures in life that were too big to pass up.

The moment he pitted the gravel shoulder with the front right tire of Janina's car in preparation for the turn into the Bloated Boar, Russ's spider sense started to crawl. He glanced sharply sideways at Janina, wondering if she felt it, too.

His spider sense came from the old knowledge inherited with his bone structure and eye color from some long-gone ancestor, some ghost who refused to take credit, or answer to blame. It came from the place inside that had connected wholly and completely with Janina, which was irrevocably tied to her, that recognized her dangers as his own.

Having just found her, he could not afford to lose her.

But she sensed nothing, felt nothing, but the enveloping euphoria she'd been wrapped in since the night she'd come to find him at the Boar and run off to become his wife. She proved that by leaning up to kiss his cheek and reaching over to caress his chest when she said, "I'm going to run by the apartment to pick up some clothes on my way back to the hotel, okay?"

"No!" Russ snapped—hardly an answer, but an order.

"What?" Janina pulled back, shocked. "What did you just say to me?"

Russ grimaced and bit his tongue. Damn. Not what he'd meant to say, do, be. Autocratic, chauvinistic ass. He pulled into the Bloated Boar's parking lot and tried again. "Uh…" Uh, what? I've got a bad feeling about something but I can't tell you what? Uh, I just don't think you should go by your apartment tonight alone, trust me? Uh, what? What? "Naked," his mouth said, independent of his brain. "You won't need clothes 'cuz you're gonna be naked the minute I get you through the bedroom door."

"Ah." Janina eyed him, believing what he said but knowing him better than he realized. "Naked, huh?"

He swallowed, gave her a lopsided, mostly lascivious grin and nodded.

"Sure it's not your spider sense?" Janina asked idly. Too idly.

Too knowingly.

Startled, Russ put the car in park, dropped his wrists over the steering wheel and looked across his shoulder at her.

She shrugged. "I didn't hang around with your brothers for nothing. My favorite subject was you."

"They don't know everything, Janie. They don't know half."

"But the spider-sense thing, that's real, isn't it? That's what's just made you sound like you were ordering me around like some husband who thinks now he's got my name on the license he can control me however he wants?" She touched his face, forced him to look directly at her. "Because you can't, Russ. I won't let you. But if it's the spider sense, if there's a reason, even if it's one you can't explain. I can go along. I can trust you—"

Russ reached for her, cutting off whatever else she might have said with a kiss that was deep and cherishing, thankful and worshipping, all at once. Janina wound her arms around his neck on a sigh and took the kiss as it was meant—a yes, pure and simple, a benediction for having read her man exactly right the first time he needed her to.

She pulled him as far into the kiss as she dared in the

busy saloon parking lot by way of congratulating herself
on a virgin effort well managed, and a prayer that future
efforts would go as easily. Her desire for him lay beyond
want or need, seemed to come from some biological im-
perative to be part of him as often as possible. To mate with
him, create with him.

Impossible, given her body's proclivity for killing off
seeds before they could be planted, but still…

The urge was there: basic, primal.

Insistent.

She wanted Russ's babies above anything. Her whole
being knew him as her perfect match, perfect mate—the
perfect father for the children she'd learned during her
time with Buddy she would be unable to conceive naturally.

But intellectual knowledge didn't stop her body from
quickening, preparing for him. Didn't stop that pleading
murmur from climbing the back of her throat and encouraging him further.

She'd stopped being a thinking adult the minute she'd
walked into the Bloated Boar and Russ had called her
Janie. Because people warned women about guys like
Buddy, but nobody warned anyone about bright, upstand-
ing, solid-citizen, marrying-kind, heroic guys like Russ
who could lead a woman straight down the garden path to
hell, embarrassment, intense public mortification and possible heartache, and never bring her back.

Except for Russ himself. And as far as Janina was concerned, Russ warning her about himself didn't count,
mostly because she hadn't listened.

Hadn't wanted to, and so hadn't bothered to.

The double *whoop-whoop* of a police cruiser's siren
broke them apart. Almost violently disoriented, Russ nev-

ertheless instinctively covered Janina's body with his own, hiding her thoroughly disheveled hair and disarranged clothing, when he raised his head to get his bearings. The fact that she now straddled his lap in the passenger seat and that the windows were steamed beyond redemption didn't help, but he shifted her sideways into the seat, away from the possibility of prying eyes, and did his best.

"Russ?" Janina reached to draw him back.

Russ let her pull him only so far back into her kiss, into the moment, before once more pulling away, far enough to touch his forehead to hers and whisper roughly, "Don't we have a room for this somewhere?"

She laughed softly. "That would mean getting into separate cars and driving there."

"It would also mean not getting rousted by the cops."

Her pride showed. "You outrank most of the cops in the area." She was pretty sure it was Russ and not his uniform that had first attracted her, but every time he'd earned a promotion, she'd stolen his meal check and taken care of it herself. "You can tell them to get lost."

If only, his libido said regretfully. Sanity sang a different, far more practical tune. "I'm out of uniform. And we've got a cop outside right now waitin' on us."

"What?"

She tried to bolt upright. Russ judiciously held her down with one hand while he pulled her dress into place over her exposed left breast with the other.

"Hang on. You're not dressed for meet and greet."

Janina couldn't help it. She turned her face into his arm and grinned, reaching between them to make sure she hadn't undone his pants as she'd intended. "You are?"

He grunted, eased away from her fingers to arrange his

own clothing. "Let me talk to patrol and then let's get out of here."

Janina maneuvered so she could plant her mouth against his ear and breathe hotly, "Be quick about it."

Russ groaned, and put the lure of temptation away from him with a heroic effort. "I'll be right back."

He got out of the car. Jonah left the cruiser and crossed to meet him halfway.

Russ glanced back at the Chevy wagon, eyed his much shorter baby brother. "Make it good," he advised.

"She found you," Jonah observed.

Russ said nothing.

Jonah nodded. "Buddy's been released. Tobi said he's been into the diner and around the apartment, making threats. Janina needs to take out a restraining order. You need to watch your back. Man's got no balls and that's where he'll shoot you, if he gets half a chance."

Jaw clenched, Russ glanced again at Janina's car, nodded once. "What else?"

Jonah didn't need clarification to know Russ meant Maddie. "Chief wants your hide. Maddie's your case, Russ, your "special." She's terrified with anyone else around. Somethin's not right an' she's not sayin', I'd stake money on it. Her girlfriend Jess is climbin' the walls, not used to no privacy and enforced claustrophobia. It's a problem." He tipped his head toward Janina, who was exiting the station wagon. "Unfortunately for you, chief's makin' it your problem. Exclusively."

Russ studied his brother for a moment. "With Buddy after my skin?" He cast a telling glance toward Janina, who slipped up beside him. He slid an at once possessive and protective arm about her, collecting her tight. "And hers." His voice was almost neutral. His eyes were not.

"Russ?" Janina asked.

Jonah nodded at the obvious relationship between his brother and the Fat Cat waitress. "Whatever *this* is, it didn't exist a week ago, Russ. No one knew. No one knows. You humiliated Buddy in front of his pals, end of story. He wants revenge. You got worse problems than a half-baked bully in search of face."

Russ glanced at Janina who gazed back, eyes full of questions. He tightened his mouth at her, shook his head slightly and offered her a single drop-shouldered shrug of "Can't explain here." To which she responded with an equally silent, huffed-breath, "We'll see about that." He gave her a one-brow grin and turned back to Jonah.

"She's not goin' home tonight. Stay with her, make sure she's all right till I get there."

"Damn it, Russ." Worry and exhaustion made Jonah explode. "I've had your vehicle staked out for forty-eight hours and I'm not up to watch doggin' anybody. You're gonna have to lay this off on someone else." To Janina, "Sorry, Janie."

She tipped her head, acknowledging the apology without accepting it, or anything else he said. He was screwed and he knew it.

Russ eyed his baby brother mildly for a moment before crossing to his Jimmy, opening the back and plucking out a sleeping bag. He turned and shot it across the lot the way he might a basketball, hitting Jonah squarely in the chest with it.

"Three points," Janina murmured to no one in particular. Jonah glared at her.

"Take that," Russ said succinctly, crossing the parking lot as he spoke and ignoring them both, "turn in your cruiser, get changed, go with her and sleep across the doorway until I get there. Don't shoot me when I come in." He poked Jonah in the chest. "Got it?"

Jonah gave him baleful. "You are so goin' down one of these days."

"Bring it on, boy," Russ shot back.

Janina rolled her eyes and stepped between them. "Idiots," she said forcefully, shoving them apart. It didn't take much of a push. "Get over the stupid macho posturing and grow up."

"I will if he will," Jonah said magnanimously.

Russ grinned wolfishly. "Ever wonder why there's never been two Levoies in the same law enforcement agency before, Janie?"

She shook her head. The brothers worked together often enough, it had never before occurred to her to wonder. But now that he mentioned it...

"Jonah hasn't figured it out yet, either. You'll be happier when you do, baby brother, trust m—"

The sudden, steadily encroaching wail of a siren cut him off. A pair of squad cars followed by Guy's truck skidded off the highway and toward the Boar's entrance. Russ knew without having to be told that this, not Jonah's announcement about Buddy alone, was what his spider sense had been warning him about.

Without thinking, he thrust Janina toward his brother. "Get her out of here." To Janina when she might have protested he said softly, "Call me Spidey."

She studied him a moment, then nodded unhappily and turned toward her car. He caught her arm.

"No. Leave it and the keys. I'll have somebody bring it. Go with Jonah. You'll be safer."

"Russ, don't be silly. He'll be right—"

He folded, put his mouth to her ear. "Shh. Humor me once."

"Once?" Janina gave him doubtful.

He gave her back serious. "I'll feel better."

"Oh." She swallowed. Lifted a hand to let her fingers drift down his cheek. And without another word put her car keys in his shirt pocket and crossed the lot to get into Jonah's cruiser.

Jonah eyed her left hand as she buckled her seat belt. "Nice ring. Looks like one of Russ's."

Janina canted a sideways glance at him, surprised herself by saying, "It's new and it's private, Jones. I want to keep it that way awhile."

He nodded, understanding where she wasn't sure she did herself. "Got it." He hesitated then asked, "Does that include everybody?"

She lifted an eyebrow.

"Tobi. She's worried about you."

Janina winced. "Damn. No. I'll talk to Tobi."

"Good." He turned over the ignition. "I'll make sure I'm out of range when you do."

"Funny." The retort was automatic, Janina's thoughts were on the two police officers exiting their squad cars, on Guy leaping from the driver's-side door of his truck and dashing around to the passenger side.

And on Maddie, obviously in deep emotional distress, hurtling to the ground before Russ reached her, stumbling, falling, picking herself up and dashing straight to him.

Jumping up to throw herself into his arms and hanging on for dear life while he swept her up tight.

The little green edge of worry crept up to frame Janina's vision. She tried to push it back, shake it away; it refused to go. She'd believed him when he'd told her there was nothing between him and Maddie, that people were wrong about them. But he'd been looking down at her when he'd said it and her insecurities hadn't been frail with him standing right there in front of her. Touching her.

I do, she thought, *trust him. I do I do I do.*

She swallowed hard. The exact words she'd spoken when she'd married him.

It didn't matter. She twisted around beneath her seat belt and watched him as long as she could until Jonah pulled his police cruiser onto the highway and her tall husband faded from sight in the invading twilight.

Russ's attention was torn between watching his wife leave with his youngest and most volatile brother, calming the hysterical woman he'd called best friend since he was six, and staying out of reach of his normally good-natured brother Guy, who seemed intent on laying him flat while the two officers who'd arrived attempted to intervene and add their own two cents to the mix.

Guy's rant had something to do with—if Russ interpreted his snarl correctly through whatever Maddie was tearfully babbling at him about her Jess—Guy's wife, Hazel, being too damn pregnant to be left to her own devices while Russ took off to hell knew where when there was one of *Russ's* serial lunatic-killer-rapist-psychopaths on the loose. Which meant it had to be serious and then some because Guy didn't swear or lose it unless provoked beyond sense.

Russ could only guess at what his local officers had to

tell him. *"Your whore's back in town. L.T. Chief wants you to do somethin' about that quick before the press gets outta line with it again."*

And hell, what would it do to Janina if the press got hold of the current story, pulled up the old files—and wrong gossip, damn it—found out he'd married Janina and decided to talk to her about Maddie?

God blast it, he shouldn't have done this to her. Should have been thinking. Should have been aware, at least, of what stories would circulate around him in the department. No matter what respect you gained through the years, the old rumors remained.

Timing was all in the wrist, and his stunk.

With effort he forced himself out of his one-track state of "I'd rather be in bed enjoying and getting to know my wife a whole lot better for another week" and placed himself back in reality central: police lieutenant in a situation he'd not only thrown himself smack-dab into the middle of thirteen years ago as a cop, but a lot longer ago than that as a friend. Not happy about where he found himself, he gathered breath.

And loosed it in his best riot-control voice, which was fairly awe-inspiring since he'd learned it from his father— a man who'd sired six children and raised five—and had been using it on his brothers since kid-dom. "Hey, dial it down, separate it and give it to me one at a time." He glared at Guy, who appeared set to act physically on the invitation without further ado. Younger by a year and shorter by an inch, his normally good-natured and deceptively laid-back sibling nevertheless outweighed him by at least thirty pounds. If he was ready to brawl there'd be a good reason, but it would get messy. "Spoken grievances only."

He swung Maddie into his arms and carried her to the nearest squad car, jerking his head *open it* at the patrol officer, who hastened to comply. "Hush, it's all right, Maddie, I've got you. Shh. Take your time then tell me. Shh."

A little at a time she relaxed, her hysteria subsided, hiccupped away. Babble turned coherent, coherence led directly to anger born of fear and she smacked him in the shoulder with a closed fist. "Where the *hell* have you been? Jess can't do confined, and your trailer...not only too cramped but too much you in it and—"

She stopped suddenly and shoved away from him, out of his lap to stalk a circle in front of him. "And she climbed the walls, and she claimed, she said, where you're concerned I was going hetero on her, which is just stupid because I don't want you, I want *her.* I love her. And then the walls started closing in on her and she started screaming at me and she ran and—"

Her face crumbled, she buried it in her hands, collapsed into a grief-stricken pile at his knee. "I think Charlie took her."

Chapter 7

"**W**hat?" Russ straightened, sent a sharp glance at Guy for confirmation.

His brother nodded. "We got an anonymous call yesterday at your place. Somebody calling himself the 'Good Samaritan' said Jess is safe for the moment but she's been 'taken out of play'—I'm quoting. He said he hopes he doesn't have to 'delete anyone else from the equation,' unquote, end of call."

Russ opened his mouth, shut it so he wouldn't simply repeat what Guy had just said with a capital *What* and an expletive on the end of it.

"I don't make these things up," Guy said flatly. "So I'm goin' home. Make sure Hazel 'n Emily aren't people who have to be deleted from the equation. Don't know why they would be, but it seems where one of us Levoies tangles these days, the rest of us get tied up, and you'll pardon me if I'm not takin' the unborn into this psycho's neighborhood. Em's already seen too much and I won't put Hazel through the possibility of her gettin' anywhere near Maddie's father, if you hear what I'm sayin'?"

Russ went still. His eyes hardened, jaw worked. He knew Charlie's handiwork far too well, too up close, to disregard Guy's concerns. Russ was the only Levoie who'd ever personally gotten in Charlie's way, either when the Thorns ran a campground down in the canyon or since they'd left, but if for some reason Charlie Thorn went anywhere near Guy's wife and teenage daughter, neither the world nor the judicial system would be big enough to protect him. He nodded. "Go. You want someone to tag?"

Guy shook his head. "I'll call."

"Do." Not an offer, an order.

"Five days, no word, now you say that?"

The long-ingrained eldest brother's sense of responsibility and its attendant guilt threatened to surface. Russ tamped it down. He would not regret a single moment that had brought Janina to him, or that he'd so far spent with her, *taken* with her.

That waylaid a path unworthy of the dreams he'd slept with, woken with, since meeting his wife as a teen. His timing might have been off, but he'd left Maddie and Jess in safe hands.

Instead of the looked-for explanation or culpability, he offered Guy nothing but a cold, "My business, I'm back, get over it."

To which Guy responded with his usual candor, "Yeah, well, more than your own life's at stake if you don't keep your mind in the game, bro."

"I'm aware. Trust me."

Guy's mouth quirked without humor. "Maybe not this time. Not all the way. We'll see how it goes. Meantime, I'll trust me. Keep an eye on your back."

"Always. And yours, too."

Guy grinned. "Don't do me any favors."

"Hmm." Russ watched his next-in-line-brother climb into his truck and peel out of the parking lot, headed toward Holbrook and home. Then he returned his attention to Maddie and the waiting officers, who all appeared more than a little uneasy. He considered Maddie briefly, turned over Jonah's concern that she hadn't told him everything.

Felt that flitter of sensation crawl along his nape hairs that told him he'd let her lie to him, experienced the twist in his gut that said *fool,* and understood that he wouldn't get an answer from her tonight.

But their friendship wasn't based in her verbal truths; he'd always known she lied when she had to. Lied to protect herself, lied to protect someone or something she cared about more than herself. So the fact that she lied to him didn't bother him.

Much.

Unless it endangered her or someone else he held himself responsible for. Or cared about.

"You sure it was Charlie called?" he asked Maddie, suddenly aware of the obvious question he'd stupidly neglected to ask Guy.

She nodded, but folded into herself and ducked away from him.

Russ caught her chin, squared her to face him. "*You're* sure. *You* talked to him yourself? No doubts?"

She jerked away. "His voice. What I remember of him

when I can't repress it well enough. I heard it on the phone. Yes."

He grabbed her arm, swung her back. "Don't lie to me, Maddie. You want Jess back, I need it all. *All,* you hear me?"

"I hear you," she said evenly, "And I heard him. You promised me, but weren't there, so back off, Russ. Now."

Good, backbone. A commodity she'd picked up at the trial by the truckload, one she'd needed to get as far as she'd come in the twelve years since, but that Russ hadn't seen evidence of since she'd arrived back in Winslow. She was still lying about something—probably something within the phone call—but at least she was putting some spine into it.

The grin he offered her showed a lot of white. "Better," he said.

She stared at him a moment, then growled under her breath and flipped a single finger in his direction before stomping off to give the tires of his truck several swift, hard kicks. Then she crossed her arms and eyed him daggers for another fifteen seconds, and finally, when he didn't give ground, put her nose in the air and turned her back on him to wait.

Russ's grin widened. Close, long-term friendships with women could be like that.

He let his thoughts skate off Maddie with his gaze, shift and intensify with his attention to the patiently waiting cops. "Fill me in on what's being done to find Jess."

Bringing him up to date on the search for Maddie's life partner didn't take long. The call had been made from a stolen cell phone. Russ's caller ID had given them that much. A little footwork had even found them the cell phone itself, disposed of near the train tracks, showing Russ's number as the last one dialed. There were no fingerprints, and the numbers had probably been punched using the eraser end of a pencil.

The cell's owner, a tourist, had discovered the phone missing three days previously when she'd set her carry bag aside while having her picture taken with her family downtown at the Standin' On The Corner Park. She'd reported it, reluctantly, at her husband's insistence even though she'd figured the phone had been taken by her seventeen-year-old daughter who was ticked at having been forced to come on the family trip when she'd rather have stayed home near her boyfriend.

When notified, the woman was both horrified by the truth, but gratified to discover her daughter was not the culprit.

Other than that, however, the police had had little luck. Searches of the usual places had turned up nothing. Russ suggested they widen the search area to include all abandoned buildings, fallout shelters and storage lockers, especially in or around recreation and camping areas. Charlie Thorn had operated campgrounds at one time and was back-of-his-hand familiar with most of northern and western Arizona despite his years of incarceration. Depending on what his "taken out of play" meant, he'd need somewhere well-ventilated to imprison Jess. Which might mean anything from a car trunk—Russ shuddered at the thought, particularly given the time of year—to an abandoned boxcar to an underground storage tank to a refrigeration unit with holes drilled in it.

For Jess's sake, and therefore Maddie's, he hoped for a nice, airy, well-ventilated abandoned building.

Given Charlie's decidedly conscienceless history, he didn't count on it.

Who the hell had judged the man rehabilitated enough to be released from prison anyway? Some damn psych-evaluation committee he'd been able to fool by taking his medication every day? Judas stinking hell in a handbag.

Older officer dispatched, Russ turned to the younger one and understood at once where suspicion and thirteen years of withheld gossip would come from: not from the guys who'd watched him come up, but from his underlings, the ones who hadn't. Because Winslow was small and their lives were in desperate need of drama they could speculate about but didn't have to live.

"L.T., was she gay when you were with her or that somethin' happened later? What's that like anyway, bein' with a whore?" It would have been one thing if the young officer was being mean or nasty-spirited, but he wasn't. He was all of twenty, still pimply-faced-young, curious, didn't know better and was therefore blunt about what he wanted to know, pure and simple. "I mean I heard she was your girlfriend or somethin' while she was doin' your whole high school for cash, plus who all else came along. And now she's got herself a girlfriend? So…" He scratched his head and worked his mouth around question and problem, trying to figure both politically incorrect things out. "So do you, like, go out with both of 'em at once n—"

There was a sudden flash of movement and before Russ could intervene, the young patrolman staggered back under a ringing slap. "Don't you talk to him like that ever," Maddie snapped. "You say what you want to me, but you leave him and Jess out of it, you flea-brained idiot, or I will—"

"Maddie," Russ said forcefully, hauling her back. "I realize this may not help, but Carson's too stupid to mean anything by what he says."

The patrolman in question stared at her wide-eyed and puzzled, rubbing his cheek. Maddie glared at him, glanced furiously at Russ. "Too many people been stupid about this."

"Yeah, well, this boy was maybe eight during the trial. He wears this peach fuzz thinking it's a beard, he's still cherry and he's truly innocent, come to that. He doesn't understand. He wants to figure it out. Goin' about it the wrong way, but he's goin' about it."

"Is he." Not a question. She stepped up toe-to-toe and nose-to-nose with Carson. "That the truth, Carson? You trying to understand what makes different people in the world tick?"

Carson gulped. His eyes showed a lot of white. "Ah…L.T.?"

"Don't ask questions you don't want answers to," Russ advised him. "Especially not when she's around."

The boy tightened his jaw, looked Maddie in the eye and swallowed again. "Okay. Then yes, ma'am. I do wanna know. I never—I ain't never talked to anybody like you afore. I don't know how to act. My preacher just says all you folks are bent wrong somehow, but that can't be right." He stopped, worked his way around something baffling—and possibly troubling. "I mean, can it?"

Something in his face, the question, the tone—some underlying need to know—made Maddie take a step back and look at him hard and thoroughly. What she found made her mouth soften, her stance slacken. She glanced at Russ. "You knew. He doesn't have a clue, but you *know*."

"No." Russ shook his head. "I suspect. Right now beyond the simple—" he hesitated "—theater of the situation he's got questions. He needs answers he can't get from anyone around here."

Maddie sucked air between her teeth, shook her head at him. "You knew so you put him on me."

"I been gone," Russ corrected her. "I didn't do nothin'."

Maddie snorted at the ungrammatical double-negative admission. "You abandoned me so this puppy could be obnoxious and work around to his questions if he could find three minutes alone with either Jess or me. You sent him in to distract me from *stuff*. And I mean all of the *stuff* including the *stuff* you don't want to talk about. Coward."

"Wasn't me," Russ said, though it was true. Taking her mind off whatever the problem was had always been the best way to handle Maddie. He'd figured distracting her with Carson's ham-handed quest for identity might also be an excellent way to sidetrack her pursuit of his personal commodities in her baby *expedition*. "Hadda be somebody else. Kid's too young and inexperienced for me to stick on Charlie Thorn's daughter when he's huntin' her." He shrugged. "Well, unless maybe my brothers are around for backup."

"Mmm." Maddie touched her emotion-reddened nose, pointed at him—*got it in one.* "Yeah, right." She linked her arm through the now wildly flare-eyed and confused, and perhaps justifiably anxious Carson's, and started to drag him away. "Come with me, child, and as dazed, scared and befuddled as I am about Jess, I shall attempt the wonders of the universe to convey—"

"L.T.?" Carson's voice squeaked.

Russ swallowed a grin of pure *hey, you brought this one on yourself,* and cleared his throat. "Mad, cut him loose, you're riding with me, after I get his report." He gave it a beat while Carson relaxed in relief and Maddie merely rocked back on her heels, blinked at him and waited. "Then you can have him."

Maddie's teeth showed.

Carson's face fell. "Aw, L.T...."

Russ shook his head, fresh out of sympathy. "Gotta learn, rookie. You're a peace officer. Don't go into situations you're not prepared to extricate yourself from, one way or another. Happens this one's benign. Another one might not be. Might involve weapons. You provoke it instead of controlling it, what're you gonna do then?"

"I—uh…" Carson swallowed, clenched his jaw. "Didn't think about it that way. It just…it came into my head and I said it. It won't happen again."

"No," Russ agreed seriously, "It won't. And to make sure it won't, all those questions I've seen piling up in your head, Maddie's the person might have some of the answers. So you help each other out, keep her mind off things, guard her good, and you learn something about yourself in the bargain, clear?"

Carson nodded once, hesitantly. "Yes, sir."

"Good." Russ let his mouth twitch upward at one corner. "Now, fill me in."

Carson's report was mostly a rehash of what Jonah had told him about Janina's ex-husband, with updates on Buddy's most recent whereabouts and activities, a creditable imitation of the police chief's manner and language when told Russ was missing and some advice about staying away from the Fat Cat until Tobi Hosey calmed down and stopped being so willing to throw hot coffee in cops' laps unless somebody did something to get Buddy Carmichael off her and Janina's doorstep—or she sure as shootin' would.

Shootin' being the operative word.

Russ cleared his throat and swallowed a grin over the mental picture of the incensed Tobi, then winced when he considered the fact that she was probably not kidding and that she was perfectly capable of following through with her scenario if she felt Janina or herself sufficiently threatened, harassed or downright provoked. Which meant, like it or not, he'd have to talk with her—and soon.

He rubbed a hand across his eyes, feeling more tired and hassled by the instant. His own fault, no doubt. Facing the consequences of whim. But no matter how much he might regret what Janina might face due to bad timing once people found out he'd married her, he still felt good about that. Good about her. Good about them. Good.

Damn it. He needed to touch Janina, to assure himself of the *good,* the *right* of it. Put his hands on her, experience what she felt to make sure she knew what he thought he knew: good, right, them, together, no going back.

Damn, who'd told him any of this was a good idea? He had responsibilities to live up to, priorities to stack and shuffle....

Hell to pay.

On a silent oath, he tossed Janina's car keys to Carson. "Get somebody to drive the Chevy wagon over to La Posada, park it out of sight, leave the keys for me at the desk. Have the desk ring me when the officers get there. We'll safe-house Ms. Thorn there tonight. The officers who bring the car can stay with her till shift change, then I want Bisti and Damiano with her till morning. We'll coordinate another safe house and a schedule from there."

The rookie nodded. "Where'll you be?"

Russ snorted. "When I'm done here, there and over *there?*"

"Chief'll ask."

Now he remembered what irritated him about nosey underlings, and this one in particular, regardless of whether or not he understood where Carson was coming from. "Chief's home in bed."

"I gotta leave a report."

Russ sucked air between his teeth. "Fine. Tell him he'll find me slouching toward Bethlehem…trying to avert the Apocalypse."

"Huh?"

"Never mind." Russ shook his head. "Maybe you didn't study Yeats in high school. Tell him I'll see him in the morning. We can get into it then."

And so saying, he headed for his truck, Maddie and the next argument.

Designed by Mary Elizabeth Jane Colter, chief architect and designer for the Fred Harvey Company and one of the female pioneers in architecture, La Posada had the look and feel of a grand hacienda circa 1869, which was exactly the fantasy history Colter had given it. It was large and rambling, as though many sections had been added on as its fantasy family grew and prospered, its roots heavily Spanish and Mexican with large, open, airy rooms, sweeping gardens and a feeling of enormity.

Opened just after the stock-market crash of 1929, it closed to the public in 1957 and had only opened its doors again as a hotel in 1997, a thing for which Janina was profoundly grateful. She'd always loved the beautiful building and its grounds, its history, its feel. The parts of her heritage that belonged to the hacienda shared a bond with this building and the story Mary Colter had woven around it, designed into it from beam to furniture, dishes to maids' uniforms. It didn't matter that they weren't the same today as they'd been in the thirties, the fact that they'd existed at all, that the stories existed were what mattered to Janina.

That and the fact that Russ had somehow known to bring her here, of all places, to continue their honeymoon while they figured out a place to begin their practical, real life together. How could he have known how she felt about this place? Did she talk so much to him when she didn't realize it? Or did he hear more when she didn't think he was listening than she realized?

Restless, unable to sleep thinking about him, Janina leaned over the balcony railing and watched the night grow late, the stars—ancient guides for lost travelers—rise clear and bright above the cottonwoods, stark against the summer sky. Perhaps if she could read them, they would tell her what to expect, where to go, how to tiptoe her way up the slender, twisty path she suddenly found herself on. On one side lay steep ravine, on the other a rocky fall toward nothing, at the end of the path, the girlish goal she'd set herself at sixteen: Russ.

Now she stood at the balcony watching the shadows, brown eyes charged with green thoughts, knowing he was out there somewhere, taking care of Maddie, the woman he could talk to the way he'd never been able to talk to her. And it upset her. She was too newly married, too newly touched, for it not to.

Too insecure in absolute trust for it not to.

Because despite "knowing" each other for the last thirteen years, she and Russ really didn't *know* each other at all. Not enough for that kind of trust. The kind where he could spend the sixth night of his marriage out with another woman, and his wife would just say, "Okay, fine, honey, see you whenever, no problem." No. That kind of trust took time. Took building. Took…

History.

A lot of history. And a lot of sleeping together. Perhaps years of it. And waking up together. And breakfasts. And stuff.

Like dating. And flowers. And maybe chocolates. And other traditional clichés like that.

Or something.

She grimaced, turned rebelliously away from whatever accusation she felt in the breeze that stirred a strand of hair across her cheek. Anyway, a lot more of everything than they'd done.

Geez—a kick directed at the balcony railing. She didn't want to be one of those women who was threatened by her man having a female best friend, damn it. For pity's sake, his youngest brother was one of her best friends, so what would that make her?

Wise, Tobi's omnipresent demon cackled gleefully in her ear. *When they look like Sharon Stone, it makes you wise.*

"Fiend," Janina whispered. But Tobi's anticipated comeback also made her laugh and feel better.

A sudden commotion in the hallway drew her attention. She cocked her head toward it, recognized Russ's voice and headed for the door. Jonah, recumbent across the portal, but only half-asleep, grabbed her ankle before she could open it.

"Stop."

"Russ is out there."

"And? It's still me out the door first, got it?"

She curled a lip at him disdainfully, giving him a raised eyebrow.

Jonah grinned. "Some other time, someone else's dime, huh? Russ is bigger than both of us."

"Leave your brother to me," Janina suggested.

"Gladly," Jonah assured her. "Next time."

"Coward," she muttered, but she stepped back out of the way when he slid out of the sleeping bag and slitted open the door.

And let in the tail end of a corker of an out-of-context argument.

"Well, it's not like I'm asking you to join the mayonnaise-jar-and-turkey-baster donation club, so just think about it once, Russell!" Maddie shouted.

"I'm not even having this conversation with you, Madelyn, so just forget it," Russ shouted back from the middle of the hallway.

"What's *she* doing here?" Janina asked, none too pleased to see the woman who was her nemesis in a room catty-corner from her honeymoon suite. Not to mention seeing her brand-new husband quite obviously having just emerged from the selfsame room.

Jonah shrugged. "At a guess? New safe-house accommodations. Ones where he can be with you and she can be near him."

"Ones where he can…and she can…" Janina gaped. Then swore.

"That about sums it up."

"Damn you, Russ, who else am I supposed to ask?" Maddie yelled now. "I don't want anybody else's baby!"

From up and down the hallway, doors of occupied

rooms opened, hotel guests poked forth curious heads, assessed the situation and retreated quickly.

"I'm not bartering my commodities with you, Maddie," Russ retorted furiously. "Get that through your thick, one-track skull. Now."

"Commodities?" Janina eyed Jonah.

"That's what I heard." Jonah nodded.

"Fine," Maddie called sweetly. "We'll talk about it later then. After you bring Jess back." She slammed her door loudly.

Russ took the steps to her door, pounded on it, ground out, "We will *not* talk about it later. We will not talk about it *ever*. We are done with this topic. Do you hear me?"

Maddie opened her door. "No. Did you say something?" She slammed it again in his face.

Jonah rubbed his chin, eyed Janina. "We don't know why they're friends. They've been arguing since they were six, ever since Russ told her she couldn't go around doing her own thing in other people's houses and she stuck her tongue out at him and flipped him off. I wasn't there, I wasn't born, but Mabel told me the stories."

"Mabel."

"It's always Mabel tells the stories."

"Hmm." Janina considered that. Contemplated the familiarity of it, the accompanying suspicion that didn't quite settle, shrugged it off in the face of other things. "Did you ever think they belonged together?"

"Who? Fuss and Bother?" Jonah assigned Russ and Maddie the brothers' favorite growing-up names for them.

Janina nodded.

He shook his head. "God forbid. Oh, once they thought so maybe, for about three days in high school when Russ took her to the prom, but that ended fast. They both knew it. They'd kill each other inside a day."

"Really."

Thoughtfully, Janina watched her husband take a frustrated swipe at the air beside Maddie's door with his foot then turn and stalk toward them, rubbing his face. When he caught sight of them he stopped short in midstep, foot in midair, a look of pained surprise on his face.

"Aw," he said stupidly, "hell." He put his foot down.

"Seems a relative place," his brother agreed obliquely.

Russ sent him a narrow-eyed *do not go there*. "What d'you know?"

Jonah straightened, said flatly, "I know better than to safe-house two women I've got feelings for in the same hotel and across the hall from each other."

"Maddie's not a woman—" Russ began, but the moment he got that far, two things happened simultaneously: Maddie's door popped open and she stuck her head out to inform him, "I am, too. I've got two X chromosomes and everything."

And Janina shoved Jonah into the hallway and told him soundly, "Go home." Then she crooked a finger at Russ. "Could I see you in here?"

"Ah." He looked around wildly, gave her a beleaguered, "Later. Gotta go coordinate the search for a missing woman and her kidnapper."

"You don't have anyone doing that already?"

"Ah. No. Sort of." Hedging. A hand through his hair in a clear attempt to rid himself of the moment. "I'm the senior. It's my responsibility. My case."

All truth as far as it went. Janina decided to tweak him—just a little. "You don't have to stay here to protect me from

Buddy. And Maddie from... What *are* you protecting Maddie from?"

Silence, more pained expression coupled with bewilderment and an obvious lack of knowledge of the right thing to say to his wife under the circumstances.

Or perhaps make that *any* circumstances.

"Fine." She relented, took pity on him. Oh man, he was cute, and in it far too deep to do more than try to unnecessarily bury history from her anyway, despite the green edges around her vision where Maddie was concerned.

"Fine," she said again. Her lips twitched. She eyed him up and down, found herself *mmm-mmm*-ing appreciatively under her breath. Even when he was getting under her skin by not talking to her, he got under her skin and heated her blood all the way from her toes to her scalp. "What were you going to do if the, er, volume of your conversation with Ms. Thorn hadn't brought every guest on this floor out into the hallway for a look-see?"

It took him a moment to shift mental gears, for understanding to hit him, but when he did, the change was instant. The defensiveness went out of his posture. His mouth curved with sensuous promise, eyes went hot and black. His entire attention focused on her, caressed her as potently, as heatedly, as physically as his hands might. Flowed back up to lock on her eyes, his own as deep as midnight, infinite as the stars she'd watched earlier and far more willing to find and guide her to secret lands into which only he knew the trails.

Janina swallowed hard, slumped against the doorjamb, and puddled under the weight of the heat in his eyes.

"I'm gone," Jonah muttered, and went before anyone had a notion to notice or hear him.

Janina held out a hand to Russ. "Get in here," she ordered hoarsely.

And predator about to take prey, wolf after mate, he came.

They took each other, and not gently. Demanded full custody of each other's spirits and souls, minds and hearts along with each thought and taste, thrust and parry, song and desire.

They didn't bother with darkness. The shadows and things half-spoken between them were enough to shroud them in dimness, enough to entertain mystery and mystique, to keep them guessing about each other and where they stood—anywhere but here. Locked together, bodies joined, his within hers around his seeding hers.

Breaths labored, mingled, groaned.

Kisses drugged and drugging, soft, deep, breaking away, skating flesh heated beyond burning. Skin rising to follow the tongue, the lips, the mouth. Bodies slipping together, flesh slapping gently, urgently, higher, tighter, faster, in and in and bursting in lightness, exploding in nothingness, hanging suspended in pure release....

Then resting in silence and awe, wondering at the magic, insecure in the sensation of security. Gathering together the moments and the strength to begin again.

Chapter 8

Dawn.

Etchings of pink low against the horizon, soft among the ridges of cloud slumbering without malice at the rim of the sky; below them sounded the clickety-clack of trains speeding east and west, forth and back, hither and beyond in an endless quest to get people and goods, commodities and shares, from one part of the country to the next.

Within the hacienda-hotel a satisfied sigh in sleep, the shift of a palm beneath a pillow, hip and thigh to a more comfortable position. The touch of a lover easing carefully out from under an arm, a leg, the head pillowed on his shoulder lest he should waken the woman he must leave.

The gentle murmur of sheets sliding against skin, the near-silent dip and sigh of Russ's body coming upright in the bed, rising to pad across the room, stooping to collect his clothing.

In semidarkness he closed the bathroom door, washed and dressed as quickly and quietly as possible. If Janina woke, spoke, touched him again, he didn't know if he'd have the strength to leave her. And he had to this time.

Part of who he was lay in what he did. If he didn't establish that between them now, at the start of their marriage, it was over. He was lost.

They were lost.

You couldn't stop being who you were because of what you wanted to add to your life or who else you wanted to become especially if you didn't want to stop being who you were at the same time.

He wanted to add *being a husband*—and one day a father, but he also planned to continue being a cop, a native artisan alchemist-jeweler and designer, a brother, a friend —but not necessarily in that order.

Right now, "husband" was the closest to his heart, the first thing on his mind, the most tempting to his soul and body. But "cop" and "friend" were the order of the day. Had to be. If he didn't put them first, he wouldn't be able to look himself in the mirror.

Sometimes, things he saw and had seen, things he remembered, things he did—especially when his temper got away from him, even if he could almost call it justified—made it difficult enough as it was to look himself in the mirror first thing in the morning.

"Russ?" Muzzy and delectable, Janina slipped quietly into the bathroom behind him, tucked her arms around his waist and rested her cheek against his back. "What are you doing?"

Russ tried to ignore the feel of her, his body's singular longing to simply sink into her and stay there forever without thought or apology. "Getting ready for work." With an effort he made himself unlink her arms from about him, draw her away.

"At this hour?" She squinted around trying to find a clock. "Is it even four-thirty yet? And you don't have your uniform."

"I'll stop for it." Janina's eyes widened with surprise and Russ winced. He sounded a little short, even to himself. He kissed her roughly. "Sorry. I don't want to leave. I have to or I wouldn't."

"Ah." A smile, slow and inviting, accompanied by her hand sliding up his chest and around to cup his head, drag him down to her. "You could wait then. I promise to kick you out when I leave for work later, too."

"God, Janie." He groaned into her mouth. "Don't do this to me. I can't. You make it too hard."

"That's pretty much the point," she murmured, wondering anew at his instant response to her. Her own need to be—to remain—part of him, one with him.

For a moment she had him.

Had him in his kiss, deep and sinking deeper.

Had him in the fingers threading her hair, anchoring her to him; in the hand slipping over her rump to bring her close, tuck her high to fit him.

And then she didn't have him anymore.

Because with an oath he set her away, left her startled and aching without a word or a backward glance until he reached the door to the corridor. Where he stopped and turned back, but didn't quite look at her leaning against the bathroom doorway in half shock.

"Someone's removing people, players from the field, to get at Maddie and me." The pronouncement was ragged, strained, almost harsh. "I doubt whoever it is knows about you but I can't take that chance and Maddie's lyin' to me about something, so Jonah's your watchdog today." He stopped, drew a breath. Sent her the look of a man bemused beyond reckoning, a cop torn between duties. "Put something on. I'll send over one of the officers with Maddie until Jonah gets here. Don't go anywhere without him." It was not a request.

Then he was gone, closing the door quietly, leaving Janina gaping after him, torn among a tumult of rising emotions: desire, frustration, curiosity, concern for him and finally, overriding the others, fury at his high-handed assignment of his brother as her watchdog for the day— or however long he deemed necessary.

Why had she never noticed this side of Russ before?

Because she'd been too busy staring at his angel's face, that's why, noting his knight-in-shining deeds, wanting his blasted body commingling with hers.

Autocratic, arrogant turkey. Well, she didn't have to do a blasted thing he said. She eyed her state of undress in the mirror. Except maybe put something on, because she didn't plan to flash the nation—even if "the nation" only happened to be another cop and Jonah—just to spite him.

But she'd damn well have a good seethe-and-plotting session while she wasn't flashing anybody. As a matter of fact...

She grabbed a cover-up and slammed out the door after her husband, intent on catching him before he left Maddie's room.

"And another thing, Russ Levoie," she said, picking up the conversation with him where she'd left it off in her head the moment she stopped banging on Maddie's door. The moment it cracked open, she shoved her way inside. "I do not care who you think you are, you do not—Hey!"

Even as she shrieked, someone grabbed her, yanked her arms behind her back, slammed her face-first into the wall beside the door and handcuffed her wrists together. She yanked hard away, twisted around and lashed out with a kick that struck her captor squarely in the side of the knee, causing him to buckle a bit—at which point she hopped up and used her other foot to kick him in the groin. He let her go and doubled backward with a harsh groan, covering up.

"Maddie!" Janina yelled, ducking between two more moving silhouettes in the shadowy early-morning light. "Maddie, are you all right?"

"She's fine," Russ snapped, snatching her up under his arm before she could do more damage to either of his on-duty officers. "What're you doing barging in here?"

"Russ?" She swiveled her neck from side to side trying to see him. "Put me down, damn it. What was he doing handcuffing me? I was looking for you."

"Well, you slammed in here like some hell-for-leather perp, so what'd you think would happen? Somebody'd open the door and say, 'C'mon in, honey, pop one in her ear?'" He dumped her upright in a chair and towered over her. "I don't care who the hell you are. Not happenin', babe."

She glared *I dare you* up at him. "Tell me you didn't know it was me."

"I was in the bathroom with Maddie. I didn't know it was you because I didn't hear you. They didn't know it was you because I hadn't told 'em you were here." He bent close to her, nose to nose, eye to eye, and dropped his voice, made it for her ears alone. "They didn't know *we* were here. Together. Do you follow me?"

"Oh, I follow you all right," she muttered furiously. "I do. You just don't want anyone to know…" Her voice trailed off. She looked at him, the warning in his eyes, the guarded expression on his face.

"Someone's removing players from the field…. I doubt whoever it is knows about you…."

He saw her realization and tilted his head in the most imperceptible of nods. She squeezed her eyes shut against it. So that's what he meant. If no one inside knew, no one outside could possibly know, either. Safer if they kept their relationship as private as possible for the moment.

Which was what she'd told Jonah she wanted to do anyway.

Fury slipped away in residual irritation, fleeting frustration, perplexity over who—or what—Maddie really was— what kind of danger she might really be in—and what she, Janina, could have missed by being simply sixteen and focused on only one thing during the trial and its insinuations, its aftermath.

"Okay," she whispered. Acquiescent now didn't mean she couldn't give him hell later, when the timing was more appropriate.

Russ leaned in close, slipped his arms around her under cover of unlocking her handcuffs and left a surreptitious kiss in her hair. "See you for dinner if I can," he muttered before backpedaling upright to toss the handcuffs to the slowly recovering Damiano. "You can stay here, but don't assault any more of my men or I'll have to run you in," he advised her dryly and headed for the door.

She picked up the nearest thing to hand—a book—and threw it at him. He caught it and set it neatly on a hand-crafted table, grinned at her and left.

Janina couldn't quite decide if she found herself truly beginning to love or hate those grins. She did, however, think she was learning to decipher them.

The thought made her shudder with…she wasn't sure what. Anticipation and recklessness, maybe. Because taciturn though he might appear, the man was Levoie to the bone.

She slumped in the chair and covered her ears. And no, she didn't need to hear George Thorogood singing inside her head a bastardized version of his lyrics to "Bad to the Bone," that had Russ as the key player.

The woman was frightened, crying again.

In growing panic the thin man paced a track in the earth in front of the shelter he'd built and tried to think. When she cried, his head hurt and that made it hard for him to focus and he knew he had to. He wasn't hurting her, he hadn't hurt her—they gave him pills so he wouldn't do that anymore, so he wouldn't want to, and he *didn't* want to. Hurting was wrong. But she had to stop crying so he could think. His head wasn't right when he couldn't think. *He* wasn't right.

He went to the shelter's entry and tried to tell her that. "D-don't c-cry. Y-you m-mustn't c-cry. I c-can't th-think when you c-cry." He wasn't sure if she heard him. The medication made his mouth dry, had given him a tick that made him stutter occasionally. He used the metal cup beside the five-gallon jug filled with fresh water to get a drink, tried again. "I won't hurt you. I'm not hurting you. I just need you to help me. She won't t-talk to me, s-see m-me. Help me. P-please."

He thought she quieted but couldn't be sure. She didn't seem as loud anyway, and that helped.

Satisfied, he resumed his pacing, his watch, his methodical attempts to figure out what would make his daughter forgive him for all the things he'd done to her so many years ago....

Feeling more than a little underdressed for the company she was in, Janina tucked her honeymoon robe more securely around herself and stood, intent on returning to her own room for more substantial clothing. A muffled sob from behind Maddie's closed bathroom door stopped her. She glanced at Damiano and Bisti, the two cops on duty. They shrugged a nonverbal *it's been off and on all night* at her. On a sigh, she eyed the door, sucked air between her teeth and grimaced an "Aw damn" at herself, and marched over to rap gently on the door.

"Maddie?"

The bathroom went silent.

"Maddie, it's Janina. Let me in."

"What did you do, make a food run from the Fat Cat?" The attempted tartness sounded pretty clogged and watery to Janina. "I'm pretty sure they serve breakfast downstairs at a reasonable hour, so you needn't have bothered."

Not in the mood for tart or anything like it, Janina punched the door with the edge of her fist. "Madelyn Thorn, I know you're upset, so I'm gonna let the aspersions cast on my job slide. Now open the damn door before I kick it in and the Winslow P.D. has to pay for it, or you do, because I sure as lightning will not."

There was a brief pause where Janina could almost hear Maddie considering the question "Can you really do that?" To which the answer was "Do *not* try me," because yes, Janina had learned to do exactly that sort of thing in her kickboxing classes, but she wasn't wearing shoes at the moment and she didn't want to have to prove herself here and now without them.

Fortunately, the brief pause passed and Maddie opened the door far enough for Janina to squeeze through. Then she slammed it closed and locked it, leaving the police emphatically on the outside once more.

The "two women in Russ's life"—as Jonah had referred to them—sized each other up.

For the first time, Janina took a good hard look at Maddie close up, and realized what she'd never seen before: that despite the other woman's best efforts, her cosmetics training and expertise, at thirty-two the brutal mileage inflicted on Maddie during her early years definitely showed. Gone was the Sharon Stone-like image. Instead Janina saw scars at the hairline and at her lip that plastic surgery couldn't hide, burn marks at the side of her face and on her arms it hadn't erased. Janina didn't want to think where else the scars existed on Maddie's body, how bad they might be, the horrors that had produced them.

Instead, she looked at Maddie's reddened eyes and said the first thing that came into her head. "Are you in love with Russ?"

"If I were," Maddie retorted promptly, "would it be any of your business?"

Janina held up her ring hand, waggled the fingers. "Vegas, the eighteenth, married. So, yeah."

"What?" Maddie grabbed Janina's hand for a better look at the ring. "You're kidding. No wonder he wasn't here. He didn't say anything." She turned Janina's hand this way and that, studying the ring. Shook her head with a wry laugh. "Trust Russ to mix something like Baltic amber with the most expensive metal he could find."

Janina took offense, immediately fingering the cross at her throat. "Why? Amber's my favorite gem."

Maddie held up a placating hand. "I didn't mean anything by that, and if it's your favorite, that'd be why he did it. It's just…" Her gaze hit suddenly on Janina's fingers, the cross. She reached for it, stopped. "May I?" When Janina said nothing, but let go so she could see it, Maddie lifted the piece delicately, held it to the light. Smiled slightly. Turned it over so she could look at the silver backing. Laughed softly. "And this is how he knew."

"What?" Janina took the cross back, shoved it into the mirror to try to see what Maddie had seen.

"See this down here?" Maddie pointed out a mark stamped into the silver. "I could tell by looking at the design, but this proves it. You found this, where…medieval fair, Renaissance festival, something like that?" Janina nodded. Maddie smiled. "Yeah. Well. He might not seem like it, but Russ likes to play. This is how he relaxes. That's his lowercase *RL*. He made this cross, too."

"He did?" Janina shoved the cross back into the mirror, moved in for a closer look. The flamboyant *RL* that she'd never have equated with Russ took backward shape in the glass, feeding her subconscious insights into the man she'd married even as her mouth softened and her eyes started to glow without her knowledge. "He did."

Maddie laughed gently and shook her head, squeezed Janina's shoulder. "You'll do." Another headshake, accompanied by a wry chuckle. "Which makes your ring vintage Russ. Unusual to see amber paired with diamonds and platinum, you know? And he's the only native designer I know who works in platinum, the only designer I've ever met who'll pair expensive precious anything with more or less inexpensive semi just because he likes the way it looks." She held out her own left hand, showed Janina the wide platinum band with the exquisitely cut figures decorating the third finger. "He designed and made our story rings, too."

Something queasy and unhappy fluttered in Janina's belly. *"Ours?"*

Maddie sniffed and nodded before she caught the accusation, the inflection on the single word. "Yeah. *Ours.*" She stepped up close suddenly, and looked Janina in the eye, all flint, steel and seriousness. "Do you love him?"

"Since I was sixteen. Yes." The answer sprang out of Janina as involuntarily as her initial question to Maddie. She drew breath, swallowed. Shuddered. "Wow. I've never said that out loud before." Then anxiously, "Don't tell him. He needs his head bounced a few times before he hears it."

Maddie's face crumpled into a genuine smile and she fingered an X on her chest. "Cross my heart he won't hear it from me." She held up her own ring hand, pointed to the ring before Janina could pursue her original line of inquiry. "And I love Russ, too, but I've got my own lover, so you needn't worry about..." She hesitated, considered the options. "Me getting in the way like that. I won't. I'm a little needy right now, that's all. Sort of goes with the territory, you know? Charlie out of prison, history catching up..."

She shrugged, looked away, spelled it out. "He took Jess, my girlfriend. My partner." Her face grew bleak. "My life. She's everything, made me everything." She breathed through her nose, blinked hard. Eyed Janina steadily. "Russ ropes the moon, he walks on water as far as I'm concerned.

But Jess…" She fiddled with the ring on her finger. "Jess is the earth, she makes the sun rise, she's the reason. Do you see?"

"Oh," Janina said, at once relieved and curiously deflated. She'd sported green-eyed monsters around the edges of her vision for a long time where Maddie was concerned. She wasn't sure what it would be like not to see things tinged in that shade anymore. But she did see. Understood completely. Because in some way, Russ had been all of those things to her for years: earth, sun, water, moon, reason. She just hadn't known him well enough to be more than "in love" with him. But six days and nights and she knew she was way beyond "in love." Hopelessly hooked would be more to the point.

Even if they still didn't know each other all that well.

She nodded once in empathy. "Yeah. I do. Oh man, do I!" Then, curiously, "Is that what Russ meant when he said Charlie—your father—was taking people from the field? Is Jess who he meant? He said but he didn't if you know what I mean."

Maddie snorted. "Russ? Explain something? So you can actually understand it? Ha!"

"You do know the same guy, then. I thought maybe it was just me. He doesn't talk around me, you know. Or quite *to* me for that matter."

"Well, it's you and it's not just you." Maddie crossed her arms over her chest and leaned tiredly against the sink. "He likes to think he knows what's best for everybody. Unfortunately, he does a lot of the time. Comes from growing up in charge of everything. But that's not the point. He also likes to *tell* you what's best for you, but not *why* it's best for you. Which is damn annoying if you ask me—which he often doesn't."

"Ah," Janina said wisely. "Hence the arguing."

Maddie tapped herself on the nose with an index finger, pointed at Janina. "Precisely."

They were silent for a moment, digesting, settling, then Janina made a soft sound of "the hell with it," screwed up her face and asked, "Do you ever get used to it?"

"What?" Maddie rubbed her eyes tiredly.

"Russ."

"It?" Maddie's attempt to swallow her involuntary grin was visible.

Janina ignored her. "And more important, have you ever found a way to get him to just stop?"

"Stop?" The swallowed grin became painful-sounding choked-back laughter. "Russ? How long have you known him?"

Russ's wife grimaced. "That's completely beside the point. Which is," she said emphatically when Maddie would have interrupted, "have you ever figured out a way to get him to tell you what he should *when* he should just because you need and want to know it?"

"Oh." Russ's best friend winced. "That."

Janina nodded. "Exactly."

"No."

"Well what good are you as his best friend, then?" Janina snapped irritably. "And a woman to boot? Aren't you supposed to be able to help me figure him out?"

For a space of ten seconds Maddie stared at Janina dumbfounded. Then she dropped her face into her hands, her shoulders started to shake and little gurgles erupted from her.

"Maddie?" Oh hell, she hadn't meant to sound so abrupt.

Janina reached out to put a hand on the other woman's shoulder in an attempt to comfort her. The moment she did, Maddie's gurgles changed to snorts and then to huge, gulping whoops of laughter. She waved Janina away, grabbed her sides and doubled over her knees in an attempt to regain control.

"I'm sorry," she said through the mirth. "I didn't expect…"

A fresh wave of amusement wiped out whatever she wanted to say. Disgusted, Janina decided she understood exactly why Russ and Maddie were best friends despite their constant bickering. Their senses of humor clearly matched.

She smacked Maddie between the shoulder blades when the other woman started to cough from laughing too long and hard. "Get a grip," she said grumpily. "You remind me of Russ."

That sobered Maddie some. "God forbid," she croaked. "I talk to people—he doesn't."

"So help me figure out a way to get *him* to talk to *me*."

The simplicity of Janina's plea, the underlying uncertainty behind it, must have spoken to Maddie's own fears and doubts and changed everything. Abruptly serious, she straightened.

"Come on," she said. "Let's get Winslow's finest to order us some room service and I'll tell you about Russ. It'll keep my mind off Jess, and if we're lucky, you'll find something in what I know about your husband that'll help you figure out what to do about him."

Chapter 9

August 3

Russ didn't make it back to Janina in time for dinner. In fact, he didn't make it back in time for anything for days.

A lot of days.

Even if he'd planned to open his mouth and say, "You know I got married, I just wanna go kiss my wife," there'd have been no opportunity to do so. Because aside from the need to find Charlie and Jess, Winslow and its environs were experiencing a sudden upsurge in violent crime due to the increasingly intense late-July-into-August heat, a couple of kids from nearby Two Guns had gone ATVing in the desert and disappeared in approximately the same area that a convict being transported to the state facility at Phoenix had escaped, and the ongoing drought had finally led to the fires they didn't need. So no one else was off kissing spouses or significant others, either.

In fact, "You go AWOL for six days and this place goes to hell in a handbasket" was pretty much the only printable thing Russ heard from his chief whenever their paths crossed, which, mercifully, wasn't often as they were each needed to direct traffic and coordinate…a lot of stuff…elsewhere.

So Russ stayed out of the chief's way and went out and turned over way more rocks than he would have liked searching for Charlie.

And came up empty every time.

Including chats with the prison warden and psychologists, who swore up and down Charlie was a changed man who stuck to his medication religiously and would never return to his old ways without the sudden removal of the meds, which would likely cause psychotic episodes, the parole officer with whom Charlie had never checked in, Charlie's few known associates and all of the campgrounds or remotely viable campable areas within a three-hour radius.

He met Guy—and the massively pregnant Hazel who insisted that as an FBI ASAC—Assistant Special Agent in Charge—even on forced maternity leave, she had connections they could use—at his trailer in an effort to go over the days' old trail in an attempt to pick up something that might have been overlooked when Jess had gone missing.

And he still came up with nothing.

Which was discouraging, and took him more outside his comfort zone than he was already. The fact that he'd stepped outside himself enough to get married rocked him. He barely understood how he'd done that, let alone how to handle it, but this…

This was Maddie's—his best friend's—life, her heart on the line. He wanted results, he wanted them last week, and he didn't like not having control over this situation. Not when he had women, plural, to protect, as well as one to retrieve.

Particularly not when one of those women held his heart in her hands. He especially didn't know what to do about that. A few days absorbing Janina followed by a few days of unscheduled apart, topped by the knowledge that because of him—well, because of Charlie and Buddy and him—she could face any sort of danger, scared him.

To death.

He had to keep her safe.

Rather chauvinistically macho of him to think of it that way, perhaps, but you didn't grow up the oldest, the biggest and the tallest brother in a family full of boys and come away thinking differently. He had to protect his younger brothers, too. Jonah, for instance, eight years his junior and too untried to be let out alone much of the time. And Russ was trying to let go, but it would be a damn sight easier if the kid read the signs and took up law enforcement in some other jurisdiction the way Guy and Jeth had.

The way Mabel had done by going into forensics. Hard for Russ, two years her junior, to overprotect her there. Harder still for him to dictate how Guy and Jeth did their jobs when they weren't under his thumb as well. Which didn't stop him trying, it simply meant he'd been forced to learn his limitations with them.

Maybe because he was of an age with them and had been up close and personal with the dangers his siblings faced, it was more difficult for him to accept, than for their parents to understand, that you can't make choices for the people you loved, they had to choose for themselves.

Dangerous situations between him and them or not.

And between finding out what Charlie had really done to Maddie, his youngest sister, Marcy, dying a few years ago on Jeth's watch, and the lives his brothers had managed to lead—especially over the last many months—there'd been enough dangerous situations among them to fill at least two books. He didn't want Janina facing anything more that could fill a book. Maddie's life was already book enough.

If he was to be completely truthful with himself, keeping Janina safe was the only way to protect himself, his heart.

His soul.

He had to see her, had to touch her, make sure she was real. *They* were real.

And he was aware that since he'd essentially abandoned her without contact roughly a week ago now, if she had any sense at all, she'd left him.

Please God, he hoped not.

In the middle of the moment when the missing Two Guns boys were located alive sixty miles from the last available escaped-convict sighting, Russ left the latest nonproductive search of an abandoned underground storage facility to other investigators, turned around and headed back to town, stalked by the uneasy sense that something he'd left undone was either haywire or about to go in that direction. Disquiet only increased when he tried to raise Jonah by radio and failed. A quick stop at La Posada to discover that both Janina *and* Maddie had been checked out by their respective keepers helped not at all and had him headed for the station at speed.

A glimpse of Jonah's multicolored pickup parked to the rear of the Fat Cat sent him skidding and squealing, fishtailing into the diner's parking lot where he barely took time to slam the Jimmy's door shut when he vaulted out and stalked inside.

"Ah, there you are," Jonah said, rising from Russ's usual booth to stretch the kinks out of his back. "I wondered when you'd show up."

Russ grabbed him by the shirtfront, prepared to shove him back into the booth. "What the *hell*—"

A hand fell on his arm, elbow linked through his, yanked him forcibly away from Jonah. "Why, hello, Lieutenant," Maddie said brightly. "How nice of you to drop by. Let me show you to a table." She shoved him into a chair at a table in the center of the room.

He eyed her up and down, the gum she chewed avidly, the pink whatever it was she was wearing to play diner hostess. Overalls, he thought maybe, tied down around her waist, with a belly shirt, and was that a diamond in her navel? Weird. Not Maddie at all. Clearly, distraught over Jess didn't begin to cover it.

Hysterical and gone mad might be closer to the point.

"Ah, here'll be fine, thanks," he said. "I guess." Though it wasn't. Because he didn't like sitting in the center of the room. He liked the back of the restaurant. The corner. Where he could see everything without being seen unless he wanted to be. But he thought it might not be good to disagree with her just now, the way she looked and all. Full of attitude.

"Good." She smiled—sort of—and patted him on the head. "I'll get you a menu. Meanwhile, digest this." She dug into a pocket, handed him a folded receipt and, nose in the air, ambled off in no real hurry to get anywhere, particularly to his menu.

Eyebrows beetled in consternation, Russ watched her go. Jess was missing and Maddie was *ambling* about a *diner*—the sort of small-town place she'd have told you she'd worked hard to get away from—*chewing gum* and *hostessing* in pink. *Patting him on the head*, for God's sake—a truly disconcerting sign—and not telegraphing any messages to him. Good, bad or otherwise.

Somehow he was certain this did not bode well.

At all.

He looked at the receipt in his hand, discovered it appeared to be more a sheaf of them, and glanced across at Jonah, who simply blinked.

"You wanna fill me in?" Russ did his best to make it a suggestion. A mild one.

Jonah worked his shoulders, sat deep in his seat and shook his head. "No."

Russ's eyes narrowed, jaw hardened. "There a reason?"

His brother studied the question a moment, shrugged his mouth then waggled the fingers of his left hand in the air. "I'm not the one wearing a promise to communicate on my wedding hand. Not the one who didn't call when I went off for better than a week on a high-stakes chase that might be dangerous. Or the one who left my brother to sit on his butt and watchdog my bride. Speakin' a' which…" He slid around in the booth and rose to stand in the aisle between tables, stuck out his rear and looked over his shoulder at it. Asked with mock anxiety, "My butt look fat to you? Been sittin' on it a lot lately. Women who won't date me have been shovin' food at me. I'm not gettin' any exercise. Not gettin' out…"

"What the hell is wrong with everyone here today?"

The decibel level was well modulated, but Russ didn't

get beyond half rising in his seat before Tobi planted a hand on his shoulder and leaned on him.

"Whoa there, big guy, where ya goin'?" She turned over his coffee mug. "Have some coffee. Oops. Well, look at that."

Stunned, Russ did. At the now-empty coffeepot, the contents of which were soaking his lap, his chair, his rear and through to his nether regions.

Tobi cocked her head, studied her handiwork with satisfaction. "Good thing I saved the cold stuff for you, huh?" she said and took the all too readily available towel off her shoulder, dropped it between his legs and started to leave. "Oh. Almost forgot." She came back and pulled a folded diner check out of her apron pocket, planted it on the table and slid it across to him with one delicate finger. "Your bill, Lieutenant. One full pot of cold coffee and five full days' worth of meals for Officer Levoie. You can pay at the register on your way out."

Then she sashayed away, swinging the coffeepot, while the Fat Cat's patrons looked on, wearing expressions that ranged from stifled mirth to shock.

Jonah studied his eldest brother with interest. Russ stared back, trying to figure out where his wits had gone—or better yet, wondering if he'd had any to begin with.

Because sure as sin he was dreaming this. Wet, coffee-stained lap and all.

"Wait for it," Jonah advised.

Russ crinkled his already crinkled, beleaguered brows. "What?"

Jonah pointed with his chin. "Incoming. One more."

If he'd paid attention to the warning, turned and ducked fast enough, he might have avoided the clip upside the head Janina gave him with her ring hand. But he didn't. Not any of it. Didn't turn, duck or avoid the ring she'd turned stone in to smack him just behind his right ear—hard.

"Ow! Damn. What the f…hell? Ring, Janie. Platinum, stone, hurts."

"You had more hair, it mighta cushioned the blow," his wife responded tartly. "But more to the point, do I have your attention?"

He regarded her with circumspection. Tipped his chin forward once—cautiously—without taking his eyes off her.

"Good." She rewarded him with a toothy grin, a lot of fluttering eyelashes and a glance at his lap. "You know coffee stains. You really oughta get out of those wet things. Here." She whisked away his empty coffee mug and dropped a huge, fluffy, new, bright *purple* bath towel the size of a blanket on the table in front of him and patted his cheek. "I brought this from home in case of emergencies. Wrap it around yourself and c'mon in the back. I mighta brought you in a clean uniform or something to change into in the event something like this happened first time Tobi saw you since, well…" She winked at him. *"You know."*

"Aw, damn." Russ slumped in his chair and scrubbed a hand across his eye. "I was worried you'd left me. Instead, you're gonna make me pay, right?"

Janina's smile this time was genuine, wicked and wholly feminine. "Ah-ah, no telling, remember? You made the rules." She pulled her bill pad out of her pocket, scribbled on it, tore off the chit and dug into another pocket to pull out a cell phone and a beeper. She handed them to him along with the chit and a list of numbers and codes. "Presents," she told him succinctly, managing to capitalize the words even in speech. "Communications devices. My new cell-phone and beeper numbers are programmed in for you already.

You'll find me listed under My Wife—just to prevent any possible confusion you might have over my being anyone else's wife. Which makes these tools Direct Links To The Little Woman, aka Your Next Of Kin. Learn to use 'em."

With a twitch of her hips that managed to say "I don't give a damn what you've been up to for the last week without a word to me, Russ Levoie," at the same time that it somehow gave full, taunting meaning to the come-hither sway-and-roll in departure mode, Janina left him without a backward glance.

None of the patrons in the Fat Cat were leaving. Live improvisational theater at one of the town's police lieutenant's expense was enough of a rarity in Winslow that everybody had to see what would happen next. Russ had no doubt there'd be a reporter with a camera soon.

He glared significantly at Jonah who, although doing an admirable job of covering, could clearly be listed among the "entertained."

"So," the shortest Levoie brother said, leaning out of his booth trying to catch a glimpse at the writing on the chit Janina had handed Russ without actually coming in range of Russ's hands, "C'n I see how much she's charging you for the lesson?"

"You're hell-bent on a short life, aren't you?" Russ snapped.

"No, really," Jonah said innocently. "I wanna know. I'm tryin' to learn from your mistakes. Educate me. You got one brand-new purple towel, a clip upside the head, a beeper and a cell phone, *her* beeper and cell phone, cleaning costs on your uniform—and whatever she got out of your trailer when I wasn't lookin' and brought in here for you to wear if Tobi dumped coffee in your lap, which we all knew she would, she's been in that kinda mood for two weeks—and whatever else she figured in that isn't comin' to mind right now." He paused for breath, leaned a little closer, gestured a finger at the check and said conspiratorially, "Anyway, c'mon. You owe me. Read it. Tell me."

Russ considered killing him on the spot, witnesses notwithstanding and entertainment value being what it was and all. Reconsidered half a tick later when Janina once again put in an appearance behind him, dappled her fingers along the back of his neck, dropped off an order at another table and disappeared once more after sending him a look that smoked with challenge: *Come talk to me or…else.*

Or…else what?

Russ contemplated his options. Precious few rose to mind. He grimaced, eyed the cell phone and beeper, the sheaf of receipts from Maddie, the chit from Tobi, the huge purple bath towel and the check from Janina's bill pad. Did a double take and nearly choked when he registered what she'd written there.

"I'm not wearing undies."

Blew out a breath and slid a finger around his collar to alleviate the sudden tightness before divesting himself of his radio and gun and passing both to Jonah, who grinned at the preventive measures. Then he got up without meeting anyone's eyes, wrapped the blasted flaming purple towel around his soaked—and sort of dripping by now— uniform pants, and strode into the Fat Cat's netherworld to make damn sure that by the time he left, his wife was wearing her panties.

Chapter 10

Janina waited for him in the doorway of the Fat Cat's small upstairs office. The suit bag containing whatever she'd brought for him to change into hung on a rack opposite the door.

She didn't let him get near it.

The moment he came within range, she snagged him at the waist and hauled him bodily into the office, shut the door and locked it behind them.

"I'm sorry," he said immediately. "I should've…"

"Later," she muttered, stretching upward on her toes, reaching for his mouth with her own even as she tossed aside the towel, undid his belt and worked open his sodden trousers, shoved them off with his shorts and pushed him off balance into the leatherette desk chair. "Sit," she ordered. "Shoes off."

He huffed uncomfortable laughter. "Janie, what—"

"Quiet. Take off your shoes. I can't get your pants off over them."

"I'm stickin' to the chair."

She rolled her eyes at him but grabbed the towel off the desk, handed it to him and went back to dragging his pants down his legs. "Put the towel under you."

Laughter was awkward, almost painful. She was nuts, he couldn't figure her out, and she was beautiful. Enticing. Exhilarating.

Enthralling.

He wanted her.

"What the hell are you doing?"

She pulled his pants off inside out with his shorts on the outside of them, and straightened and said impatiently, "Undressing you, duh. Now your shirttails are probably wet, too. You want me to get that for you, too, or you want to help?"

Russ figured it was probably best to just sit back and enjoy the ride, so he did. Sat back, parked his elbows wide over the arms of the chair and said judiciously, "No, you got a bug in your ear, you'll get to it eventually. Go ahead, help yourself."

The "bug in your ear" part might not have been the wisest thing he'd ever said, but Janina only paused a moment to narrow her eyes, work her jaw tightly over her neck and suck her teeth in irritation before reaching for his top shirt button.

By the time she got to his third button, she'd wedged her knees in between his thighs and the arms of the chair so she could straddle his lap. On the fourth button she took his mouth, and on the fifth she took him.

She never did finish getting his shirt off him.

* * *

Slumped heavily, forehead beneath his chin, a short while later, Janina felt Russ's pulse pound beneath her skin while she waited for her breath to catch up with her. Her knees were starting to cramp, but she didn't want to move, the rest of her was too comfortable, too situated, too right. *He* was right, finally, where he belonged. With her. If she moved, she'd destroy that, have to get on with…reality.

The things that made him stupid. The things that made her want to crack him over the head with a pot to see if that wouldn't brain some sense into him. Because for the love of God, what made him think he could just marry her then tell her they were all in danger then go off for a week into who knew where…without a word. Without a blankety-blank-blankety *word*.

It made her want to shake him.

Especially when she thought about the part where nobody knew to call her if he got hurt so she could be there, damn it. Because he didn't get to get injured in the line of duty anymore without her having something to say to him about the outcome.

And no, she didn't care that it'd been an especially overtaxing week at the P.D. Sally Kamiski knew where her husband was and Don Chaney had heard from his wife and everyone she'd asked had heard from spouse, fiancé, significant other or what have you.

Except her. And she was definitely *not* in the mood to excuse him on the grounds that he might have forgotten because they were simply too new for him to have *remembered* or *thought* to have called. Stupidity was the only explanation.

That or he thought that if he didn't contact her she'd worry less.

Which led her directly back to stupidity.

As if sensing what she thought, Russ lifted a hand, let it drift through her hair and down her back.

"How much sorry do I owe you?" he asked softly.

She puffed out a half laugh, half sigh, and pushed herself up to lean her forearms against his chest. "It's not about sorry, Russ. This one's about more. You left me hanging. You didn't let me know anything one way or another. And you didn't let anybody else know about me. If anything happened to you, I'd want to know. I'd want to be there. That's what I've had to think about this week. The fact that I wouldn't have been notified if you'd been hurt, that nobody would have come for me."

He stared at her stunned, while the truth hit home for the first time. If anything happened to her, too, under the present circumstances, the reverse would also be true—unless the thing was violent, and then he'd know early only by virtue of the job, and that didn't bear thought. He swallowed. "Okay."

"No. Not okay."

She tried to push herself farther away from him to make a passionate point, but her knees got stuck. It was frustrating for her—and she was funny, but he was wise enough not to laugh. She looked daggers at him to make sure he didn't. Because it wasn't hilarious funny. Just sorta…off-kilter humorous in a disrespectful you-had-to-be-there dark-cop-humor kinda way if you could stand outside and look in or weren't directly involved in it.

Mostly.

"It's not okay," she repeated, struggling to push herself off him.

He ached to give her a hand up, but she wasn't looking

for one, didn't want it. This point was hers alone to make, not his to put so much as a finger in.

"You said it was dangerous for anyone to know about me because of Charlie, but you know what? That's bull. Because Charlie's looking for you, not me. He wants to talk to you. Whatever he wants, he wants it from you and Maddie, not from me. In which case he'd only come to me to get to you if he knew about me, right? So don't be stupid about it. Quit staying away from him. And me. Let him find you. Let him reach you. Find out what he wants."

She paused, poked a finger at him. "And tell people we're married, damn it. Because I'm not losing you just 'cuz people don't know I'm your person to call in case of emergency." She stopped, swallowed. Eyed him seriously. "So change that on your work forms today, okay?"

It hadn't even occurred to him to change his emergency contacts. He was an ass. He nodded. "Okay, yep. Absolutely. But you, too."

"Did it my first day back to work." Her mouth quirked a half smile. "But I wasn't out hunting kidnappers and escaped cons and lost boys and directing traffic around fires."

His grin was slow and appreciative. "See, you knew where I was."

"Everyone knew where you were. But I didn't know *from you.* Didn't hear from you. And no specifics." She paused, stabbed a finger at him for emphasis. "And no one woulda told me about you just because it was *me.* Your wife. Understand?"

He nodded. Loud and clear. "Yeah."

She pointed at the cell phone and beeper dumped on the floor with his pants. "So now you've got technology, you can keep in touch."

There was Levoie in his grin this time. "Yes, ma'am."

"And there will be actual speaking when you call," Janina said severely. "Not any of this vintage nonspeaking Russ Levoie we all know and love."

"Speaking," Russ agreed. Then curiously and with deliberate innocence, "How many minutes did you sign me up for? Only enough for me to fix on the topic of where I am and get off, or can I, ah, veer off topic to things like whether or not you're wearing panties and so on when I'm talking to you?"

For a long moment Janina simply stared at him in disbelief. Then she started to laugh, long and hard and with unadulterated delight.

Her idiot husband might turn out to be trainable after all.

By the time Russ was dressed in the clean uniform Janina had brought from his trailer, they'd worked out a series of beeper codes for her to use if she wanted or needed to contact him and he was either out of range on his cell phone or having it on would be unwise.

Janina had also filled him in on the particulars of the restraining order she'd gotten against Buddy—he wasn't allowed within one hundred feet of her—and some of the things she and Maddie had started to remember about being neighbors "back in the when."

"It's not like it was much," she said, watching him thoughtfully. "Until I brought up Buddy."

He cocked his head and she made a throwaway gesture.

"You know the way you do when you're getting to know someone and talking about past relationships and how they were the most idiotic thing you ever did—"

Russ swallowed a grin.

She rolled her eyes. "Yeah, well, the jury's still out on you."

He laughed and made a grab for her, pulled her close. "Not from where I'm standin'."

"Yeah, well." She cupped him. "This jury's brain is constantly in your shorts."

He kissed her, thoroughly, intensely. Muttered seriously, "Not all of it."

Janina caught her breath and for a minute time stopped, she forgot everything in the heady, terrifying, powerful wash of him around her, *through* her.

And then the moment passed and she was sane again, able to step back and see him for who he was, who he could be—who he'd forgotten to be this last week, and it steadied her.

He was everything she wanted.

He was also only human, fallible.

Only Russ.

Which was exactly everything that made him special. And which would undoubtedly aggravate her to pieces until the end of time.

"Anyway." She drew a breath and steadied herself, brushed a hand across his mouth and pressed away. "I was saying…"

"Buddy," he prompted, moving in behind her and sliding a hand along her stomach to bring her back against him at the same time that he dipped and nuzzled aside her hair to plant light kisses on the back of her neck.

"Well, he… Oh, don't," she moaned when a particularly electric sensation whipped through her. "You don't have any more time—*we* don't have time. You have to get back to work. So do I. Come home tonight for this."

He slid a hand beneath her uniform and up her bare hip.

"Hard to concentrate while you're not wearin' anything under here."

"You have a one-track mind." She slapped his hand away, yanked herself out from under his arm, and he laughed.

"You're the one who said communicate."

She snorted, unlocked the office door and headed downstairs toward the group of minilockers where the employees stored personal belongings. "My mistake."

"Where're you going?" Russ followed her.

"Clearly, if you're going to hear what I have to tell you, I'd better put my panties on. They're in my purse."

"Hmm. Interesting. I'll have to remember that for future traffic stops. So what kind are they? Silk thong? Crotchless? Lace? Something I should inspect before you wear it to work?"

Poised in front of her locker, Janina stared over her shoulder at him, mouth agape. "*What?* Are you out of your mind? Thongs are like dental floss for regular wear as far as I'm concerned. And *crotchless*? I don't even want to know where that's comin' from. Go back to not communicating, would you please." She turned and gave him a full-force hands-on-hips glare. "And FYI? For work I wear industrial-grade cotton, nothing sexy."

"There's nothing you could possibly put on that I wouldn't want to strip off of you," Russ assured her wickedly.

With a wink.

Torn between laughter and disbelief, Janina fish-mouthed him for an instant. "What has gotten into you?"

"You." He reconsidered that. "Well, no, actually, that would be the other way around, wouldn't it?"

Mirth sputtered out, refusing to be contained. "That's

it," she said. "You're outta here. Go sit with Jonah and be-
have. *He* can tell you about Buddy. So can Maddie. Meantime, I'm going to clean up—alone. Without help from
you. And then I'll bring food. Maybe that'll fix your brain."

"Probably won't," Russ said tragically. "Might sidetrack it momentarily, but not much gonna fix it now I've
gotten a taste of you."

Glowing inside, Janina shoved him toward the front of
the restaurant. "You are so full of it."

He gave her soulful, pathetic. Hang dog. "It's true."

She held her course, but her heart fell for it hook, line
and sinker. "Out."

"Can I at least stay and watch you put on your panties?"

He was impossible. She had to laugh. "No. Now go. *Out!*"

Swinging doors finally between her and him, she sagged
against the wall, exhausted. "Geez Louise." And started a
second later when his face appeared in the small window
in the nearest door. He grinned at her, waggled his eyebrows and left.

And he was the serious one of the brothers. The one
who'd been unable to even speak to her two and a half
weeks ago.

She put a hand to her head and shuddered. Even when
she had the upper ground—for half a second—he was a
handful. His mother must have spent their formative years
wanting to kill him and his brothers one and all.

Especially him.

Good God, what had she gotten herself into?

Clearly more than she'd bargained on.

Ah well. She grinned slowly to herself. At least it wasn't
more than she was willing to learn to handle.

So far.

Humming the melody to Uwe Fahrenkrog Petersen's "Insanity Is Relative," Janina went to sort herself out, touch herself up—and fix her husband the first meal she'd be able to personally prepare for him since they'd married.

In complex times, it was the simple moments that got you through.

"Wha'd'you mean, Buddy Carmichael might have some sense of where Charlie's buried himself and Jess?" Russ snapped at Jonah not ten minutes later. Roller coaster didn't begin to describe the ride his insides were taking at the moment. When his brother rolled his eyes left and didn't respond immediately to his question, he snarled, "Maddie," and straight-armed himself out of the booth. Two long strides put him in the way of her delivering an order to a tableful of Janina's customers. She looked into his face and nearly dropped the plates she juggled. He caught the most endangered ones.

"These go here?" he asked evenly, motioning his head at the table nearest them without taking his eyes off her.

She worked her jaw around something that resembled a wordless affirmative.

"Good." He put the plates down, relieved her of the remainder, set those down, too, said, "Eat hearty, folks, enjoy your food," and grabbed her upper arm to propel her toward Jonah's booth.

"I didn't know then for sure, Russ, I would've said," she protested weakly. "For your own sake, keep your voice down."

"I don't think so." He swung her to face him, amazed and terrified to find himself shaking. She was afraid, he got that, but he had too much to lose now. And whether he wanted to protect her or not. *She* had to put herself on the line to help him do it. He sure as hell wouldn't put Janie there, not for history, not for Maddie, not for anyone.

"Don't lie to me this time, Maddie. I can't do that with you anymore. This is my *wife* in it now. Buddy's her ex. His contacts run deep, but he's wrong. And if he's been mixed up with Charlie, ever, he's more wrong than I knew. So if there's anything, *anything* between him and Charlie or you, and you know it or remember it, tell me now. And you tell me *exactly* what Charlie said to you during that phone call. And I mean exactly. No quibbles, you got me?"

"Russ." Jonah left the booth. "Soften it."

Russ's attention shifted half a click and settled.

"No," Maddie said quickly, grabbing Jonah's wrist, sliding into the booth and dragging him in behind her before Russ could get to whatever it was that was running through his head. "He's right, Jones. Buddy's got more to do with Charlie. More than I said. More..." She swallowed, eyed Russ. Shivered. "More."

He sat heavily. "How much did you girl-talk to Janie?"

"Some." Small voice. Her body shrank toward the window, away from Jonah, away from what she didn't want to say. To admit.

To own.

"I couldn't tell her what I didn't tell you, could I?" she whispered. "You're my best friend. But I gave her more than I did you, maybe." She ducked a frightened, apologetic look at him. "Girls, you know, getting to know each other? My best friend's new wife? She's good people, Russ. But because of you, she didn't like me. Means I gotta get to know her, have her like me, right? Let me in?"

She swallowed, hugged herself together. "But I couldn't

tell her what I was afraid to tell you. Couldn't do that to her. Didn't seem right. Fair. And I couldn't tell her what I haven't told Jess either."

She folded into herself. "And not what I wanted to hide from myself."

Smoke soiled the air with a thick, ash-filled haze, making it hard to breathe.

Wired to the gills, Charlie Thorn finished soaking down their shelter with the last of the ready water and sent a glance west toward the crackle of approaching wind and fire. They'd have to move soon, and he didn't know where. He'd expected contact by now, expected to hear somethin', but either that boy was stupider than he thought or Maddie hadn't done what he'd told her to, not even for her friend.

Between the migraines, the dry mouth and the tinnitus, things were gettin' real bad again, and his prescriptions were running low. He'd been tryin' to stretch 'em best he could, 'specially the headache pills, but he'd have to fill his other meds if he didn't want to run the risk of psychosis. Doc had made sure he understood that. Made him read the little pamphlet on it and everything. And he understood, least he did for now. Turn a man outside himself he didn't stay on his pills.

Turn him back worse'n what he was before he went on 'em. Pretty damn foolish, but there it was.

He turned at the clink of chain and a dry-voiced croak from the entry of the shelter.

"Mr. Thorn?"

Maddie's friend. Jess. He'd finally gotten that much out of her. She looked thin, hollow-eyed, bruised. He hadn't touched her. He hadn't. Some women just got to looking that way when they didn't sleep and wouldn't—or couldn't—eat under stress. Did things to their skin. She was apparently one of them.

He nodded at her to indicate he'd heard. His mouth was too dry from taking in smoke and floating ash to allow him to speak without stuttering incomprehensibly.

"We can—can't—" She stopped and cast a frightened but fleeting look at the swaying treetops, swallowed painfully and tried again, obviously more terrified of the rising wind and what it carried toward them than of him. "We can't s-stay here. The f-fire…I—I don't…I c-can't… Please. No one's coming and I'm afraid of fire. Please."

He took a step toward her, held out his hands, palms down but fingers spread wide in an attempt to calm her. Inside his gut he understood this fire, this wind. The air was thick, but they were all right here a bit longer.

Long enough, he hoped. But he had to give them— Maddie—more time. He understood if she was scared, but she'd come to it, work it out. It was taking time, that was all. And when Maddie figured it out, she had to be able to figure out where to find them.

The way his tattered mind saw it, redemption had to be earned where hell had first been meted out.

Still unable to word what he had to say, he took another step toward Jess, and another. A fourth and a fifth.

The sixth step was the mistake.

He was in range by the fifth, but she faltered and waited out the extra beat to make sure, gathering courage with the chain she'd finally managed to unscrew from the floor. When she swung, she threw the force of surprise and all her weight behind it, hurled at him her passion to keep

Maddie safe and her own desire to escape, the time she'd spent hating him for the havoc he'd wreaked on his own daughter and for the trust it was clear Maddie still hadn't given over because of him.

And she did it finally with the patience and skill born of the years of training in self-defense that had deserted her in her claustrophobic panic the night he'd been able to pick her up and render her comatose too easily.

When he was bruised, bleeding and unconscious on the ground, she didn't stop to see if she had time to get rid of the chain. She picked up her feet and ran.

Chapter 11

Russ dragged a heavy chair moaning and squeaking out from the interrogation-room table and dropped down beside Janina, opposite Maddie. "Spill it, Madelyn," he said flatly.

He'd packed her up before she could say another word at the Fat Cat. Packed up a shocked and initially somewhat ticked Janina, too, leaving the Fat Cat short on waitresses—and Jonah to explain what he could to Tobi—and hied them off to the comparative quiet and privacy of the department for the details.

"What's Buddy got to do with it? And where's Charlie got Jess? If you know, tell me. We go get her, bring her back. Keep it simple."

God, all he wanted to do was settle down with Janina, put his—*their,* damn it—house together, figure it out from there. But it all kept coming back to here. Then. The things that time would not let go of.

How could you possibly move forward if somebody else's history insisted on shoving you back?

Your history, too, memory whispered. *You were there. Janina was there. Your history, too.*

In truth, it was where he and Janina had begun. And long before that, by the look on Maddie's face.

"Russ." Janina touched his arm, drawing his attention. "I still don't quite follow," she said quietly when he finally turned to her. Looking at her made it difficult to concentrate on everything else he was supposed to focus on. She was the center of his universe and that's what he wanted to let her be. And right now he couldn't.

Damn it.

"Maddie remembered Buddy. And his father. I remembered, too, when we talked about it. Oh, not Buddy, or I'd never have…" She swallowed, looked away embarrassed. If she'd ever noticed Buddy stopping over at the Thorns' she'd have run the other direction, fast.

"Janie." Russ caught her chin. "Look at me. Listen to me. It doesn't matter. It. Doesn't. Matter. Buddy's nothin'. We start counting the stupid things I've done? We'd need a Dumpster to file 'em."

"This is true," Maddie chimed in tiredly but determinedly, reaching across the table to pat Janina's hand. "And we could start with how long it took him to get to you."

"Not finished with you," Russ snapped, "so butt out."

"Better," Maddie returned with asperity, "why don't I leave, you can do this in private, call me back when you're through."

"Your timing always did suck," Russ said pointedly.

"No more than yours—"

"Children!" Janina slapped the table and pushed herself

erect, no longer a fragile piece of her past but a present force, a fury to be reckoned with. "No more squabbling." She swung on her husband, pinned him with a look. "If you can't stay on target due to circumstances you're too close to, get somebody in here who can. Jess's getting farther away from you, Charlie's not getting any closer, and I'm wearing your ring but sleeping alone at night." She leaned into his face, made sure he got the message. "Which is not fun, since I know what you're capable of. So *alone*, dreaming about you? Not even close."

She swung around, out of his face, breathing hard. "And you!" Maddie's turn for the skewer. "Suck it up, put some courage behind it and tell the man—*your best friend,* as you keep telling everybody, damn it—what he should be and needs to be trusted with—what the hell he needs to know to get his job done to find the person you say lights the sun for you, so I can have my husband to myself and get this marriage on the road, because we haven't even actually had a first date. As in him asking me out or vice versa, and the things we don't know about each other would fill—" she hunted for an adequate analogy "—months or even *years* of daily soap opera episodes focused mainly on us. And I am *tired* of the not knowing. Especially him. Because there's stuff he thinks is gonna happen that—" her voice broke "—won't, and can't and he needs to know that."

She turned away to collect herself.

Worried…confused…completely befuddled, Russ started to reach for her, but she slapped him away.

Cleared her throat.

Came back strong.

"So all things considered? The two of you? Get. Finished. With. It."

And with that she gathered up her dignity with her purse, sent her chair skidding recklessly and noisily away from the table and slammed out of the room.

Leaving Russ and Maddie to first stare after her, stupefied, and then, somewhat self-consciously, at each other. Russ winced, shoved out of his chair.

"Damn. I need to…I should…"

Maddie grimaced, shook her head. "Not yet. Experience says wait, I promise."

He didn't want to be here, didn't want to do this. He wanted to be out there, chasing Janina, doing whatever it took to make it good.

Even if that meant fighting with her. He could do that.

He swallowed and headed for the door anyway. Wrong way, right way or some way down the middle and bullin' through like the proverbial beast in the china shop, he was going after Janina.

"Damn it," Maddie interrupted painfully. "Russ, we need to do this, like Janie said, all right?"

He stopped. Turned around. Studied her.

Gave the door a last long look, sighed and cursed. She was right. He had to stay and do this. Like it or not, his job, the responsibility he still felt toward Maddie, and therefore by proxy to Jess that consequently couldn't be handed over to a third party for wrap up, took priority over everything else at the moment.

Everything.

"She's waited this long," Maddie said softly, wisely— deliberately. "She'll give you a few days longer."

He opened his eyes and looked at her then, really looked, without letting himself offer up the automatic excuses his psyche always seemed hell-bent on finding for her. And it all crystallized in front of him in that moment.

Who she was. Who he was. Who they were. Victim and rescuer. Sparring partners.

And, occasionally, addict and enabler.

But who was which in that last was oftentimes more than a little bit up for grabs: him as the control freak-some-time-adrenaline junkie and her as the one who handed him the rush and the reins, or her as the lost soul-psychic-pain devotee and him as the one who wouldn't let her go, kept scraping her up, patching her together, preventing her from finding her whole self on her own.

She'd been injured yes, horribly. Scarred visibly and in some places invisibly beyond repair. She'd fought back, made a life—*created* a life—for herself, one whose finding he'd aided and abetted.

She'd also found love, discovered happiness, but it hadn't kept her from seeking his protection the instant things went wrong.

Or prevented him from offering it. Because he liked taking care of things, people—women. Making sure they were safe, well, happy.

Liked being needed.

Liked being the only one capable of handling situations for certain people, especially—as Jonah put it—*his* women.

Maddie.

Janina.

There were undoubtedly other women he took care of, too. Elderly or older women alone in town or around it, abused women of all ages, and all those other female crea-tures-in-jeopardy he'd somehow communed with and understood then rescued throughout his life. He was big. He had a gift.

He could beat things into submission. Make things go away and leave the women—and children, couldn't forget them!—alone.

Some things anyway. And maybe even most things, or at least the bad things, the things that needed to be sent packing.

That was why he'd become a cop. Why he'd always wanted to be a cop. Because as a cop he'd have a right to fix things. Get in the way of things. Bad things. Stop them.

But perhaps where Maddie was concerned, he really…shouldn't anymore.

Maybe he should set her free and let her learn to finish rescuing herself while he tried to figure out how to do something of the same for himself.

He stared at her a long time, coming to terms with that one, playing it over in his head.

"It's only a windmill, Russ," Maddie said softly. "Not like you haven't jousted 'em for me before."

He blinked at her, trying to make it easier for him at the same time that she made it as difficult as possible for him to walk away. "You were always so good at tough. Damsel-in-Distress never did suit you, Mad."

"But you're always so good at Knight-in-Shining, even a girl like me can't help herself in times of need. And I need, Russ, make no mistake. I'm terrified."

It was hard, but he did it—or made a start toward it anyway.

"I know you are, but—" He sucked his teeth, dropped to her level and eyed her directly. "Until you're ready to play it straight with me, I'm outta here."

Flabbergasted, Maddie nearly tipped out of her chair. "What?"

Russ straightened, turned his back on her and crossed the room. "Get some paper from the front desk and write it down, Maddie." He opened the door. "Make it clear, because I got work to do, but I can't let Janie sit around and wait anymore on account of my history with you."

Then he went to look for his wife.

Without noticing the wan but distinct smile Maddie sent after him. It was time, as she'd admitted, albeit somewhat diffidently, to Janina, to let him go, also.

And just as soon as he brought Jess back, she'd correct a longtime mistake and make sure her partner, her lover, her life's mate and heart's desire understood the truth of that, too.

If Jess ever forgave her for leaving her to Charlie this long in the first place, that is.

"Oops, excuse me."

Janina fast-footed it out of the way of one rushing clerical officer only to be buffeted straight into the path of an oncoming patrolman, and then bounced smack-dab into another. "Sorry, sorry."

She collected herself and sidestepped into the wall, flattened herself there and stood, breathing hard. Urgency filtered around her, filled the halls, spread fingers everywhere, including in thoughtless drifts through her nape hairs and the fine nerves along her spine. She hadn't counted on finding this, *feeling* this when she left Russ to sort it out with Maddie. Hadn't planned to *touch* what he experienced on the job: that sense of *gotta do it now or else!* That need to be here in it and nowhere else. That adrenaline push.

This was *Winslow*, for God's sake, not Phoenix. They didn't have high-speed car chases, serial killers, major gang wars or daily murders to solve. They had *stuff*, but not…this.

She swallowed and realized from the blur of activity around her that they did indeed have *this* here.

At least sometimes.

She understood suddenly that while the faces about her seemed familiar, many of these people probably didn't recognize her—and wouldn't—not out of her pink uniform and out of context. All her life in this town didn't matter. In this milieu she didn't belong and didn't fit. Russ did. Which left her the stranger here.

Wife of the city's favorite junior police lieutenant or not.

Ruthlessly she squinched her nails into her palms, letting the pain bite out the sensation of being out of her comfort zone. She didn't allow herself that road anymore as a rule. Wherever she was, she could be comfortable. She'd made that her plan, her mantra, years ago—the minute she told herself she didn't have to apologize for where she came from.

The instant she'd stopped apologizing for where she came from.

The second she'd caught Buddy's attention and encouraged it, and learned too late that he was the one who should have apologized for his origins even as he'd attempted to beat hers into her.

But she wasn't at the police station this time because of Buddy—well, only indirectly—but because of Russ. Which was a whole lot of reason to find a way to make herself not only known but comfortable on the premises. No doubt she'd find herself here a lot.

Something big parted the tide of people flowing back and forth in front of her, then blocked all but the bit of light that haloed around him. "Janie."

She sighed and squinted up at him. "You get what you needed from Maddie?"

He gave his lips a negative twist. "I'm done dancin' with her. Told her to get paper, write it down and leave it for me at the desk if she wants my help."

Janina licked suddenly dry lips, wondering exactly what that meant. "I see."

Russ offered her a wry grin and shook his head. "I doubt it." He reached for her hand, towed her toward clerical with him. "But you will. Jennifer," he stopped at Secretarial and drew Janina forward, "you know Janie, yeah? From over at the Fat Cat?"

Jennifer's frazzled look cleared and she smiled and held out her hand. "Oh yeah, right. How you doin'?"

Janina smiled back. "I'm doin'. Thanks."

Jennifer grinned, let her gaze sink to the hand Russ still held, and transferred it up to his face with a blink of outright curiosity. The subheading "Station Gossip Columnist" seemed to appear as if by some divine hand, and print itself across her forehead in bold black, albeit invisible, letters where Janina couldn't fail to read it. "So, anything I should know? You two an item?"

Down below the counter where Jennifer couldn't see, Janina kicked Russ almost gently in the ankle.

It was the *almost* that made him pick up his foot and unobtrusively rub the sting out of the injured limb against his calf even as he grinned down at his wife and said, "Um, as a matter of fact, we are. Married. Two weeks ago. The uh…"

Janina gave him a look. A very incredulous, very wifely

how could you have forgotten the date already, you idiot look. "Eighteenth of July," she supplied.

"The eighteenth of July," he repeated innocently, which made Janina want to kill him, because that's when she realized that he hadn't forgotten the date at all and probably never would. "Which means I need my personnel file updated ASAP. Especially the next of kin, the—"

"Address and phone," Janina put in.

"We have those?" Russ eyed her, surprised.

Janina looked all the way up at him, her back teeth ground together. After the talk they'd had at the diner he was apparently not housebroken yet.

Aware of Jennifer as her avid audience, she unclenched her fists with an effort. Undoubtedly it would be best to continue as she meant to go on. Even as she fiddled her wedding ring around on her finger, she offered up a loving smile and beckoned Russ down with her other hand.

He wasn't that stupid.

Even as he bent, Russ anticipated the ring clip she intended to give him and caught her hand before she had a chance to raise it. "Fool me once," he chided. "I take it you've been busy while I've been..." He considered language. Narrowed his eyes and settled somewhat carefully, even a little dangerously on, "Out."

Somewhere, almost deep enough for her to ignore it, a chill sidled through the light hair on her arms. It was the *almost* that caused her to pause, left her breath fiddling cautiously in her lungs for a pair of heartbeats. *Buddy* didn't *take to this side of you.*

"You want to find out real fast exactly how paper-trained I am, think of me as Carmichael just once more," Russ suggested softly, reading her mind.

Startled, she took an involuntary step back. His eyes were guarded, but there was also a warmth that lurked in their midnight depths, a fury that was not directed at her but at Buddy—or Charlie or any man who'd treat a woman the way they had. The fingers of her right hand went unconsciously, instinctively to twist her wedding ring round and round.

Pain scudded across Russ's countenance when Janina continued to fiddle with her ring, unspeaking. He straightened slowly. "I see."

"No, you don't." She grabbed his shirtfront, dragged him back. "You haven't been around enough, with me enough, to *see,* so don't even think about going there without a battle."

"Tell me you didn't just compare me to Buddy and spend at least two seconds afraid."

She scuffled one foot behind the other and had the grace to look mildly chagrined. "Guilty." She glanced up at him slyly from beneath her lashes. "On the other hand, you *do* tend to go all macho-alpha-guy on me sometimes, plus you disappeared without a trace last week when we should by rights still have been honeymooning, so really, maybe you could cut me some slack on the momentary brain damage?"

He stuck his tongue in his cheek and considered her. "Not lettin' go of that any time soon, are you?"

She gave him cheeky coupled with determined mixed with give-me-five-minutes-alone-with-you-and-you-won't-remember-who-I-almost-compared-you-to look. "Not as long as I can get mileage and your guilt out of it, no."

"Hmm." He appraised his wife slowly, thoroughly, *hotly*, and glanced sideways at Jennifer. "Better make sure we put her on my medical insurance and predate it to the eighteenth," he said dryly. "Way she's got me goin', we'll need the maternity benefits sooner rather'n later."

Maternity benefits, pregnancy.

Babies.

Janina swallowed hard. Things that he could never give her no matter how much she wanted him to, how hard she loved him, how often they tried, or how badly he wanted them.

Something she could never give him, no matter how desperately she ached to, longed to, felt somehow deep inside, beyond the place where science and doctors told her she could not, that she had been born for exactly this purpose beyond all else: bearing Russ Levoie's children, creating a new generation with him.

It might not be a modern thought, but inside her it existed, burned, seared.

Russ's babies.

Her knuckles rubbed at the place high beneath her breastbone where everything suddenly hurt so hard she thought her chest might cave in. She couldn't breathe.

"Janie."

She must have made a sound, pulled a face, something—or maybe it was merely that damn supersensitive connection thing he did around her, because from some distance outside the strange hollow she'd suddenly disappeared into, Janina heard Russ say her name urgently, felt rather than saw him reach for her.

Without meaning to, she shrank back an infinitesimal step—not far, but far enough—a movement so small it should have been invisible.

The instant waver of his hand, the sudden uncertainty come and gone about his mouth, telegraphed the fact her withdrawal was blatant to him.

Panic set in. She had to tell him, now, before it was too late. Before they were too invested in each other—before *he* was too invested, because she was already gone, lock, stock and nothing saved for a rainy day.

Before she loved him more.

She had to tell him before Jennifer broadcast their marriage to his law enforcement brotherhood and the rest of the Winslow universe and he looked like a fool when he wanted to back out of this precipitous union because his wife couldn't deliver the children and the life he'd assumed they would have together.

She scrunched courage into her fingers, tagged his. "Russ, don't. Stop. You don't understand—"

"Russ?" With her usual incomparably bad timing, Maddie rounded Jennifer's station, head down, expression troubled, mind on other matters, pen, paper and a detailed map of the fire area drifting through her hands. "I think I've got where Charlie might have Jess. It's got to be one of two places. Buddy's father had one and Charlie had—"

Russ raised a finger at her, concentration on Janina. "Give it a minute, Mad." He drew Janina toward an office. "Tell me."

Around them the air seemed to buzz, electric and intense. *It's the overheads,* Janina thought nonsensically. *The fluorescents.*

"Janie." Russ's voice was rough, soft, encouraging. He stepped close to her and cupped her waist between his hands to get her attention, and her mutinous body felt alive, flagrantly so, demandingly so.

She gulped and shoved at him.

He didn't go anywhere.

She tried again, a little harder this time, but he merely

anchored her more tightly to him and caught her chin, forced her to look at him.

"*Tell* me."

She yanked her chin out of his hand. "I could maybe do it easier from the other side of the room."

His grip slackened. "It's that bad?"

She looked away. "Worse."

"Aw, c'mon." He stroked her arms, cajoling. Bent and placed his mouth beside her ear, murmured, "Thought you were the one supposed to be able to communicate."

She sputtered and almost laughed at that. It was true, she was, and here he was, the one doing most of the talking. She opened her mouth. Nothing came out but a wisp of air trailed by a grimace.

"Hey," Russ said gruffly, only half kidding, "when did you quit trusting me?"

Janina compressed her lips, her emotions. Truth was, they didn't know each other well enough for her to trust him to react the way she needed him to: as though what she had to tell him, what she was or physically couldn't be, didn't matter and wouldn't matter to him ever.

Especially in the long run.

"I—" she had time to say—to gulp—when once again into the fraught moment rushed Maddie.

Almost as though she'd been listening and heard her cue to crash in.

Fully fraught herself and near to panic.

"Russ, damn it, you've got to look at this." Her voice pitched high, nerves clearly dangling from its edges. "We have to *go*."

She was shaking, trembling, unable to still herself when she shoved the map at him. He started to say something, but she rushed on, terror for Jess overriding whatever he might have said to shut her off.

"Carson came in. I showed the map to him. He said the fire's about reached the area where I remember Charlie having his shack and—"

"Lieu-ten-ant!"

The drawn-out yell accompanied by pounding feet and the sudden slam of a body into the office door frame shut Maddie up the way nothing else would have. As one, Russ, Janina and Maddie turned to Carson. The young officer swallowed, keeping his inexperienced countenance as blank as possible, his eyes on Russ, without looking at Maddie once.

"I'm sorry, Lieutenant. Fire team out near one of the new homestead sites toward Show Low just called in. They found an abandoned bomb shelter. We got bodies."

Chapter 12

She couldn't breathe, but one look at Maddie, and Janina abandoned all thought of wobbly knees and her own seemingly worthless lungs to reach for the other woman.

Instinctively, Maddie reached back, looking for comfort not from her usual lifetime source but from this more recently discovered one: uniquely feminine, inherently more supple and resilient—and so, possibly, even more permanent than Russ had proven to be.

Russ glanced at neither. The nature that informed who he was had also caused him to step forward at the sound of thundering feet, plant himself unflinchingly between Janina and Maddie, and the doorway, then between them and Carson and the news he brought.

Made him herd the youngster out of the office almost more quickly than he'd entered.

He might not be able to contain the damage, but he would distill it as soon as possible. He could...

Janina was on him before the decision to leave her and Maddie behind took shape in his head. He swung about, managing to stay half a word ahead of her even so.

"Don't even think about it," he told her flatly.

"Don't you," she shot back, startling him with her ability to read him. "This is Maddie's family and we're coming."

"No," he said. "This is my job, not yours. Fire victims..." He didn't finish. "She doesn't need to see this, and neither do you. Especially if it's not them."

"And if it is?"

"I can identify them." His mouth worked. "If there's enough to identify."

"And what about her? What about..." She fiddled her tongue between her teeth. "What about us?"

His guard went up high. "Which us?"

She snorted. "Maddie and I. Clearly, you and I get tabled for later. Again." She waved it off as of no consequence when he might have said something. "Anyway, what about her, what about us while you're off gallivanting, identifying? Or not?"

He shrugged. "You stay here, out of the fire, where it's safe. In case it's not—" He stopped, turned what he'd been about to say around. "In case Charlie's still out there hunting Maddie." He stared long and hard at his wife. "And maybe out looking to get to me through you."

"Really." Soft, clearly enunciated, but understated enough that Russ relaxed and let down his guard.

He blew out a pent-up breath. "Yes." He nodded. "Really."

"Who the *hell* do you think you are?" Janina gave him a resounding flat-handed smack in the chest that surprised him enough to send him rocking back on his heels half a step. "What deity laid down and put you in charge of all that's holy and everything that's not? Because I've got to tell you, buster, not so much endearing right now, you want to know the truth.

"Frankly, you want to know what I think, you could go right ahead and protect me and Maddie a heck of a lot easier and more personally if we were with you. I am sick to death of being shuffled off to Buffalo every time you think you've got a more important piece of business to deal with somewhere else. So you just put us in your damn bulletproof SUV or squad car or whatever, have Carson or Jonah ride shotgun and take us with you. Got it?"

Russ blinked at her.

Twice.

Then while Carson stared wide-eyed after him, he turned without a word and strode from the office.

Anger rose inside Janina with tidal force. Fifteen minutes or so ago he'd talked to her as if it was the easiest thing in the world, and just like that, not even a finger snap later, when it was far more important that he speak, he was gone.

Her throat tightened, chin jutted and lifted. She turned her head stiffly, glanced at Maddie alone and emotionally naked across from her. Where Maddie stood there were no longer any barricades, no walls or protections, and the ramparts had long since been blown apart. Charlie had stolen her childhood, her youth, her adolescence, then they'd let him out of prison to tear away her heart, too. And Russ just walked away? Oh no. Not on *her* watch.

Not while she was still married to him. This much Janina knew for certain: job to do or not, Russ Levoie did not get to stalk away from this. Not *this*.

Not without at least some explanation.

Sucking in a breath full of determination that was well on its way toward deeper, more treacherous waters, Janina headed after her husband, maintained focus on her objective: Russ and getting out of him what she knew Maddie needed.

What she herself needed on behalf of the other woman—and in some strange fashion on behalf of herself and her marriage. As though that way lay some sort of proof. Kinship. Irrevocable…linkage.

The true bonds of their matrimony, for want of a better term. For better or worse.

More determined, ticked off and confused than ever, she stepped into the teeming police department hallway—and ran smack into Russ.

With his arms full of clothing.

On his way back for her and Maddie.

"You're not going anywhere without us," Janina snapped, putting out a hand to catch herself against the wall before she crashed into it.

Russ caught and steadied her, looked her up and down, then maneuvered her back into the office and shut the blinds. "What size boot you wear?"

She glared at him, off balance. "What?"

He dumped the clothing—jeans, T-shirts, lightweight police-issue jackets, belts and thick socks—on the desk and glanced at her bare legs.

"You got nothing covering your legs, and not that you're going to, but if it happens that you get out of the vehicle in a hot zone, your shoes'll melt. Now, boots. What size? Maddie, you, too."

"Nine," Maddie said hoarsely but promptly. "Wide."

"Oh." Wind taken effectively out of Janina's sails, her rising indignation had nowhere to go. It fell into her belly like heavy canvas and lay there flattened and becalmed. "Seven and a half. Regular, er, medium, I guess that'd be."

Russ clipped a nod at her. "I'll see what I can find while you change."

She stopped him leaving with a hand, asked him for an explanation without saying a word.

Insisted on knowing why getting exactly what she wanted from him wasn't enough to kill the niggling rise of self-doubt that batted against her temples, the newly persistent qualm that said marrying him in haste might not have been exactly what she'd thought it would be after all, or the right—or best—thing for either of them.

But the midnight eyes were unrevealing, filled only with an alien knowledge when he looked at her.

He squeezed her fingertips and released them, headed for the door. "Get changed," he said brusquely. "I'll see about boots. Then if we're goin', we've got to go."

For all the effort, argument and agony, it wasn't them.

In the loudest silence Janina had ever experienced, they traveled to the build site where the bodies had been discovered.

Outside, the sky was so smoke-filled it was nearly black despite the fact it was still late afternoon, and the air was so thick with drifting ash, a thin coating of it covered the department's Yukon long before they'd reached their destination.

As Janina'd suggested, Jonah and Carson came with them.

The drive to Show Low took close to two hours. By the time they arrived, the bodies were ready for transport. Refusing even the thought that Maddie might accompany him before they knew for sure what they were looking at, Russ went alone for a first look.

The sight was grim, even for someone who'd dealt with similar events before.

Russ's stomach rolled at the stench the instant the body bags were unzipped. He shut his eyes and turned to find a breath of cleaner air, then drew on a pair of latex gloves and went after what he was looking for, starting with the woman and relieved beyond believing when he knew it wasn't Jess.

It was more than hard after that to turn to the male, the body he knew wouldn't be Charlie's. Brutally difficult, in fact, because as badly as he'd needed the dead woman not to be Jess, he wanted the other body to belong to Charlie. Wanted Charlie to somehow have simplified things for all of them and wound up here beyond his own control, and so now out of Maddie's life for good.

But then, where would that leave them looking for Jess?

He didn't know. He just knew that something, somewhere along the way, needed to get simple because where he stood now with Janina—who was getting tougher to figure out by the second—and with Maddie continuously locked into the picture wasn't good.

He was torn. Duty, honor, friendship, family, life and now wife…all the pieces of himself stood to lose big if he couldn't sort his priorities into their proper and exclusive cubbyholes soon.

And the fact that they weren't only priorities he had to pigeonhole, but constant everyday choices he had to make, didn't help an iota.

Again he breathed it all into himself and tamped it down deep the way he always did—had always done.

Had learned to do when he'd discovered himself the oldest son, the leader by default, the heir to whatever examples had to be set for his brothers and Marcy when she'd come along much later and the one responsible for keeping them and his sisters safe.

Guardian, keeper, watcher, custodian and sentinel.

More often than not when he'd opposed them, they'd referred to him as "warden."

Because as it had turned out, he was not only the oldest but also the biggest. He could pound on them until they did what he said because he knew what was best for them. And damn it, he'd done what was best for them as long as it was possible.

As long as they'd stayed near enough for him to get hold of them and run their lives for them.

And Mabel, despite the three years she had on him, didn't count. It wasn't a matter of gender or chauvinism in this case, the way he'd often been accused, but of size and personality: he had almost fifteen inches and a good hundred and thirty or better pounds on her, and she had the owlish personality of a science geek, which didn't go with, well, leading, warding or guarding.

Or herding.

Russ glanced half-resentfully over at the SUV full of people—women—he'd rather not have had with him just now. For a Pai he'd done an awful lot of herding instead of riding and peach farming—and other things his people were known for—in his time. Which meant that, like it or not, he'd been born with the traits and abilities for taking care of people.

With a silent snarl that was directed at himself for letting a moment of self-indulgent intemperance get away from him, Russ short-chained his temper two links closer to the floor and proceeded with his examination of the male corpse. The body didn't belong to Charlie.

Hearing a commotion erupt from the direction of the SUV because Janina had decided to come see what was taking him so long and Jonah was doing his best to prevent her, Russ gave a quick thanks to the EMTs on the scene, stripped off and disposed of the latex gloves, and advanced on his wife and youngest brother.

"Damn it, Russ," they shouted at him in perfect—and comical—unison. "Would you do me a favor and remind him—*her*—that she—*he*—is not the boss of me?"

Russ glared at them. "Then who is?"

Clearly they'd spent too much time together lately if they could squabble at the scene of a tragedy that might have been Maddie's like a couple of six-year-old siblings who'd no respect for the dead. They were getting on each other's nerves.

His had been jangled all to hell and back long ago.

He glanced into the Yukon where Carson hugged his door and tried to pretend he didn't know anyone and Maddie actually bit her lower lip and almost smiled.

It was a pale travesty of a smile, to be sure, but even the caricature of her usual lightning-laced effort appeared genuine. As if she couldn't help herself.

Even as a little kid, Jonah'd had an uncanny knack for being able to make Maddie laugh when things were roughest.

Thoughtfully, Russ eyed him and Janina again, but with a touch more discernment. Yep, there he caught it this time, the intentional steps Jonah took to bait Janina, rile her—and *there*…

Russ coughed to cover startled laughter when Janina took Jonah so off guard he suddenly didn't look as if he knew whether he was coming or going in their brangle. Then with a wink at Russ that made him choke, she wrapped an ankle behind Jonah's and toppled him into a pile of ash on his butt, stuck her nose in the air and climbed back into the Yukon—into Jonah's place in the front seat— dusting off her hands of the entire affair and leaving Jonah fuming in real outrage.

Russ understood exactly to what lengths his wife would go to keep a friend's mind off her troubles.

His heart expanded to fit around her more securely and he winced over the thoughts he'd been thinking, the druthers he'd had that made him want to be out here doing his duty alone. He had a duty to fulfill, yes, but he wasn't alone. Not this time.

He crossed to her door, opened it and leaned in, took her face between his hands and startled her to bits by kissing her soundly.

In front of everybody.

Or at least everybody present.

Janina's amazingly shiny brown eyes shimmered up at him all puzzled and curious, liquid and full, anxious and…

Almost forlorn.

Then she blinked and the not-quite image disappeared.

Disturbed by what he couldn't be sure he'd seen, Russ scraped his thumbs across his wife's cheekbones and kissed her again, gently and with circumspection. Eased away and murmured, "Thank you."

Her head tilted, and where she'd been bold back at the Fat Cat and at the station, she now tried to shrug shyly away, unsure. "For?"

He smiled and let her go. "Being you."

Again that fleeting confusion coupled with sadness disturbed her features. Jonah advanced on the department vehicle. "I take it the news is…good?" he said to Russ.

Russ glanced at his baby brother, his wife, stuck his tongue in his cheek by way of washing his hands of whatever was about to happen, and stepped over to the back door of the Yukon to confirm his news to Maddie first. "It wasn't them."

She swallowed, nodded gratefully. "I didn't think it could be, but thanks for saying."

"You know I'd wish it was him if we knew where she was."

A tiny blink of affirmation followed by a glance away when her eyes began to tear. "Me, too."

And from the direction of the front seat, "Hot damn, Janie," Jonah howled, once again sprawled on his butt on the ashy earth. "You won't know when or where, and you're not gonna know how but, *sister*—" there was heavy, almost blackmail-weight stress placed on the single word "—you are goin' *down*."

"Oh, you think you're gonna take me?" Janina shook her head, turned on her dignity and climbed back into the SUV, slammed the door behind her. Looked over her shoulder at Russ and Maddie. "You wanna get this show on the road? I need a shower, playin' with your baby brother. Boy needs a nanny…"

She faced front again, planted her back hard against the seat, muttering more imprecations against her youngest brother-in-law.

Behind her, Maddie pressed her lips together and cleared her throat hard, twice, before shakily losing her battle with a sobbing sort of laughter.

That didn't take long to turn into just plain sobs.

Hearing them, heart aching in empathy, Janina turned to find Russ already reaching for the woman within whom Janina had discovered her own sort of kinship. She held out a hand to him, shook her head and hopped back out of the truck to climb in beside Maddie, take Russ's place and fold the other woman in her arms.

Russ squeezed Maddie's shoulder and cupped Janina's face gratefully then let his hand drift through her hair before he shut them carefully in, jerked his head at Jonah and got them the hell away from one more dead end.

Chapter 13

August 12
The new trailer, approximately forty miles
southeast of Winslow

Night drifted down, still and restless with the summer's heat and drifting smoke clouds from the distant fires, sprinkles of ash and an uncertainty that grew more cloying with every single lost hour of each unproductive day.

Maddie's nerves, long past raw, had simply frayed then frazzled, and had to be pinched back together and cauterized. She'd have sold her soul for a call from Charlie that didn't come, had groveled on her knees to gods—any gods, including the one she'd long since stopped believing in—for some sign of them at the hovel she'd finally remembered Buddy Carmichael's daddy sharing with Charlie.

But by the time a team had been able to reach the place, the fire had gotten there ahead of them and erased almost all traces of human habitation, except for some utensils' remains and the chains.

They'd also found the underground vault she hadn't chosen to remember, the place where she'd been used and degraded unspeakably. And the reason, Russ decided grimly, sickly, when he saw it, was that Charlie had wanted Maddie to find him and Jess there. It would be the place where the horror had begun and would, therefore, in the man's sick, twisted mind, be where redemption would have to take place.

At the least, it would hurt Maddie unimaginably to be there.

But again, they found no bodies, living or dead. And the tracks that weren't destroyed, that showed the woman running away before the man followed, only led deeper into the forest, into the fire, and vanished.

Discovering that, Russ had resolved to set Guy tracking the pair ASAP. His brother was the best tracker he knew under the worst possible conditions, but since Guy had sent word that Hazel was finally in labor and he was taking paternity leave, ASAP became a relative term at best.

Which meant finding a second-best substitute fast.

That had been days ago. And second best was turning out to be nothing short of disastrous in terms of turning up leads.

And to top that off, he was pretty sure Janie was pulling away from him just as he was letting down more and more of his guards and letting out more of himself with her.

A *crack* deep to the west drew his attention, made him cock his head and wait, listen for follow-up, for echo, for anything.

When nothing came he wrinkled his mouth wryly, relaxed muscles automatically gone tense in anticipation of come-what-may-be-wrong, of protective instinct gone into overdrive. Hot damn he was getting sensitive to the slightest incident. His freaking skin was *crawling* with the heebies.

The jeebies had eaten him alive days ago.

With a rip, he tore the chains on his temper loose from the floorboards he'd shackled them to and slammed out of the trailer, making the door bounce violently on its hinges. Strode forcefully around and gave the propane tank a pair of savage punches. It banged up his knuckles and hurt like blazes, but he was prepared for that—he'd battled propane tanks in lieu of deadlier, less cooperative, less available demons before.

He hated this. Hated the wait, the not knowing—the inability to just be able to go out and make it better.

He wasn't good at standing still. Wasn't good at holding back.

Wasn't good at not being able to make it right.

Whatever *it* was.

Especially not where certain women were involved.

And now he had the two most special women he'd ever met to take care of. His best friend *and* his wife.

His wife, damn it. His *wife*.

And he couldn't seem to do anything significantly right for either of them.

Especially not Janina.

It was bad enough watching Maddie's eyes sink and go dark and bruised-looking, to know that she was losing weight because she wouldn't, couldn't eat. See her nose chapped and red from too much blowing, too much crying. Witness his toughest friend in the world act as though she'd finally given up, given over, give in and lose her battle with despair because she no longer believed Jess was either alive or would ever be found.

But Janina...

Whatever was going on there wasn't so blatant. He could simply see her fade, and knew deep inside himself he had to be to blame. In fact, he could pinpoint the day, the hour, the minute, if not the specific cause—at the station, somewhere among his asides or requests to Jennifer the day the bodies had been discovered in Show Low.

Desolation cut serrated slices deep enough to knick bone. His heart—no, his *soul*—would die if he couldn't make things right for Janie, whatever these things were.

While he'd been out on the job, she'd set up this place for them. And little as it was, short a time as they'd been in it together—anywhere together—it was home now. *She* was home. He couldn't bear the thought of her shutting down and pulling away from him—and everybody else, if the looks and comments Tobi'd been casting his direction lately were any indication.

He couldn't stand the thought that he—or something unsaid between them—might be the cause.

Or that his job, his *identity*, or simply some gossip out of the past that he'd somehow missed hearing could be hurting her now because she'd found him drunk and uncustomarily romantic, he supposed, and had run away with him on the basis of...

A moment out of time that had looked like a bright shining truth they'd both wanted to believe in.

What the hell had he done—had had the time to do? What could Jennifer or anyone else possibly have said?

Nothing sufficient to keep her away from him at

night, that was something. No, their lovemaking was more intense than ever, almost ferociously, desperately so, but the sadness that seemed to engulf and accompany her every time she looked at him—kissed him—made him wonder whenever she touched him if it was for the last time.

And if it was… Hell, he really didn't think he'd survive if he could never squeeze her hand, stroke her cheek, curl her hair around his fingers or—his entire body ached with the very thought—love her again.

Inside, the sounds and shadows of the encroaching night squeezed tight around Janina's lungs, made paranoid forays along whichever nerves made the fine hair on her arms and neck stand on end, sent gooseflesh racing from fingertip to toe.

When she'd rushed blindly, recklessly, happily into her life with Russ—into setting up *their* life together out here on the acreage before civilized living conditions were fully met—she'd never dreamed it would be like this.

So dark.

So full of sound and scent.

So unknown, so uncivilized and so…

Not human.

She hadn't realized.

Growing up, there'd been a fair amount of visiting wildlife, especially around the trash bins where the raccoons were bold and sassy, the skunks were clumsy and tended to knock things about, snakes collected on warm flag and had to be watched for especially after dark when the stone along walkways held the heat after the sun went down. But this was different. There it was never dark, never absent of people. There had been lights everywhere, from other trailers, on poles, wherever someone had strung up Japanese lanterns, or left Christmas lights up all year.

And the noise! The noise was constant. Crying babies, screaming children, laughter, shouting, sobbing, talking, arguing—*people* noise, *human* sound—and always someone within shouting range.

At her apartment there was constant evidence of human activity even on the quietest days, including those days on which neither she nor Tobi saw another living soul between their place and the parking lot. Because from within the apartment they could hear not only the neighbors above them, but also the ones through the walls on either side, the street traffic or passersby from out front, the sounds kids made playing out back. Human racket was everywhere.

And the smell! Scent, flavor, stench, fragrances—the air was laced with them. Mingled food—the mouthwatering flavors of peppers or spice or paella or overripe fruit. Perfume, bodies, asphalt, paint, cars overheating in the summer, the peculiar odor air conditioners gave off in the summer, furnaces in the winter, wood fires, laundry—both clean and dirty. Whether foul or fresh it was still human, someone, somehow to be seen, touched, known. But here…

Janina swallowed, stepped away from her kitchen window and into the brighter puddle of light the overhead cast and wrapped her arms a little more closely around herself before she allowed herself a quick glance in the direction of the room at the far end of the trailer where Maddie spent most of her time—or tried to—and another in the opposite direction where she thought she detected her husband outside beating up…something.

Again.

Here there was not only Russ to get used to, but the intense darkness, the sounds and smells, the lack of a certain civility, a lack of amenities that she'd never before even considered.

Here there was Maddie struggling with an ever-increasing sense of hopelessness and despair, of grief and loss, fear and desperation, trying ever more desperately not to get in the way of her friends' less-than-month-old marriage.

But despite her best efforts, she was smack-dab in the middle of it most of the time simply because she was here.

Here was darkness so intense that Janina, who'd never thought herself afraid of anything, found she was afraid of it.

And the sounds it made.

The sounds she didn't recognize.

The inhuman ones.

The cries, the screams, the emphatic sneezy barks and yowls, the growls and tremulous wails, the *kee-yows* and the *waows*.

But mostly she was fearful of the noises she didn't hear.

The silence could be deafening.

The fear was legitimate, she assured herself, because she'd grown up with skin-walker stories, the tales of evil native witches who could turn themselves into anything and cause all manner of havoc. It didn't matter that she hadn't grown up on the Big Rez but merely adjacent to it, that she wasn't Navajo, only a mixture of Spanish and Mexican and Incan or Aztec or Mayan or something equally hair-raisingly superstitious, and that she told herself she didn't believe in any of it anyway. It didn't matter because it was difficult to outgrow the little niggly bits from your childhood when you were suddenly plunked down into so much darkness, so many weird sounds.

When you added in Charlie out there in all that blackness somewhere, and—though she hadn't told Russ yet because she had no concrete proof—Buddy out there some-where, taunting her from his requisite hundred feet or bet-ter as required by the restraining order, well, it sort of all added up to too much.

So *too much,* in fact, that she hadn't yet been able to bring herself to talk to Russ about the whole baby issue, or rather the lack of baby issue. She knew it was coming between them, but she just wasn't ready to risk losing him…not when the world was so chaotic and she needed him so much.

And on top of that she'd been flat out feeling weird lately. Like Russ's spider sense, kicking in or something. But she didn't do spider sense.

Oh hell, she was paranoid, that was all. It was simply the Buddy thing on top of Charlie and…whatever…and all the rest. She'd just seen Buddy too often lately to be coin-cidence, that was all, especially on top of what Maddie'd told them about his father—that he'd been there that night, too, that he'd wanted Janina brought in. But she couldn't be clearer.

Now wherever she went, Buddy seemed to be down the block or across the street, or exiting Bashas or Safe-way as she entered. He'd done his shadowing clumsily but well.

As though, she'd decided uncomfortably, someone had schooled him so that his being that close to her could and would appear accidental.

Accidental her eye. Especially not when he'd brushed up against her on her way into Wal-Mart, deliberately leav-ing through the entryway when she came in a little ahead of her constant companions so he could do it. Bumping his shoulder into her so that Maddie, who'd been with her, had only caught the exchange from the corner of her eye and couldn't be sure of what she'd seen. And while Jonah's back had somehow managed to be fully turned to them both.

Janina hadn't enlightened either of *them* regarding that incident or any of the others. And she sure as hell hadn't told Russ. She'd seen him react to Buddy once. She didn't think even Jonah would be able to intervene if Russ reacted the way she thought he would to her ex-husband stalking her with intent to harm.

Which meant she'd handle the bastard herself.

A certain amount of grim satisfaction came with the thought, reduced her fears momentarily. She looked forward to dealing with Buddy once and for all—and on her own—as soon as the proper time and opportunity presented themselves. Finally being able to defend herself against something—no, some*one*—specific would be a relief after too long spent living with the unseen.

A sudden skin-creeping scream shattered the twilight, caused Janina to jump and tremble and emit her own inadvertently shuddering, "Oh, God, I hate that," in response.

She knew what the sound was: something—fox or coyote probably—had taken a rabbit for supper. But knowing didn't make the cry easier to get used to. A rabbit's scream was like no other, and no matter how often Russ tried to assure her it was merely life cycling onward, she just couldn't deal with it.

And it only served to remind her that she and Maddie were sitting out here in the middle of nowhere with no neighbors to spy on them, no gossipy town looking in on them. Prey.

And damn Maddie for filling her in on what Charlie— and Buddy's father, which meant, if she thought about it, which she never intended to, Buddy, too, possibly—was capable of doing—

"Janie?"

"*Gaaaaah!*" Startled, Janina yelped, clutching her heart, and turned to find Maddie behind her. "Don't *do* that."

Jumpy in her own right, Maddie sucked air and recoiled, too, put out a hand to catch the edge of a counter and squeaked, "Damn, what the…? Are you all right?"

"No." Janina glared at her. "Why do you think I yelled?"

"Ah…" Maddie's mouth made weird movements into her cheeks, while her dark-circled, sunken eyes moved wildly, and deliberately, about in their sockets. "I don't know?" A definite question.

One that had some reservations about more than merely Janina's current state of mind.

"Why," Janina said pointedly, "are *you* all right?" Meaning she, for one, doubted it. In the extreme.

"I'm—"

She gasped, grabbed for Janina when a large moth, attracted by the light, fluttered crazily against the kitchen screen. Janina clutched her back, until they both calmed enough to recognize what they were doing, laugh weakly in embarrassment and shove away—though not far.

"I'm a lit-little jumpy tonight, thanks," Maddie finished feebly.

Janina gave her mouth a self-conscious twist. "Make that me, too." She shrugged unhappily. "I've got the weirdest sensation something's about to happen, but…" She tossed her hands. "I don't know where it's coming from. I don't do this sort of thing—have this sort of feeling."

Maddie eyed her speculatively. "It's a Levoie thing, you mean? A Russ thing?"

Janina hesitated, nodded, shook her head, nodded more decisively. "Yeah. Sort of. Kind of. I just know it doesn't feel like...*me*."

Intrigued out of her own problems, Maddie cocked her head and studied her best friend's wife.

And started to smile.

An instant later she flung her arms around Janina and hugged her hard. "Oh, my God," she said, delighted. "It would explain everything."

Janina simply inhaled deeply, shook her head to clear it, then patted Maddie on the back and muttered something about both of them having lost their marbles along with everything else.

Maddie laughed dizzily, pulled back a bit and shook her head. "No, I haven't," she said firmly. "And neither have you. Really. I thought Russ had been sniffing around you differently the last couple days, weirdly, you know? Treating you like glass. I bet it's because he knows, but he doesn't want to spoil it for you so he's waiting for you to find out and tell him. Or maybe he doesn't know but just senses something fragile about you. Either way you're pregnant, Janina. And you really don't have a clue, do you?"

Massaging his bruised knuckles, Russ stepped out from under the trailer's awning and flicked perspiration from his chest and the back of his neck. He grabbed his shirt off the nearby picnic table and wiped himself down with it.

Damn it was hot. Almost too much heat in the air to breathe.

Though the temperature would probably drop into the seventies later tonight, it was still a sweat-soaking one hundred degrees even with night finally crawling in. His temper and frustration level were short enough these days, he didn't need the heat index adding to the already strained links on his chains.

An abrupt movement at the corner of his eye piqued not only his curiosity but his spider sense, and he stilled, ducking into shadow to study the scrub to the south, waiting. Excellent night vision gave him the advantage. When whatever it was shifted forward a few paces then flattened itself into the brush, he dropped his shirt and got rid of his shoes before slipping silent and crablike into the nightfall with astonishing speed.

It was too much.

First, all Russ seemed able to talk about was keeping her safe, catching Charlie or how soon they'd need maternity benefits.

And now Maddie thought she was pregnant.

The unfairness of it welled up and stung Janina's throat, pricked fire behind her eyes. She blinked, stretched her jaw in an effort to hold back emotion.

And failed.

The tears welled, big, hot, flash floodlike, and spilled. Unwilling to share them, she shoved by Maddie and darted for the bedroom. Maddie was quick, and reached the room before Janina had a chance to shut her out. Too exhausted to fight, Janina simply heaved herself into a cross-legged ball at the head of the bed, grabbed a pillow, shut her eyes and let the tears fall.

Maddie sat on the edge of the bed, reached out and touched her hand. "Janie?"

Janina squeezed her eyes tight and tried not to pull away from the aching sympathy in Maddie's voice.

"I'm sorry, Janie," Maddie said softly. "I got so excited for Russ that it never occurred to me you might not want to have a baby so soon."

"What?" Janina lifted her head. "Not want to have…" She looked at Maddie incredulously. "Oh, God. Oh, God, Maddie. If I thought I was pregnant, I'd be dancing. *Dancing.* I want his babies—our babies—more than anything. But I can't. My body won't let it happen. And he keeps talking about it. And…I don't know how to tell him. And now you… And you think he…? But how can he when it's a lie? It's not possible.

"We got married too fast." She let her chin fall into the pillow again. "And I am such a coward. It's just not possible."

Maddie poked her on the point of her chin. "You lookin' for someone to talk you out of that?"

Janina smiled wanly. "Okay, I'm not a coward. I will tell him. But if kids were in his plans with me all along and we can't have them together, I don't know him well enough to know what to expect from him."

"Neither do I," Maddie said.

Janina viewed her with dismay.

Maddie grinned. "If I had to guess," she suggested, and waited until Janina nodded warily at her before continuing. "Well, if I had to guess, I'd guess that he wants kids but that he married you and not whatever fertility goddess you might or might not be connected to. I mean, hell, he waited long enough to get around to it, right?"

Janina tipped her chin hesitantly.

"And unless I miss my guess…" Maddie paused, cleared her throat delicately. "He's yours, exclusively."

Janina smiled slightly without meaning to.

"I knew the first time I saw him look at you he was gone,

and he wasn't comin' back. This seems like maybe the wrong thing to say right now but it's why he's the only man I want to father a child for Jess and me. He's got all the quality and none of the crap. I like his brothers, but he's the only man I've ever loved—in a nonhetero kind of way, you understand," she amended quickly.

"That's what you two were yelling down the public hotel hallway about on *my* honeymoon?" Janina gave her full-blown, screwed-up-face disbelief. "*Those* commodities? As in…should-be-mine-exclusively-'cuz-we're-married-now commodities?"

"Well, he turned me down," Maddie protested, "You heard him. And…" She looked away sadly, seeing something Janina couldn't. "Anyway, I asked him before he married you—before any of this happened. He said no then, too. Nada. Not happening. And it wasn't for me to carry. I can't—it's Jess. But now…"

Silence washed between them, a moment shared wherein they each recognized themselves for what they were: Russ's *women*. In different capacities, certainly, but belonging to him—or him to them—nevertheless.

It was Janina who ended the hush with a watery laugh. "I get it now, Mad. You love him, don't you? Not like I do, and not so I have to worry about him with you, but you do."

"Yeah, well." Maddie shrugged. "I told you, Jess is my earth, the world. I can't love Russ that way even if we need a donation from him so Jess can get pregnant. I never wanted him to deliver it in person, but he got spooked anyway."

Janina grinned. "Big baby."

Maddie snorted. "Some days." She turned serious. "You know, I think you're the best thing's happened to him." She smiled. "And if he's too big an idiot when you tell him you can't have kids to realize it doesn't matter 'cuz he's got you and that's all that does, then you come see me and I'll hog-tie him and remind him why it doesn't matter. Not compared to losing the person you love like I've lost Jess."

Janina leaned over and hugged Maddie. "Thank you."

"No." Maddie hugged her back hard. "Thank you."

A yell from the direction of the kitchen door brought them both around.

"Janie! Janie, get the door."

"Russ." Janina scrambled off the bed and headed for the kitchen, Maddie on her heels. "Russ? What is it?"

"Jonah!" She heard him order their out-of-sight but omnipresent watchdog. "Call the station. Get a team out here. I want a full sweep of the area. Lights, ATVs, the works. Now."

"What? Why? Russ?" Janina banged the door open, held it wide to find her husband carrying what appeared to be a body into the shadow of the awning. She slipped out of the trailer to let him inside. "What's going on?"

He eyed her grimly, jaw clenched. A muscle ticked in his cheek. Then he showed her the woman in his arms.

"I found Jess."

Chapter 14

"Jess? Jessi?"

Maddie rushed forward, all at once anxious and fearful and trying to relieve Russ of his burden.

With a mild eyebrow lift, he shouldered Maddie out of the way and let her flutter apprehensively ahead of him into the bedroom she'd been using and get underfoot while he settled Jess on the bed and Janina made sure Emergency Medical Services was on the way.

Securely ensconced at last, Maddie seated beside her, more than a little weepy and babbling, Jess roused herself sufficiently to smile weakly but affectionately at her companion. Then the smile faded, her eyes snapped, and the woman who'd survived three weeks of both Charlie Thorn and an arduous flight from him lifted her right hand and slapped Maddie hard across the face.

"Damn it, don't you ever lie to me by omission about

anything I might be able to help you with again, you hear me, Maddie?" she croaked.

Then her face crumpled, her entire body folded in toward Maddie, she buried her face in her partner's lap and sobbed.

Maddie bent over her, surrounded her, stroked her hair, shushed her, crying, too, making emotional promises, soft vows, swearing whatever oaths Jess needed to hear.

Russ shut the door behind them when he and Janina left the room.

The instant they were alone, Janina stepped into him, slid her arms around him. "How?" she asked simply.

He didn't need a translation to know what she meant. "I saw movement. I went to find out what it was. She said before the fire got too close Charlie'd been keeping watch on this place, knew it was mine. Saw us here the day we came back from Vegas, watched you and Maddie and Jonah get this place set up. But he kept waiting for Maddie to catch on to the hunt, bring me and come to him. She finally got loose and brained him. Took off in the wrong direction until she figured she lost Charlie, then worked her way back around here."

"What is she, some kind of Navy Seal or something?"

Russ shook his head. "Spends a lot of time Orienteering as a sport. She's pretty good. Got a bunch of awards, from what Maddie's told me. Not Maddie's thing though—and way she was treated when she was out in the woods, I don't blame her."

"But it was still you who had to go out and bring her in." Janina hugged him tightly, rested her cheek against his torso. "My hero."

He snorted. "She'd have made it under her own steam,

if I hadn't seen her. Woman's stubborn. Wouldn't be with Maddie if she weren't."

"Doesn't matter. You still did the deed." She stepped on his foot and grinned. "In your bare feet no less."

He chuckled. "Shoes are too noisy."

She sighed, pressed a kiss into the center of his bare chest.

He cupped her head, stroked her back. Told her wryly, "You might not want to get so close. I'm pretty sweaty."

"We could shower together." Janina circled one of his nipples with her tongue then the other, making him shudder. "Because I want to get a lot closer than this right now."

His laughter was low and smoky. "Hold on to that thought? We're about to be inundated with company."

She reached up, laced her fingers behind his head and drew him down into a kiss filled with promise and passion.

"Later then," she whispered when she let him go.

She would take Jess's admonition to Maddie to heart and tell him all tonight, the minute they had the bedroom to themselves and she had his full and undivided attention.

For a change.

A thorough sweep of the thirty-five-acre property, of the surrounding area led to no sign of Charlie.

Which didn't make Russ happy in the slightest.

Particularly not when Jess was able to fill him in on the facts of how low Charlie's medication had run and how serious it had become the minute he'd stopped taking enough of it.

But Russ kept his concerns as tightly bound as he could, put himself on hyperalert, lit a fire under Jonah now that they had three women to guard, pulled in Carson full-time, and intensified security around his perimeters as best he could.

Beyond that, there was little more he could do besides ride it out, and he knew it.

"Oh my…Russ. *Russ! Pleeeaasse…*"

Nearly sobbing with pleasure, Janina twisted, lifted her hips off the bed, either trying to get closer to or escape from her tormentor's wicked mouth, she was too far gone to know which.

He tucked his big hands around her, anchored her against him with a murmured, "C'mon, love, give it to me. You know what I want. What we both want."

Oh sweet heaven, did she! And that's what it would be: heaven. To give him what he wanted—what *she* wanted, as well.

To give up, give over, give in and then unite and fuse.

To join and become one. Become whole.

The same thing he was willing to do for, and with, her every single time he joined her in their bed, or wherever else their loving took them.

Regardless of what she still held back.

And suddenly, she knew she couldn't hold back any longer. Had to tell him what she was hiding from him—all of it, babies, Buddy, everything—before they finished this.

She grabbed his head between her hands and tried to lift it. "Russ?"

And gasped.

And lost her train of thought when her all-too-perceptive husband chose that precise instant to tongue the exact, most exquisite spot designed to drive her mad, send her over the edge, and start her body on a course of spiraling climaxes that only increased in intensity when he surged up her body and plunged into her to join her.

3:13 a.m.

Russ sought solace in Janina's body, comfort, respite, relief.

He also simply couldn't stop himself making love to her.

She smelled different lately, sweeter, headier, incredibly more luscious and ripe. Her skin glowed from the inside, and her nectar...

Heaven.

She was his and he couldn't believe his luck.

When she came for him, he lost himself, let himself go, didn't have to think about chains linked to the floor. He was simply free, unfettered.

Unbound.

So when they finally slept, he wrapped himself around her, as much to protect himself as to protect her. Because losing her would be losing more of himself than he could possibly spare.

He crouched in darkness smelling the thick, rusty scent of iron and knew someone nearby was bleeding. He rubbed his head with the hand that didn't hold the gun and tried to remember what had happened. It didn't help, so he tried pounding his temple with the heel of his gun hand, but all that did was make his headache worse.

"No." He shook his head, a sort of rapid tick from side to side. "No." Trying to assure himself. Of what he didn't quite know. "Wasn't me." But he had the feeling it had been. Some person connected to him. Using his hands. His arms. A piece of his unhealthy brain. "Is he dead? I can't tell."

"No."

The assertion was sudden, definite. For an instant the frightened part of him peeked out of his head, then that other person shoved him back in, stuck him out of the way.

"No," he said again. This time he said it with purpose and authority.

This time he wiped the blood from his hands using the back of Carson's uniform, noting with detachment that the boy was still breathing as he hauled him quickly into some brush where he'd be out of sight.

Then he zigzagged silently in the direction of the trailer, alert to the presence of whatever other interference he might need to deal with as he went.

Maddie moved restlessly in sleep, tried to fit herself closer to safety, to Jess.

But even in slumber, Jess, bruised and hurting, shifted uncomfortably away from her, muttering incoherently at first then with greater clarity, *"Wakey-wakey, my girl, Daddy's here. Time to get it done."*

"Russ. Russ!"

He was awake and alert before she'd finished saying his name once. Maddie, calling him in a voice little short of a scream.

"Don't let him take her again."

He reached under his pillow and started to come off the bed in a single movement, dropped back when he felt Janina stir and scooted her groggily off her side of the bed and onto the floor where out of sight could mean safer.

"Stay down, keep quiet and cover your head," he whispered. "I'll be—"

Trying hard not to lose it completely, Maddie stumbled backward into the patch of moonlight that silvered a path across the bed and onto the floor inside the bedroom door. Fingers of one hand laced tightly in Jess's hair using it as leverage to shove her along, and visibly trembling gun tamped behind her right ear with the other, Charlie Thorn followed his daughter.

"You'll be a while," he said, blinking rapidly, but verbally coherent for the moment. He glanced at Russ's hand, still under the pillow, and his mouth twitched. "Leave the gun. Don't want any accidents. Had enough of those." Turned to Janina, not quite on the floor. "You. I seen you before, haven't I. You take the pillow. Do it slow. *Slide* it, that's the way." Back to Russ. "Fingers off the weapon, one at a time. Raise your hand. Good. No fuss, no bother, no accidents." He shifted, keeping Jess in front of him. Gestured with his head. "Get over there with my baby. My girl. Keep plenty of space between you, hear?"

When they'd done as instructed, he dragged Jess over to the bed and collected Russ's weapon. His mouth twitched again. "Kitchen," he said. "Haven't eaten in days. I'm hungry. March."

Dawn brought full bellies but no relief.

It also brought Janina a full-on case of unwanted-but-forced-breakfast-at-gunpoint post-breakfast nausea.

Grimly Russ held her head at the kitchen sink and shot Maddie's sire a look that, were there justice in the world, should have killed him on the spot. He wrung out a clean dish towel in cold water, applied it to the back of her neck.

"Better?"

"Yeah."

She started to nod weakly then loosed a wretched invective and returned to the sink as her stomach clenched again.

Russ's jaw tightened and he looked at Charlie.

"You've eaten. Let's get to it, Thorn." He relaxed one hand with an effort and placed it protectively on Janina, gestured at Jess with the other, making sure to include Maddie even though he knew that was pushing it. "You don't want them, you came for me. So let's us guys get out of here and leave the women to it, how 'bout it?"

For the tick of an instant, clarity wandered across Charlie's face and through his eyes. For that same fractional sweep of the clock's second hand in the passage of a minute, his gaze slipped toward his daughter and registered what for him Russ thought must pass for emotion.

Then it was gone. Clarity shattered. Simply left Charlie's face, his eyes, his person.

What remained was frightening—a psychotic episode created by the abrupt and prolonged absence of chemicals his brain had come to rely on for creating proper thought and behavior. His hands wavered, body trembled, gaze turned inward as if he listened to something outside their experience. The gun that had lifted toward the ceiling and almost ceased to be an immediate threat dropped back into position, aimed at Janina.

"No, Charlie. *Charlie.*" Though he said it sharply, Russ tried to keep both voice and demeanor calm and focused. A bare toe at a time, he inched forward, maneuvering to get between Janina and his confiscated department-issue .45. "Charlie, look at me."

But Charlie was elsewhere, awareness keened on one night thirteen years earlier on the girl who might have been Janina, or maybe someone resembling her.

"I know you," he hissed. "You were there that night. You saw it all. You know what happened." His voice was a harsh drawl. His eyes burned, his skin flushed, ran with sweat. "They wanted you over, too, you know. But me, I said no, leave that one outta it." He laughed, a skin-creeping sound. "Yeah. I know you. I know all about you. Saved you from hell, you don't even know."

His gaze wavered over her with something akin to ownership, and Russ knew without doubt, that Charlie was indeed seeing Janina at sixteen—and younger.

Instinctively he put out an arm to block her from the monster's view, but Charlie anticipated the younger man and moved faster than Russ guessed humanly possible, if in a wholly different direction.

Almost before anyone could blink, he'd knocked the table out of the way, lunged across, laced his fingers through a fistful of Maddie's hair and dragged her to him.

As though caused by the sudden exertion, a handful of epileptic-appearing tremors spasmed through him the moment he straightened, jerking control of the muscles of his face and left arm, stuttering into his left leg until the chair beside him rattled the floor.

His eyelids fluttered, but he didn't lose consciousness and his grip on Maddie didn't loosen.

In fact, if anything, all it did was contract, causing him to tighten his grip on Maddie.

And Russ's gun.

Charlie's seizure naturally produced multiple contractions in his left hand. The one slung around the butt of the gun, index finger through the trigger guard and around the trigger, flexing on and off that sensitive little item with every flicker of his nerves and muscles.

Coming up a hero took considerable concentration, great reflexes, a fair amount of timing and more often than not, victim cooperation. So when Russ shoved Janina to the floor, she went, devising her own plans on the way down. And Jess, having "been there, done that" as recently as a few days ago simply dropped at the same time. But Maddie...

Russ pivoted forward and flipped her heels out from under her in order to unbalance Charlie and get her out of the way, then moved in to head butt Charlie in the face and take back his gun, Maddie, being Maddie, moved in the wrong direction. And got in the way, unbalancing Russ instead.

In which case Charlie's finger contracted fully around the trigger and Russ was shot point-blank in the upper left chest nearest his shoulder.

"No. Oh nonononono*noooo!*"

Janina heard the screaming from a distance and wished someone would take the shrieking woman away and shake her so she could get to Russ. Because if she could get to him, he'd stop leaking red all over the place and be warm when she touched him.

If only the screaming would stop.

And then she reached him where'd he'd staggered back against the sink cupboards, slid down them and sagged.

Touched him. Stepped outside herself. And knew she was the one screaming.

"You *bastard!*"

She scrambled for towels—paper, cloth, it didn't matter so long as they'd stop the bleeding—not sure if she yelled at Russ, certain she shrieked at Charlie. Unwisely, she kicked out with a foot and flung a chair in his direction.

"If he dies I will kill you personally."

The seizure left Charlie weak. He lolled his head in her direction, a margin of clarity once again written in his eyes. "I know." He worked his mouth, trying to swallow as though his tongue felt thick, his mouth dry and cottony. "Couldn't save her, but I saved you."

He'd said that before, Janina realized, and it still didn't make sense. Right now she didn't care. Right now all that mattered was Russ.

She pressed towels down hard on his wound and he groaned. His glassy eyes turned her way.

"Janie?"

"Stay with me, damn you, Russ. Do you hear me?"

He coughed. "Pretty bossy way to talk to the man who's bleedin' all over our brand-new kitchen floor." He swallowed convulsively. "Know a good crime-scene cleaner you might wanna get in here—"

"God…" Crying, she bussed him hard so he'd shut up. "*Damn* you. This is not a joke."

The too-small towel soaked blood, squished it up between her fingers and over her hands. She'd lose him before they ever had a chance to tell each other anything important if she couldn't stop the bleeding.

"Janie?"

She blinked at him. He tried to lift his good arm so he could stroke her cheek, but he was already too weak to do it. Choking back a sob, she did it for him. Pressed her cheek into his palm. He ran the pad of his thumb over her lips. Offered her a grim travesty of her favorite Levoie grin.

"Trust me?" he asked faintly.

She eyed him incredulously. "You're dying and you ask me this *now?*"

He shrugged his mouth, grunted in pain. "I know you

think—" He coughed, tried to adjust himself so he could breathe. Charlie was on him instantly, one weapon wavering undecidedly on Russ, another half drawn in the direction of Maddie and Jess. Russ ignored him, let his attention stay exclusive to Janina. "I know you think you can't get pregnant and it doesn't matter a damn to me."

He paused to draw a winded breath, ran his tongue around his mouth looking for moisture. "But you need to know, you *are* pregnant. I smelled it on you, *tasted* it on you tonight, Janie. I'm not plannin' to, but if I die today, I want you to marry Jonah. You like each other and you'll be good together and you could do a lot worse—"

Janina's mouth dropped. "You arrogant, autocratic... If you don't die today I am going to kill—"

In the middle of the word, while Maddie and Jess, mouths agape, were starting to sputter in disbelief, and Charlie was momentarily distracted, she surged to her feet, caught up the cast-iron skillet off the edge of the sink with both hands, spun about in one of the lightning-quick turns she'd learned in her martial arts class and brained Charlie solidly with it.

Then while Russ lost consciousness, and Maddie and Jess found Russ's handcuffs for Charlie, she 911'd for a medevac helicopter and the troops to come get Russ—and whoever else might be down.

Fast.

Chapter 15

Winslow, Arizona.
August 20. Standin' On The Corner Park

It was a hellaciously long and scary few days.

Janina sucked frozen mocha frappalatte between her lips and studied the hot brick morosely. Russ had been in the hospital nearly a week now and despite her druthers she couldn't spend every minute at his bedside.

For one, from practically the moment he'd gotten out of surgery and regained consciousness, he'd steadfastly refused to allow it because he worried she wasn't getting enough rest, enough to eat, enough time off her feet, enough you name it for every minute she spent with him. He *wanted* her, he said—and she, idiot that she was—believed him. He wanted her with him, wanted her around.

He just didn't want her watching over him while he slept, while he burned with fever, while he ached, lay shot up and trying to heal from the inside out.

Didn't want—or maybe that was *need*—her next to him while his teeth chattered and he mumbled or cried out in fevered dreams, and muscle and bone, ligament and fiber and tissue went through the initial stages of draining, straining and mending.

He didn't want her sitting there while they gave him transfusions against the blood he'd lost, and for which hers was a perfect match.

In muttered incoherence he'd begged Guy—who'd turned up immediately when called despite having to leave Hazel home with their barely ten-day-old daughter after Jonah'd been found concussed at his post not far from the trailer—not to let them use her as a donor.

Guy had taken one look at her, sized up the situation, and particularly her fury at Russ's doltish heroics, taken her adamant "I am his *wife*" with a snort of "It's about damn time" and gotten out of her way.

And for two...

Well, for two...he was *Russ*. She adored him. Loved him to pieces. Heart, soul, body, mind and all the other places nobody'd ever thought to name. Loved him.

And he was an idiot. A big, studly, macho, card-carrying idiot.

And she'd nearly lost him because of it.

A drop of emotion slipped off the end of her nose and landed in her frappalatte.

Because he had to protect everybody and he wouldn't back off.

Which had left her, in the space of a month, wedded,

bedded and… Well, okay, so "nearly widowed" didn't rhyme the way "him nearly deaded" did.

She blinked and another unaccustomed bit of eye-weather skidded down her cheek and dripped off her upper lip. She blotted her face with a hand. God, what was the *matter* with her? She didn't do this. Ever. As in *never* ever. And since the evening Buddy'd tripped her and Russ had stopped him and married her, she'd gotten weepy…

A lot.

As in all too damn frequently.

She sucked more frozen ice cream and coffee and let herself wallow a little deeper in self-pity.

Today she'd finally gotten up the courage to buy and take a pregnancy test, and well…it had minused out.

Damn it.

Exactly as she'd predicted.

And not only that, but she was two weeks late for her period, no doubt due to all the stress from Russ and Maddie and Jess and Charlie and Buddy and…God knew what else. And she was so bloated she'd had to take off her wedding ring and leave it on the kitchen table.

She sniffed. Thank God there was no one around to witness her self-pity party, because if there had been she'd have had to bag her head and hide in a barrel.

Or maybe she should simply shoot herself.

In the foot, of course.

Her lips twitched with self-deprecating humor at the thought. No sense doing the shooting somewhere it might actually accomplish some good. Like maybe in the butt.

Grinning outright now, Janina turned at the sound of her name.

"Janie, hey, Janie!" Tobi leaned across the seat and

gunned the engine on her elderly Ford pickup in an attempt to keep it from dying in the middle of the street. "You on your way to the hospital or to work?"

Janina moved in to lean over the door and made a *thpppt!* face. "Russ is weak and can barely talk but he said I make him nervous, fussing around him. So he kicked me out of his room. The idiot can't see it scares me to death to not be there. I'm on my way to work. Maybe it'll take my mind off him."

Tobi nodded sympathetically, not even commenting on the fact that she was babbling.

"Where's your car?"

"Garage." Janina nodded vaguely in the direction of the place that did her tune-ups. "I was on my way to get it."

"Get it tomorrow." Tobi pulled her door latch. "I'll drive you to work, you can stay with me tonight, be like old times. We can talk, you can relax, let Russ miss you for a while." She grinned her demon grin. "Make sure he does."

Janina bit her tongue on a half smile. The idea had a certain appeal even as she automatically went to reject it. Even married to him, Janina couldn't see herself running after Russ forever, tending his wounds and being shoved out the door every time he got hurt just because...well, she really didn't understand the "just because." Just because he was Russ, she supposed. And she had no intention of losing him just because he was an idiot, but if he wouldn't listen to her say that...

Maybe she'd better figure out a way to demonstrate it.

She nodded at Tobi. Pitched the remains of her frappalatte toward the nearest trash bin, walked back to the truck and started to climb into it. "Okay," she said. "Let's do it—"

"Janie?"

The hitch in her friend's voice and the look on Tobi's face stopped her cold. The expressive Navajo features and bright black eyes were frightened—an unusual expression for her in-your-face pal. She swallowed. Hesitated. But didn't look back. If you didn't look, if you acted normal whatever was there, it couldn't see your fear.

"What?"

Tobi grabbed her wrist, dragged her bodily onto the seat. "Buddy," she chattered hoarsely, and made an effort not to point at him. "Out there. Exactly where you were standing. Drinking the drink you threw away. Watching you. I didn't see him before. I don't know where he came from."

Refusing to be spooked, Janina turned her head and gave him back stare for stare. He winked boldly at her and cupped his crotch crudely, sucked from her discarded drink.

And laughed.

Then he cocked an imaginary weapon at her, popped off a make-believe round and blew her a kiss. "See you," he said.

She swallowed a lungful of fury and snapped face front to stare out the Ford's windshield. Said in a voice so soft and menacing it scared Tobi, "I look forward to it."

"You did what?" Jeth Levoie stared at his oldest brother in something like astounded pity.

Russ blinked crankily out at him from amid the tubes and bandages running around his left arm and shoulder, the oxygen tube chapping his nose that they'd promised might be able to come out two days ago but that was still in because he'd developed a bit of a cough with fever.

"Sent her home," he breathed a bit unsteadily.

"You jackass," Jeth said succinctly.

Russ glared at him.

Jeth clarified. "When the woman who loves you wants to stick around and tend to your shot-up hide, you *let* her."

"Like you?"

"You know damn well I let Allyn take care of me when I was shot," Jeth said patiently. "In fact, you know freaking well she's the only one took care of me when I was down." He eyed Russ meaningly. "Bathroom breaks and everything."

Russ grimaced. "Go away."

Jeth grinned. "Not till I've fluffed your pillows." The grin faded. "Seriously, Russ. She wants to be here, don't shove her away. She'll think you don't need her or want her."

"I can't let her…be here all the time. She's pregnant. She'll wear herself out."

"After growing up with Mom, I can't believe you said that."

Russ laughed roughly, winced at the pain. "Yeah. Well. Ma's not Janie. Janie's sure she's *not* pregnant and that she never will be. She thinks she needs to convince me that I won't want to stay married to her if I find that out. I tried to tell her. She thinks it was an act to distract Charlie. Some of it was. But I still know it. It's on her skin. I can—"

"Smell it on her," his brother finished, nodding. "Yeah. I know that one. So does Guy." He thought about it a moment. Shrugged. "Okay, what do you need?"

"Find a wheelchair and get someone to pull these tubes so I can sign myself out of here," Russ said promptly.

"Ah…" Jeth eyed him dubiously.

Russ raised a finger to forestall objections, forced strength into his voice. "Charlie said something that night that I've finally remembered and I have to know what he meant."

Jeth raised an eyebrow.

Russ swallowed. "He told Janina, 'I couldn't save her, but I saved you.' I have to know what that means. He wasn't entirely lucid at the time, but he said it more than once. He also said something about her knowing everything even though she doesn't realize it." He moistened cottonmouth, reached awkwardly for his water glass, sipped at the bent straw. "He might have meant Maddie, but Janie was there that night. She and her mother lived in the trailer across from the Thorns. She got out a shotgun to back me up when there wasn't anyone else there and she doesn't know I saw her. I never mentioned it to her. Didn't want her involved. She never volunteered anything, so I figured she didn't see anything more'n anyone else coulda seen from the front of the place. But maybe…"

He took another sip of water. Looked at his brother. "I have to know. Make sure she's okay. Will be okay. Permanently."

"Sh—" Jeth started, and blew out a breath. "Why didn't you mumble this on your deathbed when they were bringing you in 'stead of all that stuff about Guy keeping Janina outta your way and safe so you don't have to worry about her? You brain-dead idiot, you'd made it clear, we'd have taken care of this a long time ago 'stead of turning Janie loose to get into whatever the hell trouble she wants."

"Russ, you can't even stand. What are you doing here?"

Hurriedly Maddie attempted to steer him to a chair in the suite she and Jess had taken at La Posada until everything with Charlie was sorted out. Jeth and Guy could have manhandled him just fine between them, but Maddie was the managing sort and almost always had been. Experience had taught them to let her lead while they got out of the way.

And picked up the pieces left in her wake—if Russ hadn't collected them first.

Russ grunted. "Judas, Mad…leave the stitches and bandages. They're all that's holding me together."

"No glue and staples?" Jess asked mildly.

"Hell, I don't know. I was asleep. Feels like a truck-load's in there though. Run me through a metal detector and find out."

Maddie wrinkled her mouth. "You signed yourself out of the hospital, didn't you?"

Russ tried to find a comfortable position in the chair and didn't answer.

"Does Janie know?"

There were no comfortable positions for a body that should still be propped up and pumped up on painkillers and not out wandering about trying to hold coherent conversations with anyone.

"She doesn't, does she." A flat statement, and not a particularly pleased one at that.

His shoulder and chest throbbed, entire body hurt, head ached. His skin felt like fire.

"Russ?" Maddie almost sounded anxious. He must have zoned out for a minute. "You in there?"

Russ gathered himself. Focused on her. "Mad, Charlie said something about Janie…about not being able to save you, but saving—"

"You dumb jerk." She was in full fettle now. "That woman loves you more than I ever thought about doing even when I thought I was straight, and you can't even let her know you pulled your plugs and went running off into the wild blue chasing some*thing* you think Charlie said when he was crazy." She poked his nowhere-near-healed shoulder and demanded, "What is she going to do if she goes over to the hospital and looks in your room and you're not there? What's the first thing she'll think? Dead, that's what. That you died and nobody called because you didn't want her there badly enough to make them."

She threw up her hands and stalked away from him. "You are such an unbelievable *idiot,* Russ Levoie. And I am glad I don't have to fall in love with men."

When she reached Jess, she touched her partner's cheek then kissed her gently, lingeringly, before tossing a look of pure loathing over her shoulder at Russ and marching into the bathroom, nose in the air, to slam the door behind her.

She opened it almost immediately. "And I'm not coming out," she informed him, "until you use the sense God gave you to call your wife and tell her where you are."

Jeth looked at Guy, who glanced at Jess, who nodded. "That seems to state it quite clearly," she said.

"We tried to tell him," Guy agreed.

"We told him to send Jonah," Jeth pointed out. "So he sent Jonah to stand guard at the hospital."

"Cowardly," Guy said.

"Stupid," Jeth put in.

"Uncommunicative," Maddie yelled through the bathroom door.

It took every ounce of will he possessed, but Russ pushed himself erect, sucked as much air into his lungs as he could manage and bellowed, "I don't freaking care what you call me, just get the hell out here and tell me what I need to know to protect the pregnant woman I love from whoever your father thinks he saved her from. Damn it, Maddie."

Then he collapsed back into the chair and allowed himself to blank out for a full three seconds.

* * *

Janina and Tobi finished totaling up the last of their evening checks and exchanged coin tips for paper cash before Manuel, the Fat Cat's assistant manager, left the office and emptied the till for the night then headed into the back to change.

"You mind if we run by the hospital before we call it a night?" Janina asked. "I want to check on Russ, let him know where I'll be in case he tries to call." Her mouth drooped. "Not that he will, or at least he hasn't yet."

Tobi huffed a breath. "Janie." Stopped.

Janina waited. Said, "What?" when Tobi didn't go on.

Tobi shook her head. "No. Never mind. None of my business."

"But you wonder if I need my head examined 'cuz I'm not acting like myself about Russ anymore," Janina supplied wryly.

Tobi grinned. "Yeah. Somethin' like that." She shook her head. "No, exactly like that."

Janina shrugged. "Join the club. I don't know who I am anymore either. It's eggshells and glass all over the floor and I don't know where to step. And the dumb thing is, I'm not sure it's actually him, but me. I'm the one all of a sudden can't think how to put words together. Simple words. Tell him what I mean, what I think, how I feel. I don't even know if I should."

She made a face. "It's like...we got married and I..." She hesitated, then, "Lost my bearings. I don't get the impression he lost his. Maybe he did. He must have. He's ridiculous as all get-out about some stuff, but the things he knows, that he understands, about me..." She blew out a long sigh. "It's amazing. And then there are those times when I'm sure I should leave him, that we did it too fast and it was wrong and…"

She tucked her tongue behind her bottom teeth to keep her lip from quivering. "Damn. And lately I cry about everything and he's shot and if I lose him…"

She sniffed. "I haven't even told him I love him yet, and I don't know why, 'cuz I do, I always have, but he's such a fool, you know?" She appealed to Tobi for confirmation the other woman wisely didn't offer. "If I told him and he didn't…and he never said it back or he couldn't live with what I can't ever be—"

There was a crash and the sound of flying glass and crunching metal and wood at the front of the diner. Then the rear door into the back room caved in and a brand-new ATV came smashing toward them. It squealed and careened and skidded to a stop sideways in front of them, bouncing on its tires. Buddy Carmichael sat astride the machine, grinning gleefully at Janina, meaty hands encased in studded leather half-gloves. He aimed and fired his imaginary weapon at her, using both hands to do it this time, then stood up on the seat of his ATV and cupped his hands around his mouth.

"Hey, Daddy, come look what I found. We got her to ourselves this time and she brought us a friend, too."

Maddie hadn't wanted to remember.

Nothing new in that, Russ reflected, doing everything in his power to keep himself focused, awake. It was more difficult than he'd anticipated, though the pain helped.

A lot.

Still it was pain. And it was distracting. He didn't need distracting right now. Because what Jess had finally gotten Maddie to remember was about more than Charlie. It was about Buddy's father. And Buddy.

And the fact that they'd *both* been there that night thirteen years ago.

And that it had been Buddy's father, not Maddie, who'd killed her brother. Murdered him, in fact, when the boy threatened to blackmail him over the things he'd been doing with Maddie up at the cabin that had burned when Charlie had held Jess captive in it. The things they'd taken photos of.

Things they'd discussed doing to Janina, too, apparently.

Which was where Charlie had drawn a line, and what he'd meant when he'd said, "Couldn't save her, but I saved you."

Sick as he was, there was a line even Charlie hadn't wanted to cross. But Buddy's father hadn't cared, and had even used Maddie's terrified and confused mind to hide what he'd done. Had put the gun in her hands and forced her to pull the trigger in order to ensure the police finding gunshot residue on her hands.

And now Russ had to know if Janina remembered seeing Buddy or his father at all that night. She'd already said she didn't remember seeing Buddy or she'd never have gotten involved with him, but he had to probe, had to make her press her memory deeper for her own sake, own protection. Because he didn't know how he could build a case, collect enough evidence to protect her from one of the area's more influential residents if she didn't know what Charlie was talking about.

"Jeth, you there?" Jonah's voice crackled through the radio.

"We're alive, number five," Guy said easily to the fifth-born Levoie. "Come back."

"Tell Russ no joy," Jonah returned. "I'm at the trailer but

she's not. And sorry, big bro, but she left her ring on the table. I'm headed for Tobi's. Out."

For a moment Guy and Jeth were silent. Russ sat in the back, closed his eyes and waited for the hollowness to set in, the finality, the certain knowledge that Janina was gone.

It didn't come.

In its place rose something else, another knowledge, a connection, the same kind he experienced when they made love, only different.

More.

And then his throat constricted, his lungs fell in on themselves and his heart started to fail. His good hand flinched, crushed the edge of the seat the way it might a windpipe. He gasped suddenly for air, struggled for it, and then he knew.

And nothing else mattered.

"Fat Cat," he ordered harshly. "Carmichael has 'em at the Fat Cat."

11:37 p.m.,The Fat Cat.

"Isn't this just the stupidest man-trick you've ever seen in your life?" Janina wheezed at Tobi.

"Geez, yes." Her friend nodded. Which set her rocking helplessly. Which set them both giggling hysterically, not wise under the circumstances, since they were both lying on their stomachs, hog-tied in plastic wrap and freezer tape with their hands behind them, wrists to ankles, heads up, necks more or less loosely connected to the entire contraption by meat-packing string, which sort of made them look like acrobatics-class rocking horses, which in turn was what was causing the giggles and making them rock. It was undignified, uncomfortable and extremely difficult to breathe because every jerk on the string made it cut into their necks.

But every yank caused another strand of the oft-wrapped string to break.

So *stupid* about covered the whole thing right down to the fact that Janina nearly had her wrists loose from her ankles because sweating beneath the plastic wrap was causing it to get slippery. Buddy had also done a lousy job of wrapping and taping their wrists to their ankles with the abysmal-quality freezer tape that wasn't really meant to stick for long periods of time.

The whole thing was too much.

And all because the half-bagged Buddy hadn't come prepared to deal with her and Tobi once he'd captured them. Nor had the drinking buddy who came along for some hell-raising but who hadn't turned out to be his "daddy." One look at Buddy's true intentions had sent the guy—who Janina recognized as having been with him that fateful evening Buddy'd tripped her—scrambling for the desert night on the double. Leaving the used, and undoubtedly out-of-town-stolen Hummer II parked in the middle of the Fat Cat's counter.

Buddy, she reflected, never had been good at the follow-through his father required. No doubt why she'd never pegged him as having been *there* the night Maddie's brother was killed.

Or why she'd never thought of him as a wife beater until he'd hit her that once.

She thunked over onto her side. Another piece of string popped loose around her neck.

"You get the feeling Buddy's daddy never let him be a Boy Scout?" Tobi sort of gasped, thonking sideways, too.

"This kitchen's sure not prepared for torture tying." Janina rasped back. She squirmed in the direction of Tobi's voice. "You ever play Mummenschanz when you were a kid?"

"Huh?"

"You know. Mime acrobats. Dressed in black. Used blocks for heads and feet, or tubes for bodies or whatever. They were on *Sesame Street.* Did a lot of tumbling. Impossible stuff. They were great. We used to try everything they did."

"Ah…"

"Never mind." She twisted her hands under the film of plastic. "Think I've sweated enough to slide my hands out of this wrap if you…"

She felt a slight tug and her hands drifted a bit then suddenly wrested free of their prison. Her aching shoulders sagged gratefully, but she gagged when the multiple loops of string unexpectedly threatened to cut into her throat. When they abruptly separated from her ankles, and her feet clunked heavily to the floor, she gasped and lay still, breathing for a moment, letting stiff muscles and joints relax back into the shape they were meant to inhabit. Then she gingerly rolled over and unwrapped and untaped her feet, found a box cutter in a nearby drawer and turned to Tobi's bonds.

"Where's Manuel?" Tobi asked.

Stricken, Janina looked at her and shook her head. She had no idea whether or not he'd come down from the office and gone out front before Buddy's arrival. Or if Buddy'd had found him or…

Tobi swallowed hard. "We should look for him."

"Yeah." Janina didn't want to find him the way Tobi was afraid they'd find him either. "Maybe we should call police and rescue first?"

"I'll call, you look," Tobi said with alacrity, absconding with the non-dirty work—as usual. "That'll be fastest."

Janina glared at her friend. "You know I hate you."

"And you know how this works." Tobi half winced, half grinned at her. "Them as can, designate, and them as forget to, look for the blood." She gave Janina a look of devilish innocence. "Besides—" she shrugged "—you know you love me. Who else would put up with you?"

Russ, Janina wanted to shout, but at the moment, she wasn't as certain about that as she wanted to be.

She went to look for Manuel.

Jonah fishtailed to a stop in the middle of the highway, then jammed on the gas and jerked hard out of the path of an oncoming semi and careered onto the side of the road, breathing hard. Damn, whatever had made him do that had come too close this time. If he kept listening to it—whatever *it* was—he'd get himself killed sooner than later.

Deliberately he shook off the remnants of the sinking, wrenching fear tumbling through his belly and focused. Sure enough, reason surfaced. Alerted by some instinct, Levoie or otherwise, he stuck his hand in his uniform breast pocket and fingered the ring Russ had given Janina on their wedding day. Gem and metal heated instantly to his touch, seemed to fuse with the skin of his palm in a manner that had nothing to do with August's high heat.

Curious, he switched on the pickup's interior lights to study the ring. Nothing.

With something akin to misgiving, and full of reluctance, he lifted his palm to his nose and sniffed the ring. Instantly his senses whirled, head spun. He shut off the interior lights and closed his eyes to the sudden kaleidoscope of impressions a single whiff threatened to drown him in.

He huffed air, shallow breaths, making sure not to breathe more of the Janina- and Russ-soaked ring than he had to. He'd worked toward this end a long time and achieved nothing like this, so why now?

Because now it was necessary, instinct answered, that was why. Now there was need.

He closed the wedding ring into his fist, held it at arm's length and took a deep breath. All right then. He would respond to the need, help his brother, his new sister, and take on the side of himself he'd hunted since adolescence.

Leaving the truck at the highway's edge, he headed into the Arizona brush, found himself a likely spot where he wouldn't be disturbed, and focused his energies not only on what he needed to do but on Janina's ring.

Chapter 16

Janina found Manuel pinned beneath the Hummer that was lodged in a lopsided slump half between the kitchen pass-through and the swinging doors into the kitchen. He was bleeding from numerous cuts, and unconscious, but his pulse was strong.

Shaking and queasy, she gulped relief. "I found him," she called when her voice was ready to cooperate. "He's alive—"

"Ain't that nice," Buddy observed.

Janina whipped around. Gun loose in one hand, his other arm crooked around Tobi's throat choking off her air, Buddy teetered his way through the debris, dragging the struggling Fat Cat waitress with him. Janina's gaze locked with Tobi's. Tobi, fish-mouthed, gasping for air, then deliberately flashed a glance downward, back at Janina. And blinked once. Janina tightened her jaw, gave her friend the slimmest curl of a smile in response. Felt around her for something heavy but hand-size.

"You're mine now," Buddy said, coming to an unsteady halt atop a pile of rubble. "No bully cops here to rescue you this time."

"No daddy here to see you either, Buddy," Janina said quietly. "And your friend from the Hummer ran. Bet he called the cops the minute he saw what you wanted to do."

"No." Buddy shook his head in momentary confusion. "My daddy didn't run. He told me…" He looked at her, rubbed his temple with the fisted weapon—and took a menacing step forward. Leveled the gun. "No. You quit now. You always did this. Tryin' to get between him 'n me. He tol' me. You need to be managed. Taken care of. I brought him to show him I can. He didn't run. Told me you were fer me. Said he'd show me how. Worked it on that other one. Showed me. Not his fault I couldn't do her like he said. But it's different now. He said—"

A vehicle skidding and screeching to a halt near the diner's destroyed front window arrested his attention, caused the gun to waver. In the same instant Tobi sank the nails of both hands into the bare forearm at her throat, and Janina came up with a full sugar container and threw it hard at his head. She followed it by surging to her feet, table leg in hand and, as soon as the sugar bottle hit Buddy and he loosened his hold on Tobi, she belted him with the piece of curved steel.

He screamed and staggered, but bewildered and enraged, didn't go down. Instead, he attempted to lunge at her across the rubble. She sidestepped him, smacked him in the ear with the pipe at the same time Tobi jammed a loose chair into his path and tripped him.

Simultaneously all hell—or heaven, as the case may be—broke loose. A large predatory bird screamed through the broken window, reversed to brake in full flight in order to come at Buddy, talons first. It descended sharply, wings spread, beating the man about the head anytime he attempted to rise, using its talons and beak to rake exposed skin whenever threatened, but lifting obligingly out of the way when Janina shooed it or made a move to continue dealing with Buddy herself. And when Russ, pumped full of dread and adrenaline at the sight of the Hummer parked inside his wife's place of employment, finally hurled his battered body through the wreckage sans help from Guy and Jeth, the big bird cocked its head as if to give him an avian once-over. Then it shook something on a leather thong out of its breast feathers, hooked it into its beak and tossed it at Russ before taking wing and vacating the premises.

"Janie? Janina?" Damn, he couldn't see her, where was she?

Too intent on staying conscious, erect and getting to Janina to notice anything else, Russ missed the wink of precious metal and gem arcing into the beam of the headlights Jeth had left on.

"Janie, please. Answer me." The object thrown by the bird hit him center forehead, staggered him. He opened his good hand, caught the ring as it fell. Dropped in his tracks and stared at Janina's ring in confusion. "What the…?"

"Russ?" Janina spun from where she'd finished laying Buddy low with the heel of her hand to his nose and a follow-up knee to his groin, and spotted Russ collapsing into the mess that used to be his favorite booth. "Oh, geez. *Russ!*"

Fast as she could move, she scrambled through the rubble to reach him, tried to catch him and ease him down.

"What are you doing here? You're supposed to be in the hospital. Who let you out? If anything more happens to you, I'll…"

"Kill me?" Russ asked weakly. "Are you—"

"Fine," Janina snapped. "Psychically demolished but physically intact. Mostly. As far as I know and no thanks to you. And no I don't want to kill you, I want to shake you within an inch of your life. You brass-plated, pigheaded, closemouthed, uncommunicative nincompoop." Then she threw her arms around his neck, heedless of his hiss of pain, and burst into tears.

Outside, the wail of sirens and honking emergency vehicles rolled through the night and into the parking lot outside the diner. In a moment the Fat Cat was inundated with firefighters and paramedics, Winslow police, sheriffs and the highway patrol. Jonah showed up last.

"Shh, Janie, shh." As best he could, Russ pulled her close, needing the feel of her living, breathing and warm against him more than he minded the ache. "It's all right. We're all right. It's done now. You got him. We're okay."

"No, we are not." She pushed back. Smeared the ball of her thumb across her cheek. Snuffled emotion away while she watched a pair of firefighters work to free Manuel from beneath the Hummer. Planted her tongue behind her bottom teeth to get control of her quavery chin and looked her husband close range in the eye. "No, we are so *not* okay, it's all out pathetic."

"Janie, I—"

"No, don't. It's my turn to tell you."

She reached out, kneading the muscles in his damaged shoulder until he grunted when the immediate throbbing turned into excruciating pain. "Janie, damn, that—"

She grabbed his chin, aiming for his attention. "Talkin' here. Listen up."

"Got it. Absolutely." He cleared his throat, worked his jaw around a groan, and nodded. "I'm silent as long as you quit killing my shoulder."

"Be glad I don't kill *you*," Janina said thickly, but with asperity. "Because after all this, you deserve it." She gulped, swiped at her face again, determined not to cry more. Failed. Took a deep breath and let it out in one long flow of anguished chatter. "I mean, you seduce me into marrying you then you don't come home, then you're the most attentive husband ever, then you get shot being stupid and you nearly die in my arms, then you *don't* die, but won't let me near you in the hospital even while you're telling me you're worried about me being alone 'cuz of Buddy and his daddy and you think I'm pregnant so I go take a damn pregnancy test and I'm not and you still won't let me stay with you, so what am I supposed to think, blast it?

"And then this happens and Buddy says his daddy always had me marked for him—did you know that? He's nuts—and you're not in the hospital where you're supposed to be and I was on my way there when Buddy got *here* and what would I have done and you've never told me you love me and I—I c-can't have babies and you want them a-and…"

"Janie." He said it softly, hoping to interrupt her, get her attention. He wanted to touch her face, but couldn't reach her with his right hand and his left was strapped to his chest with his arm. "Janie, don't."

He knew what she needed—hell, what he needed, too—but he had a couple of things that had to be gotten out of the way first. "Buddy's father was picked up tonight. He's the one who really shot Maddie's brother, put it on her. That, on top of everything he did to her…" His gut twisted again over the *everything* he hadn't known about, including how Maddie had been torn up so badly inside that bearing children was out of the question for her.

He worked his jaw. "She said she told you what she asked me and how I reacted."

Tears flowed like rain, threatened to become a late-summer monsoon. Janina lifted her face and didn't hide from what frightened her. She nodded. "She told me before you got shot. And while you were in surgery, we talked about it again. She wants Jess to have the baby. I told her…" She bent her head. Whispered, "I told her if I couldn't have them, someone should." She met his gaze, cognac brown to midnight blue. Loneliness spilled out of her, through him. "It'd be a beautiful baby, Russ. You could baby-sit. Maybe I could be its favorite aunt, if not its mother."

He heard it in her voice, felt in his gut the statement she didn't make, *"While you find someone who can have kids with you."*

He shut his eyes, sank away from her. Was that what she believed about him, thought of herself? His stand-up, never insecure, talk-back or take-'em down bride? The woman he'd felt part of from the moment he'd entered her? Knew without a doubt…

"Judas, Janie." Him and his vaunted sensitivity to women and all creatures female. Damn it all to hell. "Janie, listen to me—"

A uniformed officer squatted beside them. "Sorry, Lieutenant, but we've gotta move you and your lady out of here so the crews can work. Paramedics want to check her out, and you're lookin' a bit rocky yourself, you don't mind me sayin'."

The skin beside Russ's left eye tightened marginally. Oh but he did. He minded a lot. Not the fact that the uniform thought he "looked rocky," but the interruption, the umpteenth million and one on top of way too many in his month-old marriage, the anniversary of which he'd not had the opportunity to celebrate because he'd been in the hospital without his wife, shot by a man who hadn't really even wanted to shoot him.

As gently as possible he eased his good arm from Janina, traced her cheek with his forefinger, and grabbed the shocked cop by the shirtfront.

"Get out of the middle of my marriage. Before I put you out of it," he said evenly.

"Russ!" Janina grabbed his hand, tried to pry his fingers open. "Stop it. Let go."

"No." He turned his head. Eyed her deliberately. "I'm tired of you thinking the wrong things, sick of the department and whatever else getting between us at the wrong times. It stops now, here."

Somewhere in the diner's superstructure something groaned loudly. Janina cast a nervous glance ceilingward.

"Ah, really, Russ, this might not be the best—"

Nearby, the Hummer shifted sideways in the kitchen's pass-through amid shouts. The rescue team slid a stabilized Manuel safely from beneath the vehicle and got him out of the building just as the massive SUV settled heavily into the spot where they'd been. Russ ignored it all.

"Hang it, Janie. It's what we've got."

Janina succeeded in tugging one of Russ's fingers out of the cop's crumpled uniform shirt. "Trust me. We could have it out there." She jerked her chin at the parking lot. "Really. All of it. Whatever you want, we can have it."

"Trust you…" He cut her a sideways glance from beneath his lashes. "And whatever I want. Hmm."

If she'd been in more—no, make that *less*—of an "I love you, we're in danger of things falling on us, now let me get you out of here" frame of mind, she probably would have noted the very devilish Levoie bent of his *"Hmm."* But she simply nodded and promised him frantically, "Anything."

"Good." He released the officer. "Got a flashlight?"

The uniform gave him ticked off. "Outside."

Janina shoved her shoulder under Russ's good one and agreed readily. "Yes, please."

Seemingly from nowhere and everywhere, all three of Russ's brothers turned up on cue and gently moved Janina aside.

"But…" she protested.

Guy shook his head. "Trust us," he advised. "You'll be glad you did." Then he hiked Russ up by the torso while Jeth and Jonah grabbed a leg each.

"No," Russ said emphatically. "Nunh-unh. Down. Put me down immediately. My own steam…I'm good. Ow, damn, watch the left side. Hell, that hurts."

"What'd you always tell us when we were growin' up?" Jeth asked, deliberately ramming his brother's right foot into an obstruction that he himself stepped carefully around. "Oh yeah." He glanced at Guy and Jonah.

"Do the crime, do the time," the brothers chorused.

"But—"

"Assault police, do time," Jonah, who'd been assaulted more than once working with his eldest brother, and all too frequently since he'd sent Janina off to find him, stated emphatically.

"Cowboy off to do it yourself, do time," Jeth, who knew all too well whereof he spoke, said pointedly.

"Forget to tell the woman you love that you do," Guy, who was exceptionally good about doing so but had almost lost Hazel anyway, offered mildly, "and you'll lose her."

"Piss me off any further by not putting me down," Russ said between his teeth, "and one-handed and half-dead or not, you're all goin' down."

"You think so?" Guy asked.

Russ canted a glance at his wife. Grinned crookedly. "Yeah. First rule for a rookie cop in unknown territory— never go in without backup. Right, Janie?"

She studied him a long moment, bewildered. Then her eyes went wide and she swallowed hard. "You knew?"

"Always." He opened his hand where her ring still sat snugly in the center of his palm, held there by the thong he'd laced around his fingers. "Thought you were pretty before, but that's when I fell in love."

"Oh." Janina blinked. Glanced around for someplace to collapse. Pointed at the back seat of Jeth's SUV. Looked at his brothers. "Put him down there," she croaked. "Gently."

"Easier if I do it myself," Russ protested.

She drew an unsteady breath, nodded. Crawled ahead of him into the heavy-built 4X4 vehicle.

She wanted his good side to herself.

When he was in, she reached across and shut the door behind him then locked them in.

He quirked a brow. "Jeth has the keys."

Janina traced his mouth. "He'd better not use 'em."

"This thing has lots of windows."

"They're tinted. No one can see in."

Russ grinned. "True. But I'm not exactly in any shape for gymnastics…"

"I don't care." Janina kissed the corner of his mouth. "If you love me even if I can't get pregnant, nothing else matters because I've loved you forever and…"

Russ reached up and switched on the interior light, threaded his hand into her hair, pulled her head back. Let her feel the ring still in his palm. "Janie, look at me. Listen up good. I knew before we married that you might not be able to get pregnant. You told me about you and Buddy, or else I heard you talking to Tobi. It doesn't matter. I knew. I know. Thing is, stuff changes. The body protects itself, kills off things for a reason. And while you might have killed off Buddy's, you're not killing off mine. That negative reading you got from the pregnancy test? Either you got a bad kit or your body's lying to you. Don't believe me, but I can smell pregnant on you, taste it on your skin, in your honey. Everything's sweeter. Different."

Her chin quivered, her eyes filled. She fitted her tongue between her teeth to steady herself. "No," she whispered. But not to him. "It can't be. It's stress."

Again, but with no interruptions in the offing this time, Russ showed her the ring. "Why did you take it off?"

"The first time?"

He made a motion for her to go on.

"Your blood." She fingered the ring, slipped her hand inside his strapping so she could touch his left hand. "I was covered in it. I had to wash it off. When I went to put my ring back on, my fingers were so swollen…" She shook her head. "I put it on when the swelling went down, but they've been like that all week. Figured between the heat and PMS, water retention…"

She ducked her head, bit her lip. "But I'd already missed my period. Even with stress, the divorce, Buddy at his worst, that never happened before." Her mouth twisted. "I couldn't hope. I had you. That would have been too much."

Russ smiled.

She shrugged. "But you were in the hospital, you didn't want me there. I couldn't worry you, tell you Buddy'd been following me. I had to handle that by myself so, you know…" A one-shoulder hunch. "Extra stress. I was worried about you, too, and I was afraid you—because you never said anything about love—and I wondered if maybe it would be better if we…or maybe I…. I guess I left it at home this morning when it wouldn't go on."

"You know why I couldn't stand to see you at the hospital?" Russ asked.

"No."

He grimaced. "You were making yourself sick and I couldn't bear seeing you that worried about me."

She rolled her eyes. "There's a cure for that, you know. Don't get shot again."

He gave her a lopsided grin. "I'll keep that in mind."

They were quiet for a moment.

"You know, you've never said anything about love, either," Russ said finally, gently. "But I know you do because it's in every damn thing you've ever done for me, and it's been in everything you've done every minute of every day from the moment you set foot in the Bloated Boar." He touched her mouth. "It's a word that's nice to hear, but you saying it wouldn't tell me louder than you're telling me now. Than you've told me for years. I was just too big an idiot not to have heard you and done something about it sooner."

"I adore you," Janina said thickly. "Love you to distraction and to the point of wanting to shake or kill you when you don't take care of yourself." She hesitated apologetically. "But in order to stay sane I'll need the words from you at least once more. And probably once in a while after that, too."

Russ laughed. Gasped in pain, but couldn't prevent the mirth from spilling out of him. So he let it. Chuckled, snickered, roared. Hard, long and with feeling.

Until a miffed Janina grabbed her ring away from him, ripped off the thong and slipped it on, stone in, and swatted him upside the head with equal feeling. Then he subsided, rubbed his skull and gave her that devastatingly devilish Levoie grin.

"You never read your ring, did you?"

She viewed him with did-they-sew-your-shoulder-to-your-belly-button misgiving. "Read my… What? What are you talking about?"

He wiggled his fingers. "Give it to me."

She took it off. "Even if it needs to be sized so I can wear it all the time after a legitimate doctor tells me whether or not I'm pregnant, I want it back."

Russ swallowed a smile. "Noted." He held the ring up to the interior light, angled it so she could see the inside. "Remember I told you I made this six months before you rescued me from the Boar?"

Janina nodded warily.

"I inscribed it then, too, just in case this damn tongue of mine tripped me up so I never got around to telling you how I felt."

All shaky again, Janina peered at the inscription. Grabbed the ring and read it again to make sure she'd seen it right. Put it back on and turned carefully to face him.

"Dear God, I love you," she said, and with the greatest care slid her arms around his neck, leaned in and kissed him.

His one good arm wrapped tightly around her, Russ pulled her close, let his heart expand, open wide...

Then he took her deep inside himself and kept her there.

For Janina, who owns my heart. Always. Russ

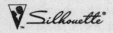

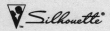

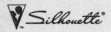

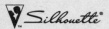

INTIMATE MOMENTS™

GHOST OF A CHANCE

(Silhouette Intimate Moments #1319)

by award-winning author

NINA BRUHNS

Could the gorgeous man Clara Fergussen found in her bed really be the infamous pirate Tyree St. James? He'd been caught in a curse for the past two hundred years, and had only one week left on earth. After a passionate night in his arms, would Clara risk everything to be with him—forever?

Available September 2004 at your favorite retail outlet.

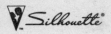